P9-CER-377

IN COUNTRY

Also by Bobbie Ann Mason

SHILOH AND OTHER STORIES
THE GIRL SLEUTH
NABOKOV'S GARDEN

IN COUNTRY

a novel by

Bobbie Ann Mason

HARPER & ROW, PUBLISHERS, New York
Cambridge, Philadelphia, San Francisco, London
Mexico City, São Paulo, Singapore, Sydney

The author wishes to express her gratitude to the Guggenheim Foundation, the National Endowment for the Arts, and the Pennsylvania Council on the Arts for support while writing this book. Special thanks to W. D. Ehrhart for helpful advice.

Copyright acknowledgments appear on page 247.

Portions of this book originally appeared in *The New Yorker*.

 For information address Harper & Row, Publishers, Inc., 10 East 53rd Street, New York, N.Y. 10022. Published simultaneously in Canada by Fitzhenry & Whiteside Limited, Toronto.

Designed by Ruth Bornschlegel

Library of Congress Cataloging in Publication Data

Mason, Bobbie Ann.
In country.

1. Vietnamese Conflict, 1961–1975—Fiction. I. Title.
PS3563.A787715 1985 813'.54 85-42579
ISBN 0-06-015469-1

89 10 9 8 7 6 5 4

For Roger

I'm ten years burning down the road
Nowhere to run ain't got nowhere to go

—*Bruce Springsteen,*
"Born in the U.S.A."

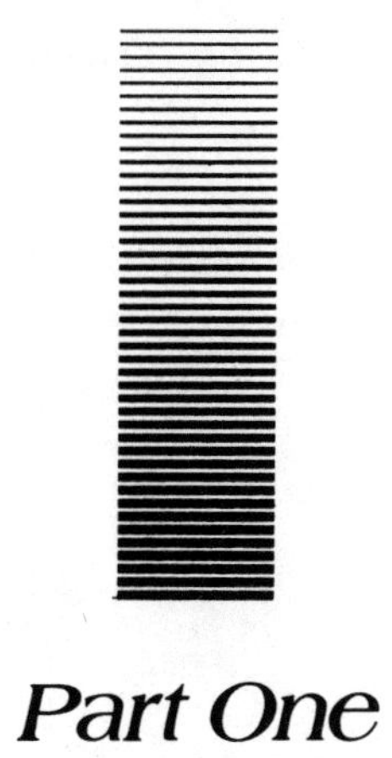

Part One

1

"I have to stop again, hon," Sam's grandmother says, tapping her on the shoulder. Sam Hughes is driving, with her uncle, Emmett Smith, half asleep beside her.

"Where are we?" grunts Emmett.

"Still on I-64. Mamaw has to go to the restroom."

"I forgot to take my pill when we stopped last," Mamaw says.

"Do you want me to drive now?" Emmett asks, whipping out a cigarette. He smokes Kents, and he has smoked seven in the two hours they have been on the road today.

"If Emmett drives, I could set up front," says Mamaw, leaning forward between the front seats. "I'm crammed in the back here like a sack of sausage."

"Are you sure you feel like driving, Emmett?"

"It don't make no difference."

"I was just getting into it," says Sam, irritated.

It is *her* new car. Emmett drove through the heavy traffic around Lexington, because Sam wasn't experienced at city driving, but the interstate is easy. She could glide like this all the way across America.

At the next exit, Exxon, Chevron, and Sunoco loom up, big faces on stilts. There's a Country Kitchen, a McDonald's, and a Stuckey's. Sam has heard that Stuckey's is terrible and the Country Kitchen is good. She notices a hillside with some white box shapes—either beehives or a small family cemetery—under some trees. She shoots onto the exit ramp a little too fast, and the tires squeal. Mamaw gasps and clutches the back of Sam's seat, but

Emmett just fiddles with the buttons on the old Army jacket in his lap. Emmett dragged it out of his closet before they left. He said it might be cold in Washington. It is summer, and Sam doesn't believe him.

Sam pulls in at the Sunoco and springs out of the car to let Mamaw out. Mamaw has barrel hips and rolls of fat around her waist. She is so fat she has to sleep in a special brassiere. She shakes out her legs and stretches her arms. She is wearing peach-colored knit pants and a flowered blouse, with white socks and blue tennis shoes. Sam does not know Mamaw Hughes as well as she does her other grandmother, Emmett's mother, whom she calls Grandma, but Mamaw acts like she knows everything about Sam. It's spooky. Mamaw is always saying, "Why, that's just like you, Sam," or "That's your daddy in you, for the world." She makes Sam feel as though she has been spied on for years. Bringing Mamaw along was Emmett's idea. He is staring off at a bird flying over the Sunoco sign.

"Regular?" a blond boy in a Sunoco shirt asks.

"Yeah. Fill 'er up." Sam likes saying "Fill 'er up." Buying gas is one of the pleasures of owning a car at last. "Come on, Mamaw," she says, touching her grandmother's arm. "Take care of the car, would you, Emmett?"

He nods, still looking in the direction of the bird.

The restroom is locked, and Sam has to go back and ask the boy for the key. The key is on a ring with a clumsy plastic Sunoco sign. The restroom is pink and filthy, with sticky floors. In her stall, Sam reads several phone numbers written in lipstick. A message says, "The mass of the ass plus the angle of the dangle equals the scream of the cream." She wishes she had known that one when she took algebra. She would have written it on an assignment.

Mamaw lets loose a stream as loud as a cow's. This trip is crazy. It reminds Sam of that Chevy Chase movie about a family on vacation, with an old woman tagging along. She died on the trip and they had to roll her inside a blanket on the roof of the station wagon because the children refused to sit beside a dead body. This trip is just as weird. A month ago, Emmett wouldn't have gone to Washington for a million dollars, but after everything that happened this summer, he changed his mind and now is hell-bent on going and dragging Mamaw along with them.

"I was about to pop," Mamaw says.

That was a lie about her pill. Mamaw just didn't want Emmett to know she had to pee.

When they return the key, Mamaw buys some potato chips at a vending machine. "Irene didn't feed us enough for breakfast this morning," she says. "Do you want anything?"

"No. I'm not hungry."

"You're too skinny, Sam. You look holler-eyed."

Irene is Sam's mother, Emmett's sister. They spent the night in Lexington with her in her new house—a brick ranch house with a patio and wall-to-wall carpeting. Irene has a new baby at the age of thirty-seven. The baby is cute, but Irene's new husband has no personality. His name is Larry Joiner, but Sam calls him Lorenzo Jones. In social studies class, Sam's teacher used to play tapes of old radio shows. *Lorenzo Jones* was an old soap opera. Sam's mother's life is a soap opera. The trip would be so different if her mother could have come. But Sam has her mother's credit card, and it is burning a hole in her pocket. She hasn't used it yet. It is for emergencies.

Emmett is in the driver's seat, with the engine running. He is drinking a can of Pepsi. "Are y'all ready?" he asks, flicking cigarette ash on the asphalt. He has moved the car, but it's still close to the gas pumps. A scene of a sky-high explosion, like an ammunitions dump blowing up, rushes through Sam's mind.

"Give me a swig of that," says Sam. "Did you pay?" She takes a drink of Emmett's Pepsi and hands it back.

"Yeah. It was six dollars and thirty cents. I wrote down the mileage. We averaged thirty-one to the gallon."

"That's good!"

The gas gauge is broken, and Sam has to estimate when to get gas. To be safe, she gets gas every two hundred miles. The VW is a seventy-three, with a rebuilt engine. Tom Hudson sold it to her less than two weeks ago. His fingerprints are still on it, no doubt—on the engine and the hubcaps and the gas cap. His presence is everywhere in the car.

"I love this car," Sam says, giving the VW an affectionate slap. "She's a good little bird." She suddenly feels strange saying that. Emmett is always watching birds and writing them down on his life list. There is a certain kind of exotic bird he has been looking for. He claimed such birds sometimes stopped off in Kentucky on their way to Florida, and he keeps looking for one, but he has never seen one in Kentucky. When Sam suggested that they could see one in the Washington zoo, he said it wouldn't be the same as seeing it in the wild.

Sam climbs in the back, and Mamaw starts to get in, but then Mamaw says, "I better check on my flowers. I should have watered them this morning."

She walks behind the car and peers through the back window.

"They don't look droopy," Sam says, glancing at the pot of geraniums wedged behind the seat.

"I reckon they're O.K.," says Mamaw doubtfully. "I'm just afraid the blooms will fall off before we get there." She gets in the front seat. "I'm still so embarrassed, spilling dirt on Irene's nice floor. I guess she thought I was just a country hick, dragging in dirt."

Emmett stubs out his cigarette and takes off, sailing into fourth gear by the time they hit the highway.

"Reckon we'll ever get there?" Mamaw asks. "We'll probably get lost."

"Don't worry, Mrs. Hughes. We've got a map."

"You can't get lost in the United States," Sam says. "I wish I could, though. I wish I'd wake up and not know where I was."

"Lands, child, where do you get your ideas?" Mamaw says.

Emmett drives in silence, intent on his job, like a bus driver. Emmett is a large man of thirty-five with pimples on his face. He has been very quiet since they left Hopewell yesterday, probably because Mamaw is getting on his nerves. He has bad nerves.

"This transmission's getting worse," he says after a while. He glances back at Sam. "It just popped out of fourth gear again."

"Tom said he worked on that transmission. It's supposed to be O.K."

"Well, it's popping out. Just thought I'd tell you."

"Well, I'm not sorry I bought the car, so don't throw it in my face!"

She leans her head against the pillow they borrowed from her mother and watches the cars fire past. On the shoulder are blown-out truck tires, scraps of rubber flung out like abandoned toys. The scenery is funny little hills shaped like scoops of ice cream. Where she lives is flat. She has never been this far away from home before. She is nearly eighteen years old and out to see the world. She would like to move somewhere far away—Miami or San Francisco maybe. She wants to live anywhere but Hopewell. On the road, everything seems more real than it has ever been. It's as though nothing has really registered on her until just recently—since the night last week when she ran off to the swamp. The feeling reminds her of her aerobics instructor, Ms. Hotpants—she had some hard-to-pronounce foreign name—when they did the pelvic tilt in gym last year. A row of girls with their asses reaching for heaven. "Squeeze your butt-*ox*. Squeeze tight, girls," she would say, and they would grit their teeth and flex their butts, and hold for a count of five, and then she would say, "Now squeeze one layer deeper." That is what the new feeling is like: you know something as well as you can and then you squeeze one layer deeper and something more is there.

Emmett's cigarette smoke floats back and strangles her. She is glad when a while later he lets her have the wheel again. She's proud of the car. It is off-white, with bright orange patches where Tom fixed the spots of rust. The rebuilt engine sounds good.

"This car will look better when I get a paint job," she says.

"What color do you aim to paint it, hon?" Mamaw asks.

"Black." Sam has been thinking that when winter comes she will get a black motorcycle jacket and dye her old tan cowhide boots black. They lace up, and they will look sinister if she dyes them black. A truck that she passed two minutes ago passes her now, with a wheeze and a honk. She slams the horn at him. Trucker-fucker, she mutters to herself.

"Why, look at that, would you!" cries Emmett, pointing to a station wagon pulling a small flat-bed trailer loaded with a dish antenna. "The license plate says Arizona. They've hauled that all the way from Arizona. Imagine having one of those. You could watch everything on earth with that."

"It probably belongs to Big Brother," says Sam.

"Yeah. He's probably got one of those, and his own satellite too," Emmett says thoughtfully.

"Whose brother are y'all talking about?" Mamaw wants to know.

"Big Brother in *Nineteen Eighty-four*. It's a book I had to read in English."

"There goes that transmission again," Emmett says.

"Oh, shit," groans Sam, not loud enough for her grandmother to hear. Cussing shocks Mamaw.

Actually, Sam never really cussed much before this summer. But now she feels like letting loose. She has so much evil and bad stuff in her now. It feels good to say shit, even if it's only under her breath.

2

On the radio, an oldies station is playing the Motown sound. Marvin Gaye, Junior Walker and the All Stars, and somebody else named Junior whose name Sam doesn't catch. The station is fading away. They are heading into higher hills, in West Virginia.

She is driving, with Emmett beside her, his long legs bunched up. He flips ashes out the window. He has smoked since he joined the Army. Sam wonders if she would smoke if she joined the Army. She decides she wouldn't. She is probably going to die of lung cancer anyway, just from hanging around smokers. Irene and Emmett always puffed away, warning her as they exhaled serious streams of smoke that it was a habit she should never start. But Irene stopped smoking when she got pregnant last year. Marijuana is different. Mamaw would have a heart attack if she knew about the pot Sam had in her purse. In case the cops stop them, Sam plans to punch the joints through the small hole in the side of the car near the floorboard. Ahead, a billboard advertises a motel with free HBO.

"We can get to Washington by night," Emmett says. "It's not that far."

"But then what'll we do? It'll cost a fortune to stay there. It's better to get there early tomorrow morning. Then we can get out of the city without having to stay all night."

"Sam's right," says Mamaw. "It'll cost a fortune."

They have had this conversation a dozen times. Emmett said he knew somebody there, an old Army buddy, they could stay with. But he didn't have the guy's address, and he refused to make a phone call because it would be long distance. He wanted to wait till they got there and then look him up.

The transmission is getting worse. It keeps popping out of fourth gear. For a while, Emmett held it in place, but his hand got tired, so Sam has been trying to hold it in place with her free hand as she drives. Her hand aches.

"If we let it go, we'll have to drive in third gear and it'll take all week to get there," Emmett says, grabbing the gear shift.

"What if the car breaks down and we're stranded?" Mamaw says.

"I'm sure we'll think of something," Sam says. She turns the radio up when a song by Bruce Springsteen comes on. She would play it louder if Mamaw weren't along.

"Imagine us, hitting the road like this," says Emmett. He starts bellowing out "Glory Days" along with the radio. Sam giggles. The transmission pops out.

"I still can't get over the way you whooshed in there at home and triggered me off on this trip," Mamaw says.

"Aren't you glad?"

"Yeah, but I don't know if I can stand real long when we get there. My legs are acting up." Mamaw takes pills to keep her legs from swelling. "I'd rather get there early when I'm rested in case I have to stand too long."

The news on the hour comes on, and they listen to some news about the presidential campaign and a hurricane in Texas. Sam twirls the dial. The Doors' "Roadhouse Blues" is on. God. If Jim Morrison were still alive, she would drive this car straight to wherever he was. "Let it roll, baby, roll . . . All night long." She pictures him in his black jacket and thinks dreamily about the time he got arrested for exposing himself during a performance.

By the time they stop at a Howard Johnson's, Sam is exhausted from holding the gear handle. When Emmett took over the wheel around four o'clock, Sam discovered that she could hook her purse strap around the handle and pull on it. That took less effort than pressing down to hold it in place. Mamaw suggested looping some baling twine between the handle and the plastic hook between the windows, but they didn't have any baling twine. It is disappointing to have bought a car with a transmission problem. Sam had longed for a sporty car like a Trans Am. Her mother has a Trans Am, and Lorenzo Jones has a Ford Cobra and belongs to a club, but he is a terrible driver.

"We haven't made good time with this gear problem," Emmett says.

They're sitting in the parking lot, trying to decide what to do. Emmett suggests sharing one room because it would be cheaper, but Mamaw is reluctant.

"Don't worry, Mamaw," Sam says. "I'll sleep on the cot and let you have one bed, and Emmett can have the other one."

"I don't know if we should sleep in the same room with a man, Sam."

"Well, I've been living with Emmett all my life. Don't you think I've seen Emmett in his pajamas before?" Actually, Emmett doesn't sleep in pajamas.

"I never slept in the same room with a man before that wasn't my husband." Mamaw laughs. "What will they think back home? They'll think I've gone wild and started running around. I didn't even bring my good housecoat."

"I didn't either," says Sam.

Emmett goes in to check on the price of the room.

"Well, here comes Emmett back!" says Mamaw a moment later. "Maybe they don't like the idea of all three of us in a room, and Emmett and me not related to one another."

"You're related," Sam says. "He's your daughter-in-law's brother."

"*Ex*-daughter-in-law."

"Or your granddaughter's uncle. That still applies."

"They want to know the license number," Emmett says through the window. "A single is fifty-four and a double is fifty-nine, with a cot for three dollars extra."

"I'll sleep on the cot," Sam says. "Are there two beds?"

"Two double beds. And it's just five dollars more than a single. Two singles would cost us a hundred and eight dollars."

"Well, I reckon we can make do," says Mamaw. "I can wrap a bedspread around me. We can turn the lights out."

The room is large and beautiful, with sliding glass doors that open to the parking lot. It has dark, striped drapes and two pictures of street life in Paris on the wall above each bed. Even the plumbing is fancy. The commode is beige, and it has a strip of paper across it that makes a satisfying pop when Sam breaks it. "What's that for?" Mamaw asks, and Sam explains. Mamaw hasn't traveled much. When they stopped on the parkway the day before to eat, Mamaw didn't even know what the little tubs of non-dairy creamer were.

Sam flops on the bed, while Mamaw works with her pot of geraniums in the bathroom. Emmett plays with the TV dial. A man brings a cot. Emmett tests out all the channels.

"The news won't be on till six-thirty," he says.

"I could never get used to that," Mamaw says. "Living in a different time zone. My time's been off ever since we got to Lexington yesterday."

Sam goes running, down a state road with not much traffic. When Sam put on her running shorts and headed out, Mamaw warned her not to get lost. Sam loves the room, so in a way it seems strange to be running away from it. The room is so clean, with no evidence of belonging to anybody, but it has a secret history of thousands of people, their vibrations and essences soaked in the walls and rug.

She passes an Exxon station. A Buick station wagon and a red Saab are tanking up. The Saab has a homemade wooden roof rack, an awkward plywood thing that looks something like a sleigh with curved pieces cut in line with the roof. The people were probably too cheap to buy a roof rack, Sam thinks. It reminds her of things Emmett does, the way he rigs up things around the house to keep from spending a dime. Emmett even made their toilet-paper holder out of scraps of wood and a sawed-off broom handle. The Saab pulls away from the pump and toots at another Saab passing by, but the other Saab doesn't toot back.

The day is humid and she is already sweating, but she aims to run at least four miles. She sets the timer on her sports watch. Huge trucks thunder past. At the previous exit, they passed a shopping mall. It is too far away, but she wishes she could run all the way there, so she could go in and see if they have that Beatles record she has been looking for.

3

After the news, they sit in an orange booth at the Howard Johnson's restaurant. Emmett orders beer.

"I'm going to sleep in the same room with a drunk man!" cries Mamaw, half laughing at herself.

Sam can't decide what to order, there are so many choices. She definitely wants fried clams because they are the special, but she can't decide between the clam plate and the clam roll. She wants to save room for ice cream.

"These prices are high," says Mamaw.

"We've got Mom's Visa card," Sam reminds her. "In case we run out of money."

"Fried chicken's five-thirty-five. I could buy nearly two chickens at the grocery for that. What are you going to get, Emmett?"

"A Gourmet Beefburger and french fries. Get that chicken, Mrs. Hughes. I'll pay for it."

"I want something I've never had before," says Sam.

Their waitress looks old and hardened, as though she has been serving Gourmet Beefburgers since the turn of the century. Sam knows how hard waitressing is. She used to work at the Burger Boy after school.

"They've deep-fried this chicken," Mamaw says when they are eating. "Doing it that way makes it tough."

"The clams are good," Sam says.

"They look like worms," Emmett says. "But that's O.K. Worms are a good source of protein."

They eat in silence, and as Mamaw mops her plate with her roll, she says, "I keep thinking about Dwayne and how everybody's life is different without him. If he had lived, he'd have a house down the road with Irene, and you would have grown up there, Sam, and I'd have knowed you a lot better, sugar. And you'd have some brothers and sisters."

Sam shudders at the idea of growing up on a farm, doing chores, never getting to go to town. She swallows clams and says, "What makes you think he would have stayed there on the farm? Maybe he would have gone to New Orleans. Maybe I would have grown up in the French Quarter."

"Why, he wouldn't traipse off to New Orleans. It would cost a fortune to live there."

"What makes you think he wouldn't have been rich? Maybe he would have made something big out of himself. He might have been an airplane pilot. Or a movie director."

Mamaw lets out a big laugh. "He couldn't wait to get back home and put out a tobacco crop."

"Is everything all right?" the waitress asks, popping up suddenly.

"This chicken's tough," Mamaw says. "It's deep-fried."

"They just ask you that so you can't sue them if it turns out there's glass in the food or something," says Emmett after the waitress whizzes away. "It's like a verbal contract."

"You know what I heard on the television?" Mamaw says later, after the waitress removes their plates. "There was a Gold Star Mother who never knew anything about just how her boy died, and her boy had a buddy who was with him when he died. And as he laid there dying, his buddy promised he would go back to the boy's mama and tell her what happened. He promised, but when he got back he couldn't make himself go look her up. Ten years went by before he finally wrote that letter."

"What happened then?"

"Well, it eased the woman's mind just to know how it happened. And the boy came to visit, and do you know it was like having a son again? He came to see her, and then they started having cookouts together, and they got to be friends."

Mamaw runs her finger down the desserts on the menu. She says, "That was such a sweet story. I couldn't get it out of my mind."

Sam concentrates on the menu, studying the ice cream flavors. She picks black raspberry and pecan praline crunch. They seem like a deadly combination, but she feels daring. Emmett lights a cigarette and gazes out the window into outer space.

4

They are in Maryland. For an hour, they have been waiting at a gas station for a mechanic named Bill to come and take a look at the car. Sam and Mamaw rode in the tow truck and Emmett hitched a ride. Mamaw lugged the pot of geraniums with her in the truck, and Sam sat squeezed between her and the driver, a talkative fat man who tried to flirt with her. But Sam was in no mood for flirting. The VW followed them on its back wheels, looking pathetic, like a little dog on its hind legs.

Mamaw is in the restroom now, and Sam paces around the picnic table where they're waiting.

"Take it easy," Emmett says. "You're working up a sweat."

"I'm going to scream if this keeps up. I'll be glad when this trip is over with. She's driving me crazy."

"Well, she's never been anywhere before, and she doesn't know how to act." Emmett seems unusually calm and considerate. Sam doesn't understand it.

"We're going to be stranded with her in a motel, I bet. That transmission job will take forever. And we can't afford separate rooms. We can't even play the radio loud with her around."

"You can listen to the Walkman," Emmett says, handing the set to Sam.

"Not now." Sam takes a drink of Mountain Dew and belches. "I wish you'd call that guy you know in Washington so we'll have a place to stay."

"I don't even know if he lives there now. I'll wait till we get there."

"I wonder if fat-sectioning would work on her cellulite," Sam says idly.

"What's that?"

"It's an operation to take fat out."

Emmett tosses his Pepsi can into a trash barrel near the picnic table. He has wet circles under his arms. The circles intersect the stripes of his T-shirt, like an abstract design in solid geometry class. He sits at the table and cradles his head in his arms. He has been touching his temples frequently today, as though the pain he has been having in his head all summer is worse.

"Should we call Tom?" she asks.

"What could he do?"

"I don't know. I just feel like calling him, but I don't know what I'd say." Sam tried to call him before they left, but she heard he had gone to St. Louis to see his brother.

"You could get him to come after you with a tow truck," Emmett says.

"Be serious."

"I am serious. A new transmission could cost a few hundred. I thought you said he fixed the transmission."

"He did. But the car's old. And transmissions freeze up."

"How do you know about transmissions freezing up?"

"I just do."

"You're making excuses for him, Sam. You won't admit he sold you a bum car."

"It's not a bum car. It's a good car. It'll look real good when I get it painted. I'm going to paint it black, so it'll look mean."

Mamaw waddles toward the picnic table. She places her foot on the bench of the table and massages her shin. "Oh, me! I've got knots from setting."

"How's your pain, Emmett?" Sam asks.

"It's still there."

"Emmett's got this pain in his head," Sam explains to Mamaw. "It comes and goes, and the doctors don't know what it is."

"It's not that bad," Emmett says. "It's just a feeling that comes sometimes, like the beeper on Sam's watch."

"I know what you're talking about," Mamaw says. "Is it a little thing that shoots up above your ear ever' once in a while?"

"Well, not exactly."

"That's neuralgia. That's like what Pap has. It's from setting in drafts."

"That's not what it is," Sam says. "This is something else."

"Pap's always got worse when it was change of season," says Mamaw. "I've had it once or twice, but it goes away." She tugs at her bra strap and glances at the highway. "How long do you reckon we'll be stranded here, Emmett?"

"Don't you worry, Mrs. Hughes," Emmett says soothingly. "We're not stranded out in the middle of nowhere. We'll get out of here."

"But it could cost hundreds of dollars to get the car fixed. I don't have that kind of money, and y'all don't neither."

"Plastic money," says Sam. She is tired of explaining the credit card.

Mamaw shifts the geraniums into a shadier spot under the picnic table. Emmett feels for a cigarette in his T-shirt pocket and strikes a match one-handed. Up in the sky, the daytime moon is a white fingernail hanging against the pale blue. Emmett sets the

Walkman earphones on his head and starts beating his hand in rhythm against the picnic table.

"What are you listening to, Emmett?" Sam asks.

"'Burning Down the House.'"

"Tell me if you hear that Beatles song."

A pickup truck roars into the station and a guy in a green jump suit gets out. Emmett unplugs his ears. "This must be the famous Bill," he says.

According to Bill, who spends about ten minutes poking around in the car, the VW needs transmission work. "I can't get around to it before about four o'clock because I have to reline some brakes, and then I've got a ring job to do. I figure I'll get this apart about quitting time." He counts on his fingers. "I figure I can let you have it early tomorrow afternoon. Are you in a hurry to get anyplace special?"

"What's it going to cost?" Sam asks.

"All depends on the labor. But I'll try to keep it under three hundred. A bug this old, sometimes the transmissions are hard to pull."

"I know about frozen transmissions," Sam says, eyeing Emmett.

They are at the Holiday Inn now, across the highway. The room costs forty-six dollars. Using Irene's credit card could get to be a habit. It is so easy. They are only a hundred miles from Washington. The hills here are long and blue, like paintings. Sam leaves Emmett and Mamaw in front of the TV, and she sits by the pool, watching the traffic—an endless river of it, families on vacation and salesmen out patrolling their territory and weirdos on the prowl and trucks hauling goods. Everything in America is going on here, on the road. Sam likes the feeling of strangeness. They are at a crossroads: the interstate with traffic headed east and west, and the state road with north-south traffic. She's in limbo, stationed right in the center of this enormous amount of energy. The whine of the diesel trucks is like the background on a rock song.

When it cools off in the late afternoon, Sam goes running

again, setting the pacer on her watch for a six-minute mile, which she cannot do in this heat, but she can sprint at that speed. She is carrying Emmett's Walkman and listening to a station from somewhere in Pennsylvania, and when a song ends and a commercial begins she lifts the earphones and listens to the highway sounds.

In the evening, they eat crackers and cheese and cookies from the 7-Eleven, with Cokes from the machine in the hall. The restaurant at the Holiday Inn is too expensive. Later, Emmett brings in more Cokes. The machine is out of Pepsi.

"Come here, Sam." Emmett is beckoning her to come behind the partition that separates the sink from the bedroom area of the room. "Do you want something sweet?" he whispers.

"Sweet stuff?" Emmett calls pot "sweet stuff."

"No." He chuckles, pulling out a bottle of Old Crow from his gym bag. "Hand me your Coke."

When she hesitates, Emmett says, "It's O.K. You'll feel better. Besides, you're grown."

He spikes their Cokes with the whiskey, and when he hands hers back, he winks at her. Mamaw is sitting in one of the beds, oblivious. Her geraniums, near the sink, are in full bloom.

Sam and Emmett sit on the other bed, propped against pillows, and sip the bourbon Cokes and watch TV. *Hill Street Blues* isn't on because of a special about the election. Some journalists are debating whether Walter Mondale's choice of a woman will help or hurt the Democratic ticket.

"She won't get elected," Mamaw says. "Nobody's ready for a woman up there."

Sam reminds her that Kentucky has a woman governor.

"Geraldine's dynamite," Emmett says when a picture of Geraldine Ferraro appears on the screen. "I like her accent."

"She wouldn't get us in a war," says Sam. "Reagan wants to go to war."

The show drags on with a lot of talk, and when some clips of Geraldine Ferraro's acceptance speech at the Democratic convention flash on the screen, Sam smiles to herself, remembering the convention. Political conventions are so funny, with all the crazy people in their party hats, all the planks and platforms and floor fights. Sam can't figure out if Geraldine Ferraro is any different from other politicians—if she's for real or for show. Politicians have to do everything for show. Sam likes Geraldine Ferraro's accent and the way she raises her fist. But she shouldn't wear those old-lady suits.

Mamaw says, "Why are y'all laughing so? Did I miss something?"

"Don't talk, Mamaw," says Sam, giggling. "This show's real good."

"Do you want another Coke, Sam?" Emmett asks.

"Not now."

"Give me a swig of that, hon," Mamaw says. "To get my pill down."

"Oh, this is empty! I'll get you some water." Sam runs to the sink and smiles at herself in the mirror. Her face is red. It is fun to fool her grandmother. Mamaw has the idea that using the Visa card is something like forging checks. Earlier in the evening, Sam helped her call home. She told Pap her legs were killing her, but that she was seeing the world. "He says it's raining at home," she reported to Sam and Emmett. "We sure needed that rain." Twice since then, Mamaw has mentioned the rain at home.

But here, in Maryland, it is a clear night. The room is nice—blues and greens, with a luxurious shag rug. The bathroom is yellow tile, and it is very clean. The air conditioner doesn't drip water on the curtains. The commode doesn't overflow.

"Johnny Carson has Joan Rivers substituting," Emmett says later. "And it's a rerun. Nothing's authentic anymore."

"I can't stand Joan Rivers." Sam has been feeling just the opposite—that everything is more real to her, now that they are on the road. She can't help wondering what would happen to her grandmother if she were suddenly stranded here alone, how she would cope.

Joan Rivers is wearing a black taffeta job with a balloon ruffle around the hips and gobs of pearls. She says her outfit is Boy George's gym suit. She is made up pretty and blond, but she isn't really that pretty or that blond. She says it is raining in L.A.—at last Willie Nelson will get his hair washed, she says. She says he wears a Roach Motel around his neck. Her first guest is Don Rickles. Don Rickles tells Joan Rivers, "Johnny hired you because you're no threat." He says Johnny is at home, posing in his swimsuit and saying, "How's the body?" Don Rickles and Joan Rivers rattle back and forth about their dates in Las Vegas. Joan Rivers says a woman needs a funny face and a trick pelvis and that's all, but Don Rickles says college would be an advantage. His daughter is going to college.

"I miss Moon Pie," Emmett says suddenly, when a cat food commercial comes on. A neighbor is feeding their cat.

"I miss home," Mamaw says. "If we ever get home in one piece, I'll be satisfied."

I miss Tom, Sam says to herself as she climbs into the cot. She is growing sleepy. Emmett goes out for another Coke, which he takes into the bathroom. Mamaw, her head crisscrossed with bobby pins, has a towel wrapped around her shoulders. She says the air conditioning makes a draft on her neck. Sam's head is fuzzy. Mamaw doesn't know Sam is a drunk and a dope fiend. In the dim room, Sam clutches at memories of Tom. Emmett is sitting up in bed, his hair crammed into his Pepsi cap, drinking from the Coke can, chasing away that pain in his head. Mamaw is snoring, but Sam fights off sleep, wanting this night to last, wishing the car repair would take forever. She dreads going to Washington.

Part Two

1

It was the summer of the Michael Jackson *Victory* tour and the Bruce Springsteen *Born in the U.S.A.* tour, neither of which Sam got to go to. At her graduation, the commencement speaker, a Methodist minister, had preached about keeping the country strong, stressing sacrifice. He made Sam nervous. She started thinking about war, and it stayed on her mind all summer.

Emmett came back from Vietnam, but Sam's father did not. After his discharge, Emmett stayed with his parents two weeks, then left. He couldn't adjust. Several months later, he returned, and Sam's mother let him live with them, in the house she had bought with her husband's life insurance policy. Emmett stayed, helping out around the house. People said Irene babied him. She treated him like someone disabled, and she never expected him to get a job. She always said the war "messed him up." She had worked as a receptionist for a dentist, and she received compensation payments from the government. In retrospect, Sam realized how strange those early years were. When Emmett moved in, he brought some friends with him—hippies. Hopewell didn't have any hippies, or war protesters, and when Emmett showed up with three scruffy guys in ponytails and beads, they created a sensation. The friends came from places out west—Albuquerque, Eugene, Santa Cruz. Boys in Hopewell didn't even wear long hair until the seventies, when it finally became fashionable. Sam had a strong memory of Emmett in his Army jacket and black boots, with a purple headband running through his wild hair. She remembered his friends piling out of a psychedelic van, but she remembered little else about them. People in town still talked about the time Emmett and the hippies flew a Vietcong flag from the courthouse tower. One bleak day in early winter, they entered the courthouse through separate doors and converged at the base of the clock tower. The county circuit court clerk saw them head up the stairs and said later she knew something was about to happen. They fastened the flag to the side of the tower with masking tape, covering part of the clock face. Merchants around the square got nervous and had them arrested for disturbing the peace. The funny part, Emmett always said, was that nobody had even recognized that it was a Vietcong flag. He had had it made by a tailor in Pleiku, the way one might order a wedding suit. Soon after the flag incident, when burglars broke into a building supply company on Main Street, using a concrete block to smash a window, people were suspicious of Emmett's crowd, but no one ever proved anything.

The friends went away eventually, and Emmett calmed down. For a couple of years, he attended Murray State, but then he dropped out. He did odd jobs—mowing yards, repairing small appliances—and got by. Now and then a rumor would surface. At one time, neighbors had the idea that Patty Hearst was hiding out with Emmett and Irene. For a week, Sam had been too embarrassed to go to school, but later she was proud of Emmett. He was like a brother. She and Emmett were still pals, and he didn't try to boss her around. They liked the same music—mostly golden oldies. Emmett's favorite current groups were the Cars and the Talking Heads.

Irene's new husband got a good job in Lexington, but Sam refused to move there with them. Somebody had to watch out for Emmett, Sam insisted, and she didn't want to change schools her senior year. The house was paid for, and Sam still got government benefits. After her mother went away last year, Sam and Emmett got into the habit of watching *M*A*S*H* every evening. Usually, they grilled something and then watched the news, two reruns of *M*A*S*H*, and a movie on Home Box Office or Cinemax. Sam's boyfriend, Lonnie Malone, used to join them before he started working late at Kroger's. Sam's favorite

*M*A*S*H* was the one in which Hot Lips Houlihan kicked a door down when she learned that her husband, Donald Penobscott, had requested a transfer to San Francisco without telling her. Emmett preferred the early episodes, with Colonel Henry Blake and Frank Burns. Burns reminded him, he said, of his C.O. in Vietnam, a real idiot. That was about all Emmett would say about Vietnam these days. Emmett had a hearty, good-natured laugh like Hawkeye's. Hawkeye's laughter was so infectious that sometimes when Hawkeye and Trapper John let loose, Sam and Emmett couldn't stop laughing, just laughing for pure joy.

Years ago, when Colonel Blake was killed, Sam was so shocked she went around stunned for days. She was only a child then, and his death on the program was more real to her than the death of her own father. Even on the repeats, it was unsettling. Each time she saw that episode, it grew clearer that her father had been killed in a war. She had always taken his death for granted, but the reality of it took hold gradually. Now, when the episode was repeated, and she saw Radar report to the surgeons in the O.R. that Colonel Blake's plane had gone down over the Sea of Japan, she felt it was poignant because Radar had looked up to the Colonel like a father. The Colonel's last words to Radar had been, "You'd better behave or I'm going to come back and kick your butt."

The summer had been wet. Early in June, a tornado touched down on the main highway south of Hopewell and knocked a few trailers together, but no one was hurt. One night a week later, another tornado watch was in effect. Emmett had been nervous all evening as he listened to the weather channel on the radio. It was ten twenty-four by the kitchen clock that sticky night before the storm. The air conditioning was grinding and thumping, and the TV was on, but above the noise Sam heard Lonnie's van turn into the driveway. The van had a faulty post-ignition shut-off jet, which meant that the engine bucked along for a few moments after Lonnie turned it off, like a stubborn child making an annoying sound.

"Did you get off from work early?" Sam yelled under the porch light. A moth flew in and whizzed around the bulb on the hallway ceiling.

Lonnie Malone was a bag boy at Kroger's. He had a six-pack of Falls City with him and an open can in one hand. He was five-eleven and muscular, and he had brown hair with a kink in it. Sam thought he had a sexy build. On his chest he had a beautiful birthmark, a splotch the shape of an Izod alligator. Lonnie had been a guard for the Hopewell Indians. When he reached the porch, Sam pushed his hair back over his ear and smacked him on the lips. He smelled like beer. Beer smelled something like a run-over skunk.

"I saw a cop on I-24, and I was going sixty," he said with a grin.

"You're lucky he didn't catch you with this beer," Sam said. The screen door slammed behind them, and like an echo, thunder scattered across the sky. "Where'd you get it anyway?"

"Down at the Bottom. I got a guy to go in for me. Crazy old coot. He was just setting out on the county line, straddling it in his pickup. He was swigging from a bottle of Jim Beam in a sack and just daring somebody to look at him wrong."

"Is it storming down that way yet?"

"No. There's a tornado watch, but I don't think it'll hit here."

Emmett appeared in the kitchen doorway, filling it up so completely that he shut out the light from the kitchen. "Hey, I'm making muffelatas, y'all," he said. "Do you want one, Lonnie?"

"Yeah, I'm starving. All I had for supper was a hamburger." Lonnie jerked one of the cans from its plastic noose and handed it to Emmett. "Have a beer, Emmett, good buddy."

Emmett opened the can and took a drink. Then with his oven mitt he swatted at the moth and missed.

Lonnie had done a double take when he saw Emmett in his wraparound skirt. He was wearing a long, thin Indian-print skirt with elephants and peacocks on it. Now Lonnie burst out laughing.

"Where'd you get that skirt, Emmett?" he asked.

"It's a joke because Klinger wears dresses on *M*A*S*H*," Sam said.

Emmett struck an exaggerated fashion-model pose against the kitchen door facing, with his cigarette dangling from the corner of his mouth. "I got it at the mall in Paducah," he said.

"Are you bucking for a Section 8, like Klinger?" Lonnie asked.

"Wouldn't hurt," Emmett said with a grin.

Sam suspected Emmett was using the skirt to draw attention away from the pimples on his face. They had been getting worse. She was dying to squeeze them, but he wouldn't let her.

Emmett shoved the muffelatas in the oven and then turned around and pranced like Boy George, modeling his skirt. Emmett had a gleeful expression that said he had gotten away with murder.

"Far out!" Lonnie said, grinning at Emmett. Lonnie emulated Emmett, and they often shot baskets together at the high school. Lonnie even had an Army jacket that he had found at the surplus store, but Sam knew he would never wear a skirt just because Emmett wore one. He wouldn't go that far. Lonnie didn't even like Boy George.

"How come you're here at this hour of the night?" Sam said, sitting down on the lumpy couch in the living room. The couch tilted at an angle.

"I quit," said Lonnie. He wasn't looking at her. He was looking across the room to a rock group riding on a roller coaster on the television screen. He took such a huge slug of beer that his cheeks bulged out.

"Oh, shit," Sam groaned.

"What happened this time, Lonnie?" Emmett asked sympathetically.

"It wasn't for me. I want to have my own business someday, and I wasn't getting anywhere there." Lonnie paused and lit a cigarette. "I'd like to do something outdoors, where I'm my own boss. I've got to be independent."

"Good for you," Emmett said.

Lonnie laughed and took a shot of beer. "At least now I can

catch up on my video games with the guys, if I can scrape up enough quarters."

"You can play with Emmett's Atari," said Sam.

"Emmett ain't got *Donkey Kong*. Or *Hard Hat Mack*."

"Hey, Lonnie, I scored over fifty thousand today on *Pac-Man*," said Emmett.

"Gah!" Lonnie blew smoke out slowly. "I'll never catch you, Emmett. You're too good."

"I've figured out the secret of *Pac-Man*. The trick is you ignore all them little vitamin pills. They're just there to distract you and make you think you can get something for nothing. But if you keep your mind on your business, you can just keep going forever." Emmett drank some beer and added, "That's the Zen of *Pac-Man*."

"I'll have to try that," Lonnie said.

"It's too bad you quit your job, Lonnie. I need to borrow some money to pay back a debt I owe the government."

"How much do you owe?"

"Over five hundred dollars." Emmett lifted his skirt and fanned his legs. "They hit me over the head with it. I'd forgot all about it."

"It was that semester he dropped out of Murray," Sam explained. Emmett had dropped his courses but kept collecting monthly checks from the V.A. all semester.

"They won't take me to court, though," Emmett said. "It's not enough money for them to fool with. And I don't have no salary to garnishee." He laughed.

"You can take my education benefits and pay for those classes," Sam said. "I don't want to go to college that bad."

"That reminds me, Sam. Your mama called this evening when you were out running. She wants to know if you're going to U.K. this fall."

"I don't want to go to the same school as my mother. That would be too weird for words. Did she want me to call back?"

"No. She just said to tell you she still wanted you to come up there."

"Don't go," Lonnie said, reaching for her hand. "I need you here to help me get started."

"I'm not going to Lexington. The track team's better at Murray than U.K. anyway. It's more personal." Sam had been accepted at both the University of Kentucky and Murray State University, and Murray was nearby. She hoped to commute.

Emmett gave Sam a can of beer. "Go ahead and drink it. I won't tell on you. It'll give you carbohydrates so you can run tomorrow."

Sam sipped the beer. It didn't taste as bad as it smelled. She and Lonnie were sitting close to each other on the couch. Sam's bare legs brushed against Lonnie's jeans and made her feel a stir of desire. The couch was fuzzy and scratched her legs. Emmett had bought the couch at a yard sale. Emmett did most of his shopping at yard sales. All their stuff was junk. She felt empty and disappointed. Lonnie didn't have a job, and he wasn't going to college. Sam had worked at the Burger Boy after school for two years, but in March she had quit so she could have more time to study. She had been promised her old job back in the fall.

Emmett took the muffelatas from the oven and transferred them to melamine plates that Sam's mother had left behind. She had taken her good dishes. He brought the muffelatas in to Sam and Lonnie.

"Thanks, Emmett," said Lonnie. "This is what I call service." He stubbed out his cigarette in Emmett's Kentucky Lake ashtray.

"Don't mean nothing," said Emmett.

Sam didn't really like the taste of beer, but the muffelata was delicious. Emmett knew how to make muffelatas just right, with lots of olives and onions. Irene never made muffelatas.

"I don't think that storm's coming," Emmett said when he brought in his own plate.

"What's on HBO tonight?" asked Lonnie. "This MTV crap is too weird."

Billy Joel was singing "Uptown Girl." He was in a garage mechanic's coveralls, lusting after Christie Brinkley. Sam said,

"HBO is pukey tonight—*Humanoids from the Deep*. But there's an R-rated movie on Cinemax at midnight."

"Oh, good!" Lonnie's parents wouldn't get cable because of all the R-rated movies. Two weeks ago, someone had blown up the cable man's mailbox with a cherry bomb.

Emmett punched the buttons on the selector box. Surfers rode by, then policemen. He settled on Johnny Carson and sat down with his plate, scooting the cat to one side. His skirt fell on the cat, but Moon Pie didn't budge. He was black with white armpits and a big saucer face. Emmett was so crazy about the cat he even slept with him. Moon Pie always woke him up at 4 A.M., and Emmett would get up and feed him, but lately Emmett had been keeping a packet of Tender Vittles under his pillow and a bowl beside the bed so he could feed Moon Pie practically in his sleep.

"How do you know *Humanoids from the Deep* is no good?" said Lonnie.

"*Hemorrhoids* from the Deep," said Sam. "I've seen it and it stinks. Oh, look at Johnny's suit!" she cried, pointing. Johnny Carson's suit made rainbows under the TV lights—soft, glistening colors like those in a puddle of oil. The colors reminded Sam of the Jupiterscope her mother had sent her for her birthday last year. She had bought it in a museum in Cincinnati. The Jupiterscope was a circle of plastic, like a large soft contact lens, that turned scenery into shimmering colors when you looked through it. It was a silly present.

Lonnie laughed. "Hey, can you imagine Johnny Carson wearing a skirt?" he said. "I dare you to wear that skirt out in public, Emmett."

"It's healthier for a man to wear a skirt," Emmett said solemnly. "He's not all cramped up and stuff."

Sam said to Lonnie, "It makes me so mad about that rash on his face. He won't see about it."

"What's wrong with your face, Emmett? I wasn't going to mention it."

"It's just adolescence. Haven't you noticed how my voice is changing?" Emmett spoke deliberately in an unnaturally squeaky voice.

"Be serious," said Sam. "You've got Agent Orange. Those pimples are exactly how they described them on the news." Agent Orange terrified her. It had been in the news so much lately.

"I wasn't exposed to Agent Orange," Emmett said.

"You might have been around it and not known it."

"Maybe you could get some money out of the government, Emmett," Lonnie said. "Then you could pay them back what you owe."

"What would be the point of that? A lot of rigamarole and we'd end up where we started. So let 'em keep the money to begin with." Emmett touched his face. "This ain't nothing," he said. He shrugged, then cocked his head. Thunder. "Socrates wore a toga," he said, petting Moon Pie. "All them Greeks and Romans wore dresses."

Sam laughed. "Are you going to wear it to McDonald's in the morning, Emmett?" Emmett always had breakfast at McDonald's with his friends.

"I don't want anybody to get any wrong ideas."

Sam and Lonnie laughed. "What would they think, Emmett?" said Lonnie.

They knew what people thought. There were a lot of stories floating around about Emmett. Emmett was the leading dope dealer in town. Emmett slept with his niece. Emmett lived off his sister. Emmett seduced high school girls. He had killed babies in Vietnam. But he was popular, and Emmett didn't care what some people said.

Ed McMahon blasted out one of his phony belly laughs, and then a loud thunderclap made the light flicker. Emmett suddenly bent over and clutched his chest.

"What's wrong, Emmett?" Lonnie asked.

Emmett was grimacing with pain.

"You've got heartburns again," Sam said. "It's those tacos you ate at supper." Sam explained to Lonnie, "He's been getting gas. I told him not to eat tacos with hot-stuff. It always makes him belch."

"I guess so," Emmett said, straightening up and shaking his shoulders. Thunder crashed again, and Emmett cringed. Sam was scared. She had never had heartburns herself, and she didn't know if heart attacks were related.

"Are you all right, Emmett?" asked Lonnie. "Don't you go kicking the bucket without making out your will first."

"It's all right," Emmett said. "It went away."

Emmett looked stately in his skirt—tall and broad, like a middle-aged woman who had had several children. Sam and Lonnie sat on the couch with their hands on each other's thighs while Emmett cautiously sat down in the vinyl chair, fluffing up his skirt to let air flood his legs.

"We'll be right back," said Johnny.

2

The storm broke soon after that and they raced around, unplugging appliances. During the storm, Emmett huddled on the stairs with Moon Pie. The rain was so hard the water rushed across the yard from the downspouts. The basement was probably flooding again.

In the hallway, in the dark, Lonnie grabbed Sam and held her close to him. "Are you disappointed in me?" he asked, after they kissed.

"I thought you liked Kroger's. You liked that job better than you liked working at Shumley's." Shumley's was the large farm-equipment plant where Lonnie had been a trainee after school during the winter. Lonnie had to buy expensive safety shoes for the job, but then he had been laid off. Now he had no use for the safety shoes, which had hard, bulbous toes.

"Kroger's was a dead end," Lonnie said. "It was boring, and I goofed off. I'd put all the cans in one sack just for meanness."

"I'm not disappointed in you. But I'm disappointed."

"Maybe I could apply at Ingersoll-Rand."

"They're not hiring."

"Mama and Daddy will have a fit, though." They had wanted

Lonnie to go to vocational school to learn a trade, but Lonnie didn't know what he wanted to do, now that he couldn't play basketball. He was famous for sinking ten out of twelve jump shots in a winning game against Hopewell's biggest rivals, the Bingley Bulldogs. People in Hopewell still talked fondly about how Lonnie had done that.

The lightning and the thunder coincided then. The storm was right there, over the house. Sam stood in the hall, clutching Lonnie. In the flash of lightning, she saw Emmett on the stairway, smoking a cigarette. They stayed there in the dark for a long time, and then abruptly the wash of rain let up and the lightning was just a flicker.

After the storm died down, Lonnie kissed Sam and said, "I know what I'm going to do now."

"What?"

"Get drunk."

In the dark, he took a beer from the refrigerator and opened it. "Hey, Emmett," Lonnie said. "The storm's let up. Let's go somewhere."

"It's almost time for the eleven-thirty *M*A*S*H*," Emmett said. He was smoking another cigarette. He and Moon Pie were on the couch now.

"Couldn't you skip one?" said Lonnie.

"But this is my special outfit for watching *M*A*S*H* in," Emmett said, flipping the hem of his skirt. "I miss *M*A*S*H*. I've been homesick for it since the series ended. *AfterMash* just ain't the same."

"They couldn't fight the Korean War forever, Emmett," said Lonnie.

Emmett grabbed his cigarettes from the end table and stuck them in his skirt pocket. "Let's go, then. Where to? The Bottom?"

"I've already been there once tonight," said Lonnie. "We could drive around and see if the storm wrecked anything."

"I know where let's go," Emmett said, taking the last beer from the refrigerator. "Let's go to Cawood's Pond."

"Are you serious, Emmett?" cried Lonnie. "I thought that place spooked you."

Cawood's Pond was Sam and Lonnie's favorite place to go parking. It wasn't really a pond but a snake-infested swamp with sinkholes. Sam had even heard there were alligators there. Emmett used to go there when he was a boy, but he stopped going. Sam was surprised that he suggested it.

"I ain't scared," said Emmett. "Let's go. I might even have some sweet stuff around here somewhere." He took a cocoa-mix can from a kitchen cabinet. "Ah-ha!" he said, looking inside.

Emmett found a sweatshirt and sniffed the armpits before pulling it over his head. He touched his face. He had one pimple about to pop.

"Let's go to the pond!" he cried. "Don't let Moon Pie out," he said as they left the house. "At night is when cats get run over. Headlights confuse them." Emmett was still wearing the skirt. He was so large he looked ridiculous in it. Sam had to laugh.

The street lights were shining in new puddles. Sam soaked both running shoes. She felt drunk on that beer. She lay down on the mattress in the back of Lonnie's van, and Lonnie and Emmett sat up front. She bounced along on the mattress, feeling like a soldier in an armored personnel carrier because she couldn't see where they were going. Emmett had once told her how claustrophobic those vehicles were, with a dozen guys packed together on benches, their rifles poking each other, and one guy in a tiny cubbyhole driving, with only a periscope to see his way. It was like being in a submarine, Emmett had said.

"There's a bulldozer over yonder," Emmett said when they reached the gravel road that led to the pond. "They're draining the swamp and rerouting the creek. The biologists are going crazy. They say it'll starve out the snakes, and birds won't land."

"I can do without the snakes," said Sam.

Cawood's Pond was named for a notorious outlaw, Andrew Cawood, who had once hidden out here and was believed to have fallen into a sinkhole. The university biologists had cleared a place for cars to park and built a boardwalk that looped out over the swamp. Sam and Lonnie had spent the night out here in the van a couple of times.

"The insects are having a conversation," said Emmett. "They're talking about me. I know 'cause my ears are burning."

"They're saying, 'Who's that weirdo in the skirt?'" Lonnie teased.

When Lonnie turned the lights off, and they sat there in the silence, they saw how the swampy woods made a black rim around the graveled clearing.

Emmett and Lonnie climbed over the seat of the van and sat down in back with Sam. Emmett pulled his sweet stuff from his cigarette pack. He lit a joint and passed it to Lonnie. The night was pleasant after the rain, and now and then a little breeze stirred and they could hear drops of water shaking from the leaves of the trees.

"Where are all the birds, Emmett?" Sam asked.

"They sleep at night. Except owls."

"Where do birds sleep, Emmett?" asked Lonnie, with a giggle.

"In bird beds."

"Hey, tell about that bird you're always looking for," Sam said. "Maybe there's one here right now."

"You couldn't see it at night."

"If it's white, wouldn't it look like a ghost?"

"What kind of bird is it?" Lonnie asked.

Emmett hesitated before answering. "An egret."

"What are egrets like?" Sam asked. "Are you sure they're around here?"

Emmett drank some beer. "I believe egrets are the state bird of Florida." He took the joint Lonnie passed him and puffed it.

Sam said to Lonnie, "This was a bird he used to see in Vietnam."

"Really?"

Emmett exhaled slowly. "Yeah. You'd see it in the rice paddies, dipping its head down in the water, feeling around for things to eat. It's a wader."

"They might be here, then," Lonnie said. "In a swamp like this."

"Why do you want to see that bird so bad?" Sam asked cautiously.

"It was so pretty. It was the prettiest bird I ever saw, all white and long-legged." Emmett worked at the tab on the beer can. "They're like cowbirds, but cowbirds aren't pretty. Sometimes you'd see these water buffalo and every one of them would have one of these birds sitting beside it, like a little pet."

"Why did they do that?" Lonnie asked.

"The bird would eat things the buffalo turned up, and it would pick ticks off the buffalo's head. Sometimes you'd see the bird setting on the buffalo's back. He didn't care."

"Won't it bring back bad memories if you see a bird like that again?" Sam asked.

"No. That was a good memory. The only fucking one. That beautiful bird just going about its business with all that crazy stuff going on around it. Whole flocks of them would fly over. They fold their long necks up when they fly." Emmett rolled the beer can in his palms, and the aluminum crinkled. He said, "Once a grenade hit close to some trees and there were these birds taking off like quail, ever' which way. We thought it was snowing up instead of down."

"Did you see a lot of action like that over there?" Lonnie asked.

"Some. I nearly got my ass killed once or twice."

"How?"

"Oh, you don't want to know."

Sam passed Lonnie the joint. She exhaled and coughed. She could almost see that bird. She felt peaceful, but her head was spinning with thoughts about Emmett. He hadn't said this much about Vietnam in years. Watching *M*A*S*H* so much must be bringing it out, she thought. Emmett used to have a girlfriend, Anita Stevens, but he had broken up with her at Christmas. He never said why. He took her out for Shrimp Night at the Holiday Inn and gave her a fancy cheese basket from the Party Mart in Paducah. Anita playfully called it her Easter basket and asked

Emmett where the sweet stuff was. The basket had so much cheese and salami in it she probably still had some in her refrigerator.

"Hey, Emmett," Sam blurted out. "I wish we had Anita with us. Why don't you call her up?"

"Sure. Hand me the phone."

"I'm serious. Why don't you call her up tomorrow?"

"Anita doesn't want a bird-watcher in a skirt," Emmett said flatly.

"Well, don't wear a skirt then," Sam said.

Emmett mumbled something. He sat propped against the spare tire in the back of the van. The glow from his cigarette reminded Sam of Mars, the way it popped out in the summer sky, burning bright orange, seeming to move toward the earth.

Lonnie turned on the radio, and Bruce Springsteen yelled out, "I'm a cool rocking Daddy in the U.S.A.!" It was from his new album. For a while, they sang along with the songs on the university FM station, Rock-95. Sam watched the moon inch from behind the broken clouds. The night was clearing, and the radio was playing "Ain't Gonna Bump No More with No Big Fat Woman," a song Emmett loved. Anita wasn't a big fat woman. She was pretty, and Sam was sure Anita still cared about Emmett. Sam felt Lonnie pulling at her, wanting to smooch with her, but her mind was whirling around in the darkness and she couldn't catch it.

Emmett and Lonnie went outside, and Sam lost track of time. Maybe she dozed off. She felt afraid. With the moon out, this was a perfect setting for a horror movie. Gradually, she became aware of a familiar yet strange sound on the radio. It was a song by the Beatles, but it was not a song she knew. Sam thought she knew every one of their songs, because her mother owned all their records. She had left them with Sam when she moved to Lexington. "You better leave my kitten all alone," they were singing. How could the Beatles have a new record, she wondered groggily.

"We've got to be quiet," Emmett muttered when he and Lonnie returned to the van. "Lonnie, keep your cigarette inside your hand. Don't show it."

"Take it easy, Emmett. It's all right." Lonnie climbed in the driver's seat and turned the key.

"Jesus fucking Christ, Lonnie!" said Emmett in a loud, hot whisper. "Be quiet! And don't turn your lights on. Cut that engine! Let's coast down to Highway 1."

"No sweat, Emmett. Just hold tight."

"What did you see, Emmett?" asked Sam, reaching to touch his shoulder.

"Don't do that!" Emmett cried, jerking away from her.

"He just got spooked," Lonnie said, backing out of the clearing. "It wasn't anything."

"Oh, shit," Sam said. "Are you O.K., Emmett?"

Emmett mumbled. "Hurry," he said. "I can't stand this."

"We're going home, Emmett," said Lonnie as they bumped across the gravel in the moonlight. "Keep your skirt on."

3

"Ow, that hurts!"

"Sorry. Hold still just a minute, Sam," Dawn said. "Let me hold that ice on your ear a minute longer. I must not have it numb enough."

Dawn held the plastic bag of crushed ice on Sam's ear lobe.

"If I get frostbite and my ear rots off, I'll sue you."

"Hold still. They wouldn't do this for you at the shopping center," Dawn said. "They'd just drive that post right through your ear without any deadening. There! I got you by surprise, didn't I?"

"It didn't really hurt that much. It was O.K." Sam shivered. Her ear was stinging.

Her friend Dawn Goodwin had pierced Sam's ears last year, and now she was making another set of holes so Sam could wear two pairs of earrings. Dawn had four holes in each ear. Her earrings made an outline of her ear lobe, like studs on a belt. Sam and Lonnie used to run around with Dawn and Dawn's boyfriend Scott before she split up with Scott and started going with Ken Williamson. Lonnie and Ken didn't get along, so they didn't double-date much. Dawn was very pretty, but she always insisted Sam was prettier. Sam didn't think so—her face was too round and she had buckteeth, sort of.

"They won't do the fourth one at the shopping center," Dawn said. "They're afraid of getting into cartilage. You can't even get a nurse at the hospital to do it. But I'm lucky to have plenty of flesh there. The only time I got infected was the first time, when I had it done at the shopping center. But I didn't dab alcohol on three times a day like you're supposed to. How's that other one feel?"

"O.K." Sam was relieved that the other needle had gone in so easily. "My ears are blood red," she said, giggling at herself in the mirror. Her round face was like Emmett's and Irene's. Her hair was short, the color of penny loafers.

"You've got big lobes," Dawn said. "You could handle four holes easy."

Dawn lived in a creaky old house, shabbier than Sam's house, but Dawn had a large bedroom with delicate gold-and-blue flowered wallpaper and a skirt on her dressing table.

"Now, if you do it right, there won't be any trouble," Dawn said. "Keep those posts in and dab them with alcohol three times a day for two weeks. And don't forget to turn the studs."

"I'm going to wear one long and one short," Sam said, admiring her ears in the mirror. "I've got some swords two inches long I'll wear in the bottom hole, and I'll put little stars in the new holes."

Dawn had on hearts, diamonds, spades, and clubs of different sizes and styles. The spades were black enamel, and the clubs were long, dangling rhinestones. The diamonds were gold wire, and the hearts were tiny studs. Dawn had such an original earring collection. She had about fifty pairs, silver and gold and cloisonné. Sam liked Dawn's earrings.

Dawn said, "What's really fun is to take some old beads and string them so they're about three-inch loops or strings and wear them. They sort of blend with your hair, and you can even chew on them if you feel like it. Here, let me give you these earrings I got at the crafts fair at the lake last year. They're made out of horseshoe nails." She plucked the earrings from her jewelry box. "I used to love these, but I'm bored with them now." She laughed. "I get bored easy, so when I get bored I just stick another needle in my ear."

"Oh, thanks." Sam tucked the earrings in her purse.

"You remember that boy that got thrown out of school for wearing that sleeveless T-shirt?"

"Yeah." Sam laughed. "It was too punk for Hopewell."

"I heard he had his nipple pierced, and he wears a little gold circle in it."

"Ouch!"

"I don't like that guy. He's a real space cadet. He was toking behind the Burger Boy and he starts coming on to me. I don't even know what that *means*. I was sure he was gay. I know I'm bad, but he's weird." Together, they looked at their faces in the mirror and giggled. Dawn was taller than Sam. "We're the baddest girls in Hopewell."

"My uncle lets me do anything I want to. He doesn't even care if I sleep with Lonnie. Lonnie stayed over three nights since he quit his job."

"Daddy would kill me if he knew I did anything like that." Dawn tossed the sodden cotton balls in the wastebasket. "Come on, I've got to clean up the kitchen before he comes home. If it's still a mess when he gets back, he'll give me a lot of shit. But if I'm not here, he'll think it's my day to work."

Dawn worked at the Burger Boy. Sam was looking forward to going back to work there, so she could be around Dawn. Dawn's father operated a dough machine at the cookie factory, and her mother was dead. Only one of her four brothers still lived at home. Both Sam and Dawn lived with no other women in the house. It was unusual, they realized. It gave them some kind of independence, but Dawn was much more domestic than Sam, and she was a good cook.

Downstairs, while they washed dishes, Sam confided her worries about Emmett's pimples. Dawn was shocked. "Girl! You don't mean it!" She had never heard of Agent Orange. "You mean it could turn up after all these years?"

"It causes all kinds of problems. I read about it in a library book. If these guys were exposed and they have kids, their kids have birth defects."

"Maybe that's why your uncle never married. Maybe he knew all along what would happen after Vietnam."

"Maybe. But they didn't figure out what Agent Orange could do until not long ago." Sam dried the glasses. All the glasses were giveaways from fast-food places.

Dawn said, "My cousin was in Vietnam, but you'd never know it. He's just like anybody else. He does shift work at Union Carbide. What can you do about this orange stuff?"

"I don't know. Emmett's got a pain in his head that scares me. Every now and then you see him jerk and twitch his forehead, and you know that pain's passing through. It's not enough to take an aspirin. It's sort of like having a hangnail, but I'm afraid it could be a brain tumor."

Dawn attacked a skillet with a rusty patch of Brillo. "I knew a boy who had a brain tumor," she said. "It was in Bowling Green, where my aunt lives and I spent the summer once. This boy used to come to the swimming pool, and he was cute. It killed me what happened to him. And I knew this other boy who *said* he had a brain tumor and only had two years to live. But he was lying. He was trying to impress me."

"Which do you think would be worse—to die from a brain tumor or be killed in a war?"

Dawn kept scrubbing the skillet, in thought. "I don't know. Sometimes I think it must be better to die all of a sudden. My mom just lingered on, and they said it was awful. I was too little to remember."

When she finished the skillet, Dawn took a quart of Coke from the refrigerator and got out some ice. Dawn's refrigerator was small and old-fashioned, with one of those freezers that didn't have a separate door. In the living room, they drank the Cokes, and Sam flipped through some old records Dawn's brothers had left—Willie Nelson, Christopher Cross, Elton John, singers Sam hated.

"I wish I could buy that new Springsteen album," Sam said. "But I have to save all my money for a car."

"I hear that on the radio all the time at the Burger Boy."

"Did you know the title song's about a vet?"

"'Born in the U.S.A.'?"

"Yeah. In the song, his brother gets killed over there, and then the guy gets in a lot of trouble when he gets back home. He can't get a job, and he ends up in jail. It's a great song."

"I like the one about the car wash—where it rains all the time and he lost his job and his girlfriend. That's the saddest song. That song really scares me." Dawn shuddered and rattled ice in her glass. "My brother took all my records," she said. "He stole the stereo I had in my room, and my radio blew up."

"I've been listening to my mother's old records," said Sam. "She's off in Lexington having a good time, and she doesn't seem worried about Emmett. That really gripes my soul."

"Do you still miss your mother?"

Sam fingered the new studs in her ears. "Yeah. I remember on Saturday nights, years ago, we used to watch TV. She'd pop popcorn and her and Emmett and me would watch about three hours of comedy shows, one right after the other. First there was *All in the Family*, then *M*A*S*H*, then Mary Tyler Moore, then Bob Newhart, and after that Carol Burnett was on for an hour. It was incredible. But the shows changed, and then when Lorenzo Jones started coming over a couple of years ago he'd talk when we tried to watch television together. He'd talk during the news too and tell his opinion on world affairs so you couldn't hear the news."

"I've got a brother like that."

"I wish you and me could do something real wild," Sam said. "We could go get jobs in Florida or somewhere and go to the beach every day. Wouldn't that be fun? We could work at Disney World."

"Lonnie and Ken would like that a lot if we went off and left them!"

"What I want is money," Sam said. "I need an awful lot of money."

"Well, you won't get it at the Burger Boy."

"I can't figure out what to do!" Sam cried. "I could go to U.K. But Emmett's depending on me, and then there's Lonnie. I think he wants to get married when he gets a job."

"And have babies."

"Not with the pill. You know, when Mom got pregnant last year, she ran me right off to the doctor and got birth-control pills for me. She didn't even ask me."

"Aren't you afraid to take those things?" asked Dawn. "I'd be afraid of side effects."

"I don't care. Having a baby would be a pretty big side effect." She giggled and touched her stomach. "A front effect!"

She flung the ice from her glass into the kitchen sink and washed out the glass.

"Do you want to marry Lonnie?" Dawn asked.

"I don't know," Sam said slowly. "I'm just in this situation, and Lonnie's not my main thought right now." She picked a wadded paper towel up from the floor. "He's so sweet to me. It would just kill him if we broke up."

"Lonnie is a hunk and a half," Dawn said. "If you married him, your name would be Sam Malone, like that guy on *Cheers*."

"Yeah. I used to think that would be terrific, but now I'm not so sure."

Dawn wiped the counter with the dishrag. She said, "You know what I wish we could do? I wish my brother would let us borrow his car so we could go hang out at one of those bars in Paducah where those traveling businessmen go. We could wear our sexiest outfits and they'd think we were a lot older. Maybe they'd buy us something to eat and give us some money."

"I'd be satisfied if we could just go to the mall in Paducah."

"Yeah. This town is dead without a mall," Dawn said, wringing out the dishrag.

4

When Sam got home from Dawn's, Emmett was digging a hole alongside the house. He was shoveling dirt furiously, heaping it on the grass.

"What are you doing?"

"I'm trying to find where that leak's coming from, and I've got to expose the foundation under the kitchen."

Emmett's T-shirt was sweaty, and his face was red. Next door, Mrs. Biggs, a widow living on social security, was watching him suspiciously from her porch. Mrs. Biggs lived in terror that Jesse Jackson might be elected President.

When Emmett saw Sam's ears, he said, "Daddy used to tag cattle that way."

"I might put a ring through my nipple next," she said.

Mrs. Biggs plunged through an opening in the box hedge. "Are you digging to China?" she chirped. She was a tiny woman, with white hair in finger waves.

"What I'm doing is excavating," Emmett explained to Mrs. Biggs. "It's noble work. The Egyptians and the Romans were all great excavators, as well as great builders. It's a grand tradition."

"Your cat messed in my petunias again," said Mrs. Biggs.

"That's good fertilizer, Mrs. Biggs. Moon Pie's got high-quality fertilizer." Emmett grunted with the effort of his digging. "The Egyptians worshipped cats too. The two things go together—respect for cats and earthwork." He tipped his Pepsi cap at her politely.

Emmett kept working till dark, taking time out only to eat some pizza Lonnie brought over. He seemed obsessed. He spaded the hard clay, and when he hit rocks he gouged them out with a pickax. Sam had never seen him work so hard. He sweated and cussed at the rocks. Sometimes he would pause and touch his temple for a moment, waiting for the sensation to pass. It was as though he were listening to some inner music. While he worked, he listened to Rock-95 on the Walkman. He said he had not heard the new Beatles song, and Sam had not heard it again either. Emmett insisted she must have been mistaken. When she questioned him about his momentary freak-out that night at Cawood's Pond, he said nonchalantly, "I'm just a wild and crazy guy." Sam had been thinking that she should encourage him to talk more about the war, the way he used to when she was little. That was before he calmed down and settled into his routines. It would be good for him to talk about it more, she told Lonnie—the way Dr. Sidney Freedman on *M*A*S*H* got his patients to talk out their anxieties. But she knew very well that on TV, people always had the words to express their feelings, while in real life hardly anyone ever did. On TV, they had script writers.

The next day, at dawn, Emmett was outside digging again. He even skipped his breakfast at McDonald's. Sam went running, and when she returned, Emmett's father, Sam's granddad, was there watching him. He had come over to get Emmett to help him haul some calves, but Emmett made excuses. Emmett and his father had had a falling out a couple of years before over some soybeans he had wanted Emmett to go halves on.

"When are you going to get a job like everybody else and stop fooling around?" Granddad Smith muttered.

"Ain't nothing worth doing," Emmett said, flinging dirt at Granddad's feet. "Most jobs are stupid. They just use up the earth's resources. Plunder the planet. How's Mama?" he asked, changing the subject.

"She's after me, wanting to go to Florida."

"You ought to go. Did the wind get you the other night?"

"No. It just stormed hard. It blowed down a dead tree along the fence line, and our dog lost his mind. We'll have to shoot him, I reckon."

"Buster?"

"No. Rusty—that bench-legged fice I traded for last year. He's real high-strung." Granddad nodded at Sam. "Sam, you come on out to the house and we'll feed you. You need a little fattening up."

"I would if I had a car," Sam said.

"We'll come and get you. Your grandma will cook you some country ham and damson pie. And we won't let Emmett have any."

"Not if you're going to shoot your dog."

"Well, I guess we won't do that. But he never did have a lick of sense."

Sam had seen a bumper sticker in town: SPRAYED AND BETRAYED. When she told Emmett, he grunted and kept digging. He had Clearasil on his face. She realized that not every soldier who came back from Vietnam was as weird as Emmett. She knew of veterans—relatives of classmates—who had adjusted perfectly well. They had nice houses and wives and kids. They didn't wear skirts, even for a joke, and they didn't refuse to get a job or buy a car. Allen Wilkins was one of them. He owned a menswear store and coached Little League. His daughter was a teen model in a Glamor Barn TV ad on Channel 6. Sam wondered if it was just her own crazy family rather than Vietnam.

The next morning, she decided to go along with Emmett to McDonald's instead of taking her usual run. She was curious about the veterans he hung around with. She had known them for years but had never thought much about them as vets.

At McDonald's, Emmett's buddies weren't there yet. A small bald man who worked with Lonnie's father at the hardware store stopped at their booth and teased Emmett about his "new girlfriend." He meant Sam.

"She keeps me in line," Emmett said, elbowing Sam.

"Emmett, I heard they're hiring at the cookie factory," the man said.

"Fuck the cookie factory," Emmett said, with his mouth full of Egg McMuffin.

The man winked at Sam. "Do you let him use that language at home, Sam?"

She shrugged. "It's on HBO."

"Does he let you watch HBO?"

"He don't care," she said, irritated.

"If I had HBO, I wouldn't let my wife watch it."

"Don't pay no attention to him, Sam," Emmett said as the man walked away. "He's got shit for brains."

Pete Simms and Tom Hudson joined them then. They had

Cokes and little apple pies. Pete worked on a highway crew, and Tom was an auto mechanic with his own body shop. Sam knew Tom had been wounded in the war, but she couldn't tell, except that his posture was a little stiff. He sat down beside Emmett.

"Do you care if I set next to you, Sam?" asked Pete. "I won't bite."

"I'll let you set here if you show me your tattoo," Sam said impulsively. Emmett had once told her about Pete's tattoo. When Pete was in Vietnam, he had had a map of the Jackson Purchase region of western Kentucky tattooed on his chest.

"You want me to show you right here?" Pete asked flirtatiously. "I might get arrested. Come on out to my truck and I'll show you."

"What kind of truck you got?"

"A Ford Ranger. Why?"

"I need a car," Sam said.

"You need a hole in the head," said Emmett.

"I wonder if anybody ever tattooed his own face on his chest," Sam said. "Like a face on a T-shirt."

"I tell you one thing," Pete said. "I wish I had a goddamn T-shirt with this map on it instead of having it on my chest." He ate a bite of apple pie. "Ow! That's hot! Emmett, how come this long-legged little niece of yours is here? What's her trouble?"

"She's got ants in her pants," said Emmett.

"*He*'s got Agent Orange," said Sam. "Look at his face."

"*I* got Agent Orange," said Pete jokingly. "In the head." He laughed and blew on his pie. "I had a place come on my leg, all brown and funny? But it went away. Reckon it ate on down to the bone?"

"Nothing can hurt you, Pete," said Tom. "You're like that guy on TV that ate a bicycle."

"That was on *That's Incredible*," said Sam. "I saw that."

"Don't you know that was bound to mess that guy up?" Pete said with a grin.

"Did either one of you get sprayed with Agent Orange?" Sam asked pointblank.

Pete and Tom sucked their Coke straws simultaneously.

"I don't think so," Tom said slowly. He tapped a cigarette from a wrinkled pack.

Emmett snapped his Egg McMuffin box shut. "Sam's got Nam on the brain," he said. "She's been reading a bunch of history books and pestering me."

"What do those books tell you, Sam?" asked Tom, staring at her.

"Nothing. They're just dull history books." She was embarrassed. The books didn't say what it was like to be at war over there. The books didn't even have pictures.

Pete said, "Hell, I remember when they used to spray it. They'd tell us to get inside because they were going to spray, but it wasn't any big deal. It smelled sweet. It smelled like oranges."

"Buddy Mangrum can't even drink half a beer without getting sick," Tom said. "They say that's Agent Orange."

There was a racket in the back of McDonald's. A kid's birthday party was beginning. Sam tried to imagine these men fighting in the jungle. She had never been able to picture Emmett with a gun, but Granddad had talked offhandedly about shooting the dog. Emmett had told her Granddad wasn't serious.

"I think my problem's I might be allergic to fleas," Emmett said with a shiver. "My cat's got fleas. And he sleeps right on my head."

"If I had a car, I'd take you to the V.A.," Sam said. "I'd march you right in there and show them your face. Boy, I'd give anything for a car."

"Tom's got a car he wants to sell," Pete said.

"That bug? Yeah, I'll sell you my VW bug." Tom and Pete looked at each other and laughed. "I'll have to fix it up some, but you can have it for six thousand dollars."

Pete laughed. "Don't let him rip you off, Sam. It's a seventy-*three*."

"I'll give you a bargain," Tom said. "You can have it for six hundred. It runs good. I just have to fix it up a little."

"I don't have that much." She had three hundred dollars in the bank, but she had to live on it for the summer.

"You can come and see it."

Tom was looking straight into her eyes, and she looked away, punching her straw in her drink. Something about him excited her, but she didn't know what it was. He looked at her as though he really wanted her to have that car. She knew her face must be red.

Emmett flattened his Egg McMuffin box and went to the men's room.

"Do you want to see my tattoo, Sam?" Pete said with a wink.

"Sure."

"That's my street," Pete said, lifting his T-shirt and pointing to his chest. "And that little red thing that looks like a ladybug is my old Corvette. My wife sold it while I was gone. It would be a classic now."

Hairs sprouted from the heart of the Jackson Purchase. The tattoo was the size of a *National Geographic*, outlined in blue, with the towns in red.

He said, "I look at it upside down, and in the mirror it's backwards. This was maybe the stupidest thing I ever did in my life." He laughed.

Tom laughed with him. "When you're that age, you do some of the stupidest things you could ever think of, and you think, Oh, wow, ain't this the funniest thing in the world!" He shrugged. He wasn't bad-looking, Sam thought. He was about Emmett's age.

"You think about that car, Sam," Tom said when he left. "Come over and see it if you want to."

On the way home, Sam asked Emmett, "Are your friends always that goofy?"

"They just like to have fun. They're good guys."

"I wish I had that Volkswagen," she said. Her mother used to have one, and Sam had learned to drive on it.

"I don't think you can buy a car. You're underage."

"I could if you sign for me."

"Since I'm so responsible and have so much money? Yeah, anybody suing me would strike it rich!"

"Would you sign for me if I bought a car?"

"You get the money first and ask me again."

Sam saw a blue Volkswagen Beetle down the street, in front of a funeral parlor. She wouldn't mind having a VW bug.

Sam suddenly remembered something she had heard about Pete. Cautiously, she asked, "Hey, Emmett, is it true that Pete chased his wife out of the house once with a shotgun?"

"No, she was chasing him. He was out in the yard shooting—not at her. He was just shooting. Cindy wouldn't put up with his foolishness, though. She told him he had to quit it or she was walking."

"What was Pete shooting at?"

They crossed the street before he would answer. On the corner was the dental clinic where her mother used to be a receptionist. Sam asked him again, "What was Pete shooting at?"

"He said it was just an urge that come over him, and he got rid of it by going out and shooting off his gun."

When they were a block from the house, Emmett said suddenly, "He had a map of Vietnam in the den, and his wife tore it down because it didn't fit her decorating scheme. It sounds crazy, but I think he'd rather be back in Nam."

"Did you ever wish that?"

"No. Hell, no! Are you kidding?"

At the corner of their block, Emmett paused to look at something off in the field down by the waterworks, perhaps a bird, but he seemed to be listening for something, and Sam thought of the way Radar O'Reilly on *M*A*S*H* could always hear the choppers coming in with wounded before anyone else could.

Emmett could look at anything—a rosebush, a stop sign, an ordinary bird, or even a circular from Kroger's—and get absorbed in it as though it were the most fascinating thing on earth. That was how he was so good at *Pac-Man*, and it was the way he watched his birds, stalking them and probably imagining a full-feathered bird based on nothing more than a glimpse of wing, a bright patch of crest or throat. Emmett reminded Sam of James Stewart in *Harvey*, an old movie they had seen on Channel 7's Midnight Theatre. Harvey was an imaginary rabbit who went everywhere with James Stewart. Sometimes it seemed that Emmett had somebody invisible along with him, too, some presence that guided him. But it probably wasn't a rabbit. It was probably a cat.

When Sam was seven or eight, she and Emmett had a stamp collection. They spent hours together poring over cellophane packets of exotic stamps sent on trial each month from stamp companies. Their stamp album was old and the countries were wrong—old colonial countries like Ceylon and the Belgian Congo. Vietnam was Indochine. While they played with the stamps, Emmett told Sam war stories, sprinkled with M-60s and grenade launchers and C-130 transport planes, and Sam's favorite—the amtrac, which Emmett laughingly described as a "yellow submarine." Sam had a picture of Vietnam in her mind from Emmett's stories—a pleasant countryside, something like Florida, with beaches and palm trees and watery fields of rice and green mountains. The sky was crowded with wonderful aircraft—C-47s with Gatling guns, Hueys, Chinooks, Skytrains, Bird Dogs. Emmett even made plastic models of helicopters and jet fighters, and he used them to act out his stories.

Irene stopped the stories. It upset her to be reminded of the war, but the reality of it didn't register on Sam until one day soon after they got their first color TV set. She was eight or nine. On the evening news, a report from Vietnam—it was during the fall of Saigon, in 1975, she thought—showed some people walking along a road with bundles on their backs. Some were carrying babies in their arms. Army jeeps chugged along the road. The landscape was believable—a hill in the distance, a paved road with narrow dirt shoulders, a field with something green planted in rows. The road resembled the old Hopewell road that twisted through the bottomland toward Paducah. For the first time, Vietnam was an actual place. As Sam watched, a child in a T-shirt and no pants ran down the road, and its mother called after it, scolding it.

5

Sam heard the new Beatles song on the radio again, while she was having Cokes with Lonnie and Dawn at the Burger Boy. It really was the Beatles—a previously unreleased cut from 1964, the D.J. said. Hearing it was eerie, like voices from the grave.

Sam sat there dazed, trying to grasp the words, while Lonnie and Dawn chattered about the construction work he was doing for his uncle. They didn't notice how far away she was. "You better leave my kitten all alone," the song went. It was great. Hearing it, Sam felt the energy of the sixties, like desire building and exploding. But there was something playful in the song, as if back then were a much better time to be young than now. Her mother knew somebody who had been to a Beatles concert in 1966.

Sam told Emmett about the song when she got home, and he still couldn't believe it. "Irene will flip out when she hears it," he said.

He was in the kitchen making tacos. He was mincing onions, making tiny crosshatches and then slicing off the bits. "Where's Lonnie?" he asked.

"Working on that house with his uncle."

"Is he coming over for supper?"

"No. His mother's having chicken and dumplings tonight."

Emmett zipped open a box of taco shells and placed six of them in a pan. He set them in the oven. He did all this with careful concentration, as if he expected to see them turn into something wonderful in the oven.

"Your mama called again," he said.

Sam took an orange Popsicle from the freezer compartment of the refrigerator. She broke it in two, then removed half from the paper and bit off the end. It was slightly mushy.

"The refrigerator's out of whack again," she said.

"Irene said to call her collect after nine o'clock," said Emmett.

Sam swallowed a lump of Popsicle. "Is she coming down here this summer?"

"She didn't say."

"She probably can't bear to leave Lorenzo Jones. He's got her snowed. He claims he's just like *this* with the Whitneys." Sam crossed her fingers and stuck them in front of Emmett's face. "But I happen to know for a fact he was just a stable hand at the Whitney Horse Farm and that was ages ago."

"You're jealous."

"I am *not*."

"I'll say this for Larry," Emmett said. "He never had a pot to pee in, but he's got it made now. Irene likes being married to an IBM big shot."

"I'm just mad that she ran out on us. And if I went to U.K., I'd never get any sleep with a baby around."

"You're jealous of the baby."

"Lorenzo Junior."

"Her name is Heather. I think it's a real pretty name."

Sam laughed. "Mom thought Samantha was a pretty name too. She never could stand it that everybody called me Sam."

"Your daddy was the one that named you Samantha," Emmett said.

"Hey! What do you mean?"

Emmett flipped a Pepsi and drank from it before he answered. "Dwayne wrote Irene once and said he wanted to name you Samantha because it was his favorite name." He belched loudly.

"I never knew that." Sam was surprised. The Popsicle dripped on her leg.

Sam used to think Irene named her after an actress named Samantha something, whose hobby was bullfighting. Sam got scratched on some barbed wire once while trying to escape from a bull Granddad Smith had rented for his cows, and she had to have a tetanus shot. "Why would you name me after somebody who fights bulls?" she had asked her mother accusingly, but Irene had denied that Sam's name had anything to do with a bullfighting movie star. Sam was confused. If she couldn't know a simple fact like the source of her name, what could she know for sure?

Emmett rattled the newspaper in her face. "Let me show you what Dr. Dobbs said today." He located the medical column in the middle of the paper. "This person wrote in with heartburns, and Dr. Dobbs says it might be Tietze's syndrome. It mimics the symptoms of a heart attack, but it's just inflamed cartilage in the rib cage. Reckon that's what I got instead of gas?"

"Maybe. Why don't you write and ask him about those firecrackers in your head? And ask him why that pimple on your nose hasn't healed in two months? And why you've got pimples creeping down the back of your neck? He'll say it's Agent Orange, I bet you money."

"Oh, them doctors don't believe in Agent Orange."

Sam sucked her Popsicle stick. The smell of the taco shells burst forth from the oven. She said suddenly, "Hey, Emmett. Tell me what you remember most about Vietnam. Besides that bird."

Emmett peeked into the oven. "What do you want to know for?" he asked.

"Just asking."

"The smell of fish sauce," he said. "And human shit in the rice paddies. And all those people pedaling their bicycles."

"What else? Tell me something that happened. Tell me about that hooch that blew up." She remembered that story. The soldiers blew up a house. The plywood covers on the windows popped off, and then it rained fire. The hooch had a bunker in it where the Vietcong were hiding. Emmett had said the scene was like the wolf and the three little pigs. There was a pig squealing. When the hooch fell down, the pig ran around in circles, squealing. Somebody shot it, but it still danced until it fell down dead. And then the pig got barbecued.

"You don't want to know all of that, Sam."

"Yes, I do."

"Your imagination is bad enough as it is. I'm not going to feed it."

"If you don't tell me, then I'll just imagine it was worse than it was."

"No, you couldn't do that."

"Well, then, tell me more about that hooch."

Emmett jerked open a cabinet door and shut it and then opened another one. "Have you seen that dooey I drain the lettuce in?"

"Moon Pie had it out on Sixth Street."

"Be serious." Emmett banged more doors. "Oh, fuck a duck! Where's that strainer?"

During *M*A*S*H*, Sam and Emmett ate the tacos and drank a quart of Pepsi. They ate on TV tables Emmett had picked up at a yard sale. On *M*A*S*H*, Trapper John got an ulcer, and Hawkeye got excited that Trapper might get to go home, but Trapper got his ulcer cured with a three-week stay at Tokyo General. Usually, whenever any of the *M*A*S*H* regulars got a chance to go home, they thought of excuses to stay in Korea. Radar believed the outfit couldn't be run without him. Colonel Potter got a chance to go home once, but he wouldn't desert his post, even though he missed his wife, Mildred, back in Missouri. Of course, the series would have collapsed if the regulars had gone home, but Sam wondered if there wasn't some truth to the idea that war was attractive. Emmett had even said that Pete preferred the war. She had been reading about how the United States got involved. All the names ran together. Ngo Dinh Diem. Bao Dai. Dien Bien Phu. Ho Chi Minh. She got bogged down in manifestos and State Department documents.

At nine o'clock, she dialed her mother, in Lexington, on the kitchen phone. She called collect.

"I just got the baby to sleep," Irene said breathlessly. "She's cutting a tooth and I was up all night last night. When are you coming up here?"

"I told you I didn't want to go to U.K." Just then Emmett went out the door in his Pepsi cap, with a beer in his hand. Sam said, "I'm going back to work at the Burger Boy."

"Sam, how many times do I have to tell you that if you want to spend the rest of your life waiting on somebody, then go right ahead. You'll be sorry if you don't go to school. Thank God I don't have to work now. I'm through being a slave."

"All I need is a car and I can commute to Murray State," Sam said. "Besides, those education benefits are good till I'm twenty-six."

It wasn't true that going to college guaranteed a better job. She knew a guy who drove a Pepsi truck and made more than most people who went to college. He was the guy who gave Emmett the Pepsi cap.

"You're the stubbornest kid I ever knew," Irene said.

"I've got a bone to pick with you," Sam blurted out.

"What about?"

"My name. Emmett says it wasn't your idea to name me Samantha. He says it was my daddy's."

"He liked the name a real whole lot."

"Why didn't you ever tell me that?"

"Didn't I?"

"You never told me anything—about him, or about Vietnam. You always wanted to forget it, like it never happened. I think that's why you gave up on Emmett."

"I put up with Emmett for thirteen years, and I think I deserve a little happiness now, so don't talk to me in that tone, Sam. Good grief."

Happiness? With Lorenzo Jones? Sam imagined him standing against the bar—they had a *bar*—admiring his collection of Jim Beam bottles. He collected oddly shaped liquor bottles sold every Christmas, and he bragged about how they were worth money. He even had a train, with an engine and a caboose, and each part of the train was a Jim Beam bottle.

"What's Emmett going to do about that money he owes?" Irene asked.

"Who knows? He got another letter from the V.A. They're charging interest." Sam explained about the basement leak and told her mother he was probably digging out the foundation to keep busy, to avoid thinking about his debt. She said, "I'm worried about his pimples."

"I'd have pimples too if I drank as much Pepsi as he does."

"Don't you think it's Agent Orange?"

"Oh, I don't know, Sam."

"I should get him an appointment at the V.A. hospital. What if he's got cancer?"

"You're taking too much on yourself, Sam. I wish you'd come up here."

"I can't leave Emmett."

Her mother's exasperated sigh sounded suspiciously like cigarette smoke being exhaled. Her mother had a nice new house and a baby. This house in Hopewell had nasty ashtrays and dead things in the refrigerator and sagging furniture. Emmett had left three crumpled beer cans on the coffee table.

Sam said, "Emmett has this weird pain in his head." She described it and said it might be a tumor.

"That sounds like what he used to have a few years ago. It must have come back. You have a horrible imagination, Sam."

"I can't help it."

"Don't fret too much over this Vietnam thing, Sam. You shouldn't feel bad about any of it. It had nothing to do with you."

Sam didn't know what to say.

Irene asked, "What's Emmett doing now?"

"He's outside hunting for Moon Pie. It's getting dark."

"It's already dark here," Irene said. "You're so far away from me that it gets dark here sooner."

Sam wanted to tell her mother about the new Beatles record, but she was afraid her mother wouldn't be interested. Irene had left all her old records behind. She didn't want to hear about the past.

Sam said, "The refrigerator's out of whack again."

Upstairs, in her room, Sam flipped through her mother's old records: the Beatles, the Kinks, the Stones, the Jefferson Airplane, Janis Joplin, Jimi Hendrix, Gerry and the Pacemakers, the Dave Clark Five. There was even an old Beatles LP on the Parlophone label, issued in England. Irene used to be crazy about the Liverpool sound. She had every Beatles record except "Leave My Kitten Alone."

Moon Pie had come in, and Sam held him under the light and picked fleas off his head. She pinched a flea in two and white goo shot out. She beheaded another one and both parts still wiggled. The flea had blood in it. Moon Pie jumped out of her lap and landed in the bed. He curled his body and then flipped over luxuriously, stretching his long body into a moon curve.

Sam turned on more bulbs in the lamp. It was a tall floor lamp with a carousel of bulbs and a dusty maroon shade. Sometimes flies landed in the lamp bowl and cooked. They smelled something like barbecued ribs. The smell would have been nice except for knowing it was flies.

Sam took her *Collegiate Dictionary* from the shelf. It was a graduation present from her mother—a hint that she should go to college. Boys got cars for graduation, but girls usually had to buy their own cars because they were expected to get married—to guys with cars. Inside the dictionary was her only picture of her father.

In the picture, Dwayne Hughes had on a dark uniform with a cap like the one Sam had worn when she worked at the Burger Boy. His face was long and thin, and a blemish on the bridge of his nose stood out like a connecting point between his eyebrows, like a town on a map. His hair was so short she could see his scalp. His ears stuck out, like Grandma Smith's hen-and-chickens cactuses in the pot with holes on the sides.

The boy in the picture was nineteen. Lonnie was going on nineteen. Sam looked at her face in the mirror—fat, sassy, stubborn. Her father's face was so scrawny. She couldn't see any resemblance to him.

6

One morning, Sam heard Emmett grumbling to himself, "Watch what you're doing, shitbird!" He had exposed most of the north wall, digging a trench about four feet deep. The crack ran the whole length of the foundation. He had mixed up a wheelbarrow of cement, and he was patching the crack when Jim Holly, who headed the local Vietnam veterans organization, stopped by. He had heard about Emmett's pimples and wanted him to fill out a questionnaire about Agent Orange. Jim, a real-estate agent, was a plump man in tan pants and a short-sleeved dress shirt. He wasn't one of the McDonald's regulars. Sam used to see him at basketball games.

Emmett backed out of the crawl space under the kitchen, where he had been inspecting the inner surface of the foundation. The knees of his jeans were muddy, and his cap was draped in cobwebs, like angel hair on a Christmas tree. Sam stood on the porch with a Dr Pepper.

"We're trying to get more vets involved," Jim explained to Sam. "We thought we'd get our families together for some social thing, like a picnic over at the lake. Everybody bring a dish. We're having a dance in a couple of weeks. Why don't you come, Emmett?"

"I don't have any dancing shoes."

"The point is to get together, Emmett," said Jim, smiling. "We need to all get together more. Maybe we'll even parade around the courthouse square—not a protest march, to get everybody uptight, just a parade. A celebration." Jim scraped his shoe on the porch step and examined the sole. He said, "We never did anything much around here. We never even had those rap groups a lot of vets used to have."

"Rat poops?"

"Rap groups, Emmett," said Sam loudly. "He pretends he can't hear sometimes," she said to Jim.

"I thought he said rat poops," Emmett muttered.

"Hell, come on, Emmett," said Jim impatiently. "Your niece here's worried about you."

"We'll never get anything out of the government for Agent Orange," Emmett said. "They're trying every way they know how to prove Agent Orange is good for you, like a big orange drink. And that settlement from the chemical companies is just a drop in the bucket."

"The money's not the point, Emmett. We need to be heard, so it won't happen again. We want to let everybody know vets are not losers. You know what I'd like to see? I'd like to see a big welcome-home party downtown. Lots of places had one the year they put the memorial up in Washington. But nobody did a thing here."

"Everything's always ten years behind here," Emmett said.

"Did you hear about Buddy Mangrum's little girl? She has to have an operation in Memphis, on account of those birth defects. Buddy's been sick too."

Sam said, "Emmett's got a pain in his head and he's got gas."

"Your face looks bad, Emmett."

"It's just acne," Emmett said, touching his cheek.

"It looks like chloracne, if you ask me," Sam said. "That's the most common sign of Agent Orange," she said to Jim.

Jim said, "You know, Emmett, there was a time when I wanted to forget it all, and I didn't want to think about what was right and what was wrong and who was to blame and all. But one day I looked in the mirror and saw a gray hair." Jim patted his head. "We were just little boys out in that jungle, but now we're grown, and it's time to take charge of our lives."

"Little boys get acne and grownups get *chlor*acne," said Emmett, like an actor in a commercial, as if chloracne were a household product, like Clorox. His face had mud crusted on it. A mud pack was probably good for it, Sam thought. Leaning against his shovel, he looked like a hillbilly guarding his land.

"You can at least fill out his questionnaire!" Sam said angrily. "It won't be any skin off your butt!"

With a shamefaced grin, Emmett took Jim's clipboard and pen.

"Your little niece sure is full of fire, Emmett."

"Yeah, I always do what she says, 'cause she's mean. *Man*, she's mean."

After Emmett filled out the form, he pointed to the crack in the foundation. "Look at that. We're lucky this house is still standing. Do you think I'm wasting my time stuffing cracks? Maybe I ought to tear this whole section out and rebuild it. Look how it goes along there."

"Are you afraid the house will fall down?" Sam asked. Houses didn't just fall down. If they did, she would have noticed.

"Yep," Emmett said solemnly. "You take a structural weakness. One thing leads to another, and then it all falls apart." He slapped his palms together and slid them apart.

"That sounds like the domino theory," Sam said. "I've read about the domino theory." It was in one of the library books. She couldn't remember which one.

Jim took Emmett's trowel and smoothed the cement on the face of the foundation, scraping it until it blended with the wall.

"I think it'll hold, Emmett," he said. "The house hasn't started to shift yet. Don't worry, good buddy."

7

"Are Emmett's pimples bigger than dimes?" Anita Stevens wanted to know, when Sam confided her worries. On an impulse, Sam had gone to Anita's apartment, a block away from the hospital where Anita worked. Anita was a nurse, and she would know what to do about Emmett's pimples.

"They're little and blistery. He put some of my grandmother's burn plant on his face, but it didn't help." Sam explained about the sensations in Emmett's head, the way he held his temples with his head bowed.

"He ought to have that checked, but it could be a lot of minor things," Anita said. "It could just be a nerve firing off for no reason. But he ought to have his eyes checked first. That's what I'd be concerned with."

"Could it be a brain tumor?"

"If it was a brain tumor, he'd be having real bad headaches and blurred vision."

Sam felt relieved. She took Anita seriously. This evening Anita was wearing dark fuchsia pants with a silver belt and string-strap heels. She had on a pale pink blouse and some silver chains. Everything about Anita was elegant. She was dressed up, and she wasn't even going anywhere. Sam had on shorts and a T-shirt with a bleach spot on it.

Anita gave Sam some brownies and a Coke. "I got Betty Crocker this time," she said, smiling. "I like her a whole lot better than Duncan Hines. That old fool." She laughed.

"They're good," said Sam.

Anita's living room had framed pictures on the walls, pictures of sailboats and flowers. Her coffee table was glass, with a stack of books. Anita said she belonged to a book club. "I like books with some substance," she told Sam. "I don't go for those sappy romance novels. I like stories with a lot of sex, a little violence—not too much—and some history. That's a good balance."

Sam loved to listen to Anita's ripples of laughter. Anita always laughed as if everything were a joke on herself. Sam remembered how Anita and Emmett used to laugh together, as if they were having more fun than anyone in the world. Irene had told Sam that Emmett broke up with Anita because he felt she was out of his class. Her father owned a paint store, and she grew up in a nice house on Edgeview Drive. But Anita wasn't stuck-up at all. Irene liked her, and they used to try on each other's clothes.

Sam told Anita about the veterans' dance and urged her to attend. "I'm trying to get Emmett to go," Sam said excitedly, picturing Anita and Emmett getting back together at the dance.

"Maybe he wouldn't come if he knew I was going to be there."

"Yes, he would. I'll make him go," Sam said.

Anita went to the kitchen for napkins. "Who are you going with now, Sam?" she called from the kitchen.

"Lonnie Malone."

"The boy who made all those jump shots that time?"

"Yeah."

"He's cute. Are you going to marry him?"

"I don't know. His brother's getting married, and I've never been to a fancy wedding, so I guess I'll see how I like it."

Anita poured herself some Scotch from a little bar in her living room. She even had ice in her ice bucket. It was as though she were sitting in a perfectly arranged setting, waiting for something to happen, like a stage set just before the curtain goes up. "I had a fancy wedding," Anita said in a hollow voice when she sat down beside Sam again. Her smile vanished. "I was eighteen, and it was just what you did back then. I didn't know what else there was to do. But it didn't work out."

"What was your wedding like?"

Anita laughed at herself. "The *works*. The reception was at the country club."

"That must have been nice."

"The day I got married, I felt nothing. Then that night, Jeff just fell asleep. I cried and cried. This was the big night, and I was scared. And he just went to sleep."

"How long were you married?"

"Four years—long enough. He was supposed to be such a fine boy from a fine family—his daddy was a doctor. He played baseball, and he was good-looking as all hell, but he didn't know what to make of me. He wanted me to be a picture. That's all I was supposed to do, just be beautiful."

Anita *was* beautiful. She had full breasts and naturally curly hair that hung down to her shoulders. Sam loved to look at her flawless skin. "Why didn't you leave town?" Sam asked. It was a shame that Anita was stuck here. She should be a model in New York.

"My sister in Nashville's always begging me to come down there, but my parents are here, and Daddy's been real bad—he has a heart condition. It doesn't seem right to walk out on them. I like it here O.K. People are good here, and it's home." She pushed another brownie at Sam.

Anita sank back into a fat pink pillow and said dreamily, "I was visiting classes at the high school once—doing a unit on hygiene?—and Emmett walks in and writes 'ORIOLES' on the board. The Orioles were in the World Series. That cracked me up. He just waltzed right in there and out again and didn't say a word."

"He might have meant birds. He watches birds and there used to be a nest of Baltimore orioles in our back yard."

"Oh, yes, I know he watches birds. What's that bird he's always looking for?"

"An egret."

"Yes. An egret. I remember." Anita sipped her drink thoughtfully. Sam realized that Anita was one of the few people she knew who didn't smoke. "Emmett gave me a peacock feather once," Anita said. "He was so cute about it. I thought as much of that peacock feather as if it had been a diamond ring."

"Do you go with somebody now?"

"I'm dating a policeman from Benton. He can talk for hours about pickup trucks. I can't remember a word he says, but it amazes me that somebody can talk that much about pickup trucks. But it's going to wear off. He's real macho, and he's getting possessive." She laughed. "When they start getting possessive, I have to get out. That's probably why I cared so much about Emmett. He was never like that. That made *me* possessive, I guess. I just *had* to have him."

"He doesn't sleep well," Sam said. "I hear him up prowling around. And he has gas and belches a lot. I just know he's got Agent Orange."

"Oh, honey, I wouldn't jump to conclusions. It's probably not anything serious. I'm going to give you the name of an eye doctor and a skin doctor I want him to see." She searched in a drawer for a piece of paper. She said, "Emmett's a good person. I hate to see him waste his life away. He's really so bright."

"I wish you'd get back together."

Anita smiled and touched Sam's hand. "I like your earrings, Sam."

"My friend Dawn's got four holes in her ears. Would you come over sometime? I'll get Emmett to make some lasagna."

Anita hesitated. "Well, I don't know if he'd want me to."

"Come over and help me get him interested in that dance."

Anita smiled. "You be sure and go to that dance yourself, Sam—in honor of your daddy. I think you ought to be proud of him."

Sam played with Anita's books. Her glass had sweated onto the paper cover of *Out on a Limb* by Shirley MacLaine. She said, "My mother never told me much about him, what he was like or what his favorite foods were or anything. I don't even know how tall he was or what kind of personality he had. He's just a face in a picture, but now I'm getting real curious."

"I know what you mean, like there's something you're not supposed to know. I've felt like that about a lot of things."

"My mother acts like the Vietnam War was back in the Dark Ages."

"It *was* the Dark Ages, Sam," said Anita. "That's a good description."

"Come over and see us."

"I'll think about it. Let me give you the names of these doctors I want Emmett to see."

Anita fumbled with her pen and paper, writing down the names. Her rings flashed in the lamplight. A grin split her face. "And then we'll see if he remembers how to dance," she said.

8

"It's digging-in-the-ditch time," said Emmett, when he brought his pickax up from the basement.

Sam recognized the source of the line: Colonel Blake saying "It's lonely-at-the-top time" once when he had to make a difficult decision.

After waterproofing the crack in the foundation, Emmett had been deepening the crawl space under the kitchen. He suspected the floor was rotting, and he was checking the joists for dry rot. He had had no more bad heartburns, but he had pointed out an instance in the newspaper of a man with a tipped heart. Sam had heard of a tipped womb, but not a tipped heart, although she supposed that if one organ could tip, any other could as well—especially if it had been exposed to Agent Orange. Emmett's face was the same, alternately scabby and runny. Sometimes he would smile and a pimple would crack.

"I wish you'd get back together with Anita," Sam said as she watched him work. "She's crazy about you."

Emmett grunted. He was stacking some rocks he had unearthed.

"Maybe I'll move to Lexington," Sam said, irritated.

"There's more opportunity there for you," Emmett said matter-of-factly.

"Do you remember that time Mom hauled me off to Lexington with that hippie friend of yours when I was little?"

"Yeah."

"Who was that guy?"

Emmett tugged on a rock the size of a boom box and upended it. "Irene was crazy about him, and she would have married him, but if she had, she'd have lost her benefits." He chuckled. "Boy, your grandma was fit to be tied—Irene living in sin!"

"What was his name?"

"Bob. He was an O.K. guy, but he thought he could make a living making clay pots, and he almost got Irene believing it, but after a month in Lexington, she knew he couldn't, and that's why she came back here with you." Emmett squatted and poked at the foundation. "I've almost got this to the point where I can fill in this ditch," he said thoughtfully.

"And then you'll have to think about paying back that money."

"Let the V.A. wait. I'll just let 'em twist slowly, slowly in the wind." Emmett cackled with a sinister laugh.

In her room, Sam tucked the picture of her father in the mirror frame. The edges were scuffed and a corner was creased. She wondered at what point her mother had been able to forget about him and fall in love with a hippie named Bob. Sam had a vague memory of going with them to a peace demonstration in Lexington. The crowd had milled around like a herd of cows in Granddad's pasture. She remembered that the hippie had given her a helium balloon, and she accidentally let go of it. She remembered seeing it float away, high over the University of Kentucky campus, and she cried because the balloon had seemed important, something to hold on to that day.

The soldier boy in the picture never changed. In a way that made him dependable. But he seemed so innocent.

"Astronauts have been to the moon," she blurted out to the picture. "July 20, 1969. Armstrong, Aldrin, and Collins. Collins didn't get to walk on the moon. He had to stay in the command module." Her father never knew things like command module and LEM, she thought, despairing at the idea of explaining to someone the history of the world since 1966. How did teachers do it?

For probably the first time now, it occurred to Sam how amazing it was that men had walked on the moon. Her father had missed so many important events. Watergate, for instance. Sam could not remember exactly what it was about. Her history teacher, Mr. Harris, had said, "The biggies in your lifetime were the moon landing, the assassinations, Vietnam, and Watergate." Mr. Harris said everything was downhill after Kennedy was killed. Sam could probably name all the other assassinations if she thought about it.

"You missed Watergate," Sam said to the picture. "I was in the second grade." She remembered Emmett absorbed in it, watching it on schedule. It was a TV series one summer. When Nixon resigned, Emmett and Irene were ecstatic, but their parents had voted for Nixon and said the country would fall apart if he was forced out. Sam wondered if that was why nobody could get jobs and the world was in such a mess.

She stared at the picture, squinting her eyes, as if she expected it to come to life. But Dwayne had died with his secrets. Emmett was walking around with his. Anyone who survived Vietnam seemed to regard it as something personal and embarrassing. Granddad had said they were embarrassed that they lost the war, but Emmett said they were embarrassed that they were still alive. "I guess you're not embarrassed," she said to the picture.

The face in the picture ruled the room, like the picture of the President on the wall of the high school auditorium. Sam set *Sgt. Pepper's Lonely Hearts Club Band* on the stereo.

"You missed this too," she said.

9

"The corn's tosseling," said Emmett.

They were riding past cornfields. Lonnie was driving, with a cigarette drooping from his mouth, and Emmett sat in the back. Sam held on to the grip on the dash. The seat belt was broken. Lonnie never bothered to lock the van after he punched out the side window when he'd locked the keys inside. The van needed paint and it rattled.

Sam said, "Emmett, I want you to remember to ask the doctor

every question I wrote down on that list. And don't be afraid to tell him about your gas. There might be some connection."

"How could there be a connection between your face and your stomach?"

"I don't know, but I haven't been to medical school. That's why we're taking you to the skin specialist."

Sam couldn't get Emmett an appointment for the Agent Orange test at the V.A. Medical Center until October 10, the day after her birthday, so she had talked him into seeing the specialists Anita had recommended. The eye doctor said Emmett's eyes were fine; he said the pain might be sinuses. Emmett bought some Allerest tablets, but they made him sleepy. Sam had read that victims of Agent Orange sometimes had their metabolism screwed up. Sam didn't like the sound of "metabolic disturbances." Agent Orange could also act on the immune system, causing it to collapse over a period of time. That sounded exactly like AIDS, she had told Dawn.

They were on the Old Hopewell Road, a curvy road that followed the crooked path of Goose Creek. They passed old farms with new house trailers in front. Farm machinery lay rusting beside lopsided barns. They saw one barn that was particularly slanted, and Emmett said, "Look at that. It'll be flat on the ground by the time we come back by." He had become acutely conscious of structures since he had been working on the foundation of the house.

Emmett was laughing now, but Sam thought he must know he had cancer. His pimples wouldn't heal. That was one of the seven signs of cancer. Agent Orange could cause any kind of symptoms.

On the way to Paducah, Emmett kept asking Lonnie about his job prospects, as though that were the only problem facing them.

"What about that trade school your daddy wants you to go to?" Emmett said as they passed a silo leaning like the Tower of Pisa.

Lonnie said, "Daddy's been pushing that electrician idea lately. The way I look at it, there won't be that much of a future in electrical work because electricity's going to go sky-high. With all this anti-nuclear stuff and plants shutting down, the price of electricity's going to double in the next five years. And people can't afford to build, so they won't need wiring. They're going back home to live with their parents. Like me." Lonnie laughed disgustedly and drew on his cigarette.

"Your parents don't treat you fair," Sam said. "Wanting you to go to trade school when your brother got to go to college."

"Well, he got a scholarship. My grades weren't good enough."

"When's John getting married?" asked Emmett.

"Labor Day. Mama's walking on clouds 'cause he's marrying that hoity-toity girl from Bowling Green." Lonnie tapped his cigarette on the ashtray and some butts fell out. "Jennifer Jenkins. Her name's like a movie star."

"That's a name Mom would like," said Sam, glancing back at Emmett.

Lonnie said, "Mama's impressed because Jennifer's daddy has a Jerry's franchise. They're having the reception at the restaurant."

"I don't have anything to wear to a wedding," said Sam.

"Wear that yellow thing you wore at graduation," said Lonnie.

Sam frowned. She wasn't looking forward to the wedding. She couldn't afford to buy anybody a present, and Lonnie had insisted she buy something nice. By Labor Day, Emmett could be bedridden. She would have to wait on him. She would fix TV dinners, since she was a terrible cook. She didn't know much about cancer. Some kinds were very fast, and some kinds lingered.

Sam's father's parents lived on a farm on a road like this, about twenty miles from Hopewell. She had not seen them in a couple of years. Her mother used to take her there at Christmas. They had given her a tacky lavender mohair sweater with glitter on it the last time she had been there for Christmas. Now she felt guilty that she hadn't seen them in so long. They had never told her much about Dwayne, so it had always been hard to make the connection between him and them, except that they had a picture of him in their dining room. Sam remembered their broad, rolling cornfields and a narrow creek that meandered through them. She suddenly recalled that in a made-for-TV movie about the Vietnam War she had been surprised to see soldiers marching through a field of corn. The tassels were outlined against the clear blue sky, and the corn looked ready to pick. It surprised her that corn grew in Vietnam. She did not know if it was there because Americans had planted it—or had given the Vietnamese the seed and shown them how to plant it—or if in fact corn was ever in Vietnam, since the movie was filmed in Mexico. They certainly had corn in Mexico because corn was an Indian plant. Maize. The woman in the Mazola commercial. It bothered her that it was so hard to find out the truth. Did corn actually grow in Vietnam?

The landscape of Vietnam was hard to envision. The library books said little about crops. When Sam asked Emmett what grew in Vietnam, he said palm trees and elephant grass and things with leaves as long as helicopter blades, and a lot of marshy grass, but he didn't remember the particulars. He didn't know about corn. He remembered the birds, but he didn't know their names until he returned and looked them up in the library.

The clinic was in a sleek new building with shiny metal sculptures outside that vaguely resembled fish. They were probably supposed to represent Kentucky Lake catfish. In the elevator, violins were playing. Sam recognized "Karma Chameleon," which sounded crazy played that way. Dr. Kresko was on the second floor. What kind of name was Kresko? Sam wondered. It sounded like Crisco. Emmett used Crisco to fry catfish.

Sam and Lonnie sat in red vinyl chairs and looked at magazines while Emmett filled out some forms. The girls at the desk chatted about their permanents. The air conditioning was ice cold. A man came through a door with a handkerchief over his nose.

"Are you worried?" Lonnie asked Sam after a fat, chirpy nurse took Emmett away.

"Yeah, but I'm glad we finally got him here."

"Will the government pay for it?"

Sam shook her head. "The doctor could say he had cancer and the government wouldn't care. Anyway, they're slow as Christmas."

"Oh, Emmett doesn't have cancer."

"It could turn into cancer."

"It would be awful to die of cancer before you're old," said

Lonnie thoughtfully. "I don't know anybody who died young except Jimmy Tibbett. You could call that a drunk-driving accident, but it was his own fault for being drunk."

Sam furled the *People* magazine she had been reading and slapped Lonnie's leg with it. "Well, then, if you go off to war, a bad war, and you believe you're doing the right thing, is it your own fault if you get killed? If the war is wrong, then do you deserve to die for believing the wrong thing?"

"That's pretty confusing, Sam."

"I can't explain what I mean."

Lonnie squeezed her hand. "Don't think about all this. Emmett will be all right."

Some new patients came in, laughing and talking. Lots of skin diseases must be hilarious, Sam supposed. She looked at the pictures in three *People* magazines while Lonnie went out and explored the building. He came back with a Coke and let Sam share it. A man brought in a little girl who had scabs on her face and hands.

Sam said to Lonnie, "My mom said not to worry about what happened to Emmett back then, because the war had nothing to do with me. But the way I look at it, it had *everything* to do with me. My daddy went over there to fight for Mom's sake, and Emmett went over there for Mom's sake and my sake, to get revenge. If you went off to war, I bet you'd say it was for me. But if you're planning on joining the Army, you might ask my opinion first. The ones who don't get killed come back with their lives messed up, and then they make everybody miserable."

"Hush," said Lonnie, brushing his hand against her lips. "People are looking."

"I don't care. It was such a waste."

Lonnie flipped a cigarette out of his pack and stared at her.

"Do you think I'm weird because of Emmett?" Sam asked. Even her mother was weird, she thought, the way she used to wear halter tops and tight jeans to P.T.A. meetings.

"You're not really weird," Lonnie assured her. "You just think you are. You're only half weird. Medium weird," he added with a grin. He pinched her leg playfully.

"I don't care. I feel like doing something really outrageous."

"Shh," Lonnie said. "Here's Emmett."

"Sixty-three bucks," said Emmett, when the receptionist added up his bill. "And he tells me to wash my face more often." He asked the receptionist, "Do you think my face is dirty?"

She smiled. "I'm not the doctor, sir, but I'm sure that's not what he meant."

Emmett paid in cash. They wouldn't let him charge it. He was pounding his fist into his palm as they waited for the elevator. "Well, I hope you're satisfied, Sambo. Sixty-three bucks."

"What did he do? He didn't charge you that much just to tell you to wash your face. What did he say?"

"First he gives me a lecture on skin. It turns out it is not unusual to get acne when you're old like me. It's not necessarily chloracne. It could be just common teen-age acne."

"It's just acne?"

"It could be."

The elevator opened. All during the elevator ride Emmett and Lonnie worked at lighting their cigarettes.

"What causes acne?" Lonnie asked as they got out of the elevator.

"Sex hormones," said Emmett, hollering with laughter. "That's why you get acne when you're a kid. Your sex hormones start acting up then. Mine are starting up again, like a volcano. It's a sign you're a stud."

"No kidding!" said Lonnie, winking at Sam. "Wow."

"He thinks it could be allergies," Emmett said. "It could be something I've been eating, or something in the house. Like a slime mold or something. He asked me a list of questions a mile long." Emmett laughed and blew smoke at the fish sculptures outside. "You know what he asked me? He asked me if I used hair spray or any kind of makeup! And he asked me if I had a cat! I said no. I wasn't going to have him tell me get rid of Moon Pie. You could tell that was coming."

"He should see your skirt," Lonnie said. They got in the van and Lonnie cranked it. The starter had been giving him trouble, but the engine caught.

Emmett seemed so jumpy that Sam wondered if he was covering up something. Maybe the doctor had said cancer and Emmett just didn't want to tell them.

"Maybe it's that basement," Emmett said. "That dampness down there. All kinds of things could be breeding, and they could be coming through the air ducts and—ooooooh! Remember Legionnaires' disease? Hey, remember that disease you get from the drip pan under the refrigerator?" Emmett shuddered as though he had just seen the creature from *Alien* creeping around the corner in the rearview mirror.

"Did he give you any prescriptions?" Sam asked.

"Yeah. Something to wash my face with and some salve. He said if it doesn't clear up he wants me to go to an allergist. That's how they make their money. They don't want to really cure anything until they work you over good. They send you on a merry-go-round and make sure their friends get theirs. They want to do their tests and run you through all their technology."

"Did he do tests?"

"Yeah. He did tests. That's what run the price up so."

Emmett pulled a wadded piece of paper from his pocket. "He gave me a list of what not to eat. Shrimp. Nuts. Chocolate. CoTylenol. Hell, I don't ever eat that anyway. Vicks Nytol. I don't eat that. Don't like it. I like Pertussin better. It's good on ice cream."

"Are Pepsis on the list?" Sam asked.

"No."

"That's what Mom thinks it is. Pepsis. What about Agent Orange, Emmett? Did you ask him?"

"Yeah, and he just laughed. I *told* you he would. I couldn't even get him to talk about chloracne. You can't even get these doctors to admit there's a problem. And you expect the federal government to jump up and clap, Sam?"

"He must have seen other vets with pimples," said Sam. "Can't he add two and two?"

"That's not the way science works, Sam," said Emmett. "They don't put two and two together, based on the obvious facts right in front of their noses. They don't make connections. They have to work ten years in a laboratory and kill nine million rats and mice, and then they might come to some conclusion. But you take anything obvious—like cats purring when they're happy? And they don't believe that's why cats purr! They say where's your proof? How many rats did you use in your experiment?"

Lonnie said, "Yeah, but when they do prove something, like some chemical causes cancer in ten percent of the rats, people don't believe it. They say, 'Rats ain't people, so I'm going to eat it anyway.' That's what they say."

"I believe it," said Sam. "Rats *are* people. People are rats anyway. That's why I don't drink diet drinks."

Emmett said, "Did you know medical science can't explain why a cat purrs? It defies all their methods. They don't think cats have minds of their own and purr when they take a notion. But a cat purrs for several reasons. Happiness. Insecurity. Bluffing. Cats are all the time pretending. Sam, remember that time Moon Pie was up in the maple tree with his paw feeling around in that birdhouse? He was looking the other way, pretending he was admiring the sunset." Emmett laughed nervously. He stubbed out his cigarette and lit another.

"Where are we going?" said Lonnie. They were still sitting in the parking lot.

"I want to go to the mall," Sam said. "I don't want to come all the way to Paducah and not get to go to the mall. At least we can do that."

"Yeah, at least we can do that," said Lonnie, backing out of the parking place.

"Let's eat at the Cracker Barrel," Emmett said. "They've got good home cooking there. I want some country ham and cornbread."

"I want some ham and beans," said Sam.

Emmett said, "In the Army we had ham and butter beans. We had so much of that we called them ham and mother-fuckers."

"I want some ham and mother-fuckers," Lonnie said with a laugh.

"They'll kill you," Emmett said.

"You know what that doctor said?" Emmett asked, as Lonnie

pulled out into traffic. "He said he'd seen a lot of vets with all kinds of complaints. He said they wanted to blame everything from a sore toe to a fever blister on Agent Orange. He just laughed at me. He said it wasn't nothing but nerves. Wouldn't that just fry your butt?"

10

Early the next morning, it was cool and Sam went running through the manicured streets of the Fairview subdivision, until recently a cornfield. All the houses there had two-car garages. The trees were still small, with support wires. Sam loved to run because it set her apart from the girls at school who did things in gabby groups, like ducks. When she ran, she felt free, as if she could do anything. She rarely met other runners. On Pleasant Point Drive, some carpenters were working on a roof, and their radio was blaring out a Kenny Rogers song. One of the men yelled from the roof, "Move them legs, honey!" Once, a guy sitting on a rock at the edge of the Hopewell cemetery had exposed himself to her, and Sam ran on, yelling behind her, "Big deal!" And one day last summer she had been frightened by a fat man following her in a rattletrap pickup, but Allen Wilkins happened to drive along and she flagged him down. He was on his way to work, and she rode with him to his store, feeling ridiculous.

She headed towards McDonald's. Emmett called the route between the Burger Boy and McDonald's the mating range. He said the kids driving their cars back and forth from one burger joint to the other reminded him of birds and their courtship dances. The kids drove the circuit in the evenings, but the traffic now was people driving to work. There were fewer people driving to work in the morning than there were kids cruising in the evening. At McDonald's, Sam spotted Emmett's Pepsi cap, but Tom wasn't with him.

She ran on, past a funeral home, a lighting store, the library, a big real-estate company, a fancy antique store, a gift shop, a junk shop, Kentucky Fried Chicken. A row of bowling trophies gleamed in the window of Lane's Sporting Goods. Sam always called that store the trophy store. Next door, in the window of the U.S. Army recruiting station, was a poster of Uncle Sam thrusting his finger out demandingly at her. She gave him the finger back and raced by. Tom Hudson's garage was near here. She slowed down.

Tom's garage was in a section of town that used to be classy, before the doctors and lawyers and merchants began building in the new subdivisions. The homes, most in run-down condition, were large and old, and the yards were dark and full of bushes. Tom's garage was behind an ornamental-iron and fence company at the end of a street of shabby old frame houses. Sam passed the wrought-iron sections of fence and lacy mailboxes on display and walked down an alley behind the building. A clumsily lettered sign, "Kustom Kollision," was nailed on the side of an old building with a yawning cave-like hole where Tom worked on cars. The clutter of auto parts and empty motor-oil cans and unidentifiable, useless-looking objects fascinated her. Mechanics could recreate beautiful cars out of a mess of greasy metal pieces and rusty pipes and screws, the way a magician would mix watches and eggs in a bowl and pull out a rubber chicken.

He was squatting, with his back to her, and he didn't notice Sam approach.

"Hi," she said when he saw her.

"Well, hello, Sam," he said, surprised. "How are you?"

"Fine. I was just out running," she said awkwardly. "What are you doing?"

"I can't get this transmission to loosen up. See that doohickey there? It's supposed to fit there, but not so tight. It's froze up, and I can't get it apart. Did you come about that VW?"

"Yeah."

"Sure thing," said Tom, standing up. He opened a small refrigerator and took out two Cokes. "You look thirsty," he said, handing her one. His hands were greasy.

"I am," she said, opening the can. "Thank you."

"That Volkswagen's worth five hundred to me, and it needs a lube job and some work on the transmission. I'll throw that in for you."

He showed her the VW, parked alongside the garage. It was beige, with rusty patches on the fenders. If she bought it, she'd have to get him to fix the rust spots. Rust could eat a car up.

After she looked the car over, Tom said, "Is your boyfriend Lonnie Malone?"

"Yeah."

"Didn't he get a basketball scholarship to Murray?"

"No. His grades weren't good enough."

Tom lit a cigarette and leaned against a rickety table covered with nuts and bolts. He had grease on his face and even on his cigarette. Sam refused his offer of a Camel Light. Then she told him about the trip to the skin specialist.

"Emmett was disgusted with the doctor," Sam said. "The doctor just laughed at him. But he got some salve for his face."

"Maybe that'll help."

"Do you think Emmett's got Agent Orange?" Sam asked. Tom was looking at her intently, making her nervous. With her fingernail, Sam scraped crud from the underside of her watchband.

He shrugged and said, "He'd have to get tested at the V.A., but a million vets could drop dead of cancer from Agent Orange and the government would say they don't have any proof there's a connection." Tom laughed bitterly. "Emmett's disillusioned with the government. He thinks they're totally in the dark about what's going on in the world. Emmett won't go out of his way to deal with the V.A. anymore."

"He's stubborn. My mom says it's a family trait."

Tom nodded slowly and fixed his eyes on a black wrought-iron mailbox down the alley. The vets she knew often got that spacey look, as though they were gazing straight into the future. When Sam asked Tom if he knew where Quang Ngai was, he gave a faint smile of recognition.

"That's where my daddy died," she said. "Or near there."

"I know. Emmett told me. I was up north of there."

"Did you like it over there?" Sam asked awkwardly. What was

there to like over there? she wondered. Did people like it, the way one would like, say, a trip to Lexington? When he took his time answering, she said, "Did you go off into battle stoned? Emmett says that after 1969 the whole Army was stoned."

Tom shook his head no. "That was a good way to get yourself blown away."

"My daddy died over there right before I was born, but everybody acts like it's a big secret. I don't know much about him."

"A lot of boys just plain got forgotten," Tom said. "And a lot of the ones who came back feel guilty that they're the ones who made it back."

"Do you feel that way?"

"Sure."

"Did you think you were doing the right thing going over there?"

"I didn't know what I was doing," he said, reflecting as he drew on his cigarette. He blew out a leisurely puff of smoke and said, "But that's all in the past."

Sam fingered a car part that looked vaguely familiar. She wished he would tell her about Quang Ngai. On the map, it was near My Lai.

He said, "There's not a day goes by that I don't think about my buddies that didn't come back. They're with me, in odd moments, like when I take a shower, or when I'm driving around. Memories come back to me, memories that had escaped for a while."

"Do they make you cry?" Sam asked, trying to recall what she had read about Vietnam flashbacks.

"Only if I'm by myself and only if it's unbearable not to cry. Sometimes I feel homesick for those memories. It sounds funny, I know."

"Emmett said something like that about Pete."

"Pete had the time of his life over there. I wouldn't say I had a blast, exactly, but it's funny, how special it was, in a way, like nobody else could ever know what you went through except guys who have been there."

"Is that true? Is that why y'all hang around together and go drink down at the Bottom?"

"Maybe." He shrugged and pulled another cigarette out of his coveralls. "Do you want to buy a dirt bike?" he asked. "I could rig you up one real good."

"No, that's not what I need."

"I know what you need," he said, but he didn't finish the thought. He toyed with a wrench. He said, "Sometimes when I feel homesick for those memories I get on a dirt bike and just go out and bump around in that woods behind the fairgrounds. I just let the memories come. It's like being back with them. It's kind of pleasant, really. But you have to go someplace like that, off to the Bottom, or out on a dirt bike trail. You can't stay in town and afford to think about what happened." He flicked his cigarette ashes on the dirt floor and said, "Sam, you might as well just stop asking questions about the war. Nobody gives a shit. They've got it twisted around in their heads what it was about, so they can live with it and not have to think about it. The thing is, they never spit on us here. They treated the vets O.K., because the anti-war feeling never got stirred up good around here. But that means they've got a notion in their heads of who we are, and that image just don't fit all of us. Around here, nobody wants to rock the boat."

"But the world's in such a mess," Sam said. "Just look at the news."

"Yeah, things will explode here one of these days." Tom nodded, as if this were no surprise.

"Emmett always says things never happen here till ten years later."

"Here, everybody's looking backward—to old-timey days. Antiques and Civil War stuff." He smiled. "My mother's got an ox yoke on the living room wall."

Sam thought of the horse collar Lonnie's mother had on her living room wall. It was a frame for a mirror. She wondered if Hopewell was just now catching up to the Civil War. When would people start putting M-16s and pictures of missiles on their living room walls?

"Have you been to see the memorial in Washington?" she asked.

He shook his head no and laughed sarcastically. "A big black hole in the ground, catty-cornered from that big white prick. Fuck the Washington Monument. Fuck it." He dropped his Coke can and stomped it with a heavy work boot. "This town's got its head up its butt, and people like Emmett find it too painful to deal with. There it is." He kicked the Coke can into a pile of twisted metal on the floor. "Do you want another Coke?"

"No."

"How far can you run? I've seen you running."

"I usually run about five or six miles. But I can run further. The furthest I ever ran was ten miles, but I got shin splints from that. I went at it too sudden."

"Aren't you afraid you'll drop dead like that race horse, Sam?"

He was teasing, and she blushed.

"What do you want a car for, Sam, if you can run that far?"

She laughed. "Everybody wants a car. To go places."

"Are you sure you don't want a dirt bike?" he asked. "What I like about dirt bikes is how reckless you can be and it don't hurt much. I put one together and wreck it and then I just put me another one together. Don't mean nothing."

"Everything means something," Sam said.

Tom bent over the frozen transmission again and tried to pry it loose. "Damn," he said. "Come on, you sucker." Sam noticed the gray in his hair.

"Do you want to go for a ride in that bug?" he asked.

"Sure. I'd love to."

"Hold on just a minute and I'll take you for a ride."

"I'd love to go for a ride."

"Well, just hold on a minute till I get this thing loose."

"Take your time."

11

Hopewell did not have a mall, but it had a small shopping center, a dozen stores between Penney's and the K Mart. Sam met Dawn at the shopping center that afternoon. On the telephone, Dawn had said it was urgent. Over Cokes in a booth at the K Mart, Dawn told Sam she might be pregnant. Sam had been dying to tell Dawn about riding around with Tom, but now her news seemed inappropriate and trivial. This was unreal, like a scene in a movie.

"Have you told Ken?" Sam asked anxiously, her insides stirring.

"Not yet."

"Will your daddy kill you if you have to get married?"

"Oh, he just doesn't want to lose his housekeeper. He can find some woman. Then he won't have to pretend he's working late." Dawn laughed. "He tries to set such a good example, but if it wasn't for me, he'd just go wild."

Sam tried to cheer Dawn up by telling her about Tom and the VW. He hadn't let her drive the car, because it didn't have insurance. They had gone as far as the Holiday Inn and turned around, and he had dropped her off at home.

"He's really sexy," Sam said. "Come to think of it, he looks sort of like Bruce Springsteen, but he got wounded in Vietnam and his back is stiff. He moves kind of jerky."

"How old is he?"

"About thirty-four."

"Wow! That's old." Dawn drank from her Coke and squirmed in the booth, her tanned legs sucking the orange vinyl. Her earrings had purple feathers on them. "Come to the drugstore with me," she said. "They've got a good jewelry counter there."

At the drugstore, Dawn whispered, "I want to buy one of those kits to test for pregnancy."

"I heard you could mix Drano with pee and find out if it's a boy or girl," Sam said.

"I heard that too, but then I heard it was just a story going around. It's not true."

"You know how the Drano can says not to put water in it when it's empty? Emmett does it all the time. He's so cheap he wants to get every little smidgen out of the can. But it doesn't explode or anything."

"It's just so they won't get sued for some freak accident," Dawn said. "Nothing's as dangerous as we're led to believe. Nothing, that is, except screwing." She examined the row of pregnancy home-test kits. "This one's the cheapest," she said. "I hope nobody I know sees me. Do you know that girl at the counter?"

"No." The cashier was a short girl in glasses, chewing gum.

"Would you buy it for me? She looks familiar to me, but I can't place her."

"So she'll think I'm pregnant? Thanks a lot."

"But you're not. So it won't matter."

"Oh, well. I don't care. It doesn't embarrass me anyway."

Dawn gave Sam a ten-dollar bill, and Sam went to the counter with the kit. To her surprise, the counter girl called on an intercom for a price check.

"I think this is on sale," she said to Sam. "I don't think it's this high."

What was wrong with it? Was it outdated? A stock boy took the pregnancy kit back to the feminine-products aisle and returned, wagging it in his hand for everyone in the store to see. Dawn was standing innocently by the toys, examining an imitation Cabbage Patch doll.

Sam wasn't embarrassed, she insisted later to Dawn, who apologized over and over. Sam said, "If you get talked about the way Emmett and me do, and the way my mother did, then nothing is embarrassing." Sam cared less and less what people thought.

"Oh, Sam, I owe you one for this," Dawn said as they walked down the sidewalk toward Penney's so that Dawn could look at maternity clothes. "How can I ever thank you?"

"Name it after me," Sam said. "Sam's an all-purpose name. It fits boys and girls both. You don't even need a can of Drano."

12

That night, Sam dreamed she and Tom Hudson had a baby. In the evening, the baby had to be pureed in a food processor and kept in the freezer. It was the color of candied sweet potatoes. In the morning, when it thawed out, it was a baby again. In the dream, this was a happy arrangement, and no questions were asked. But then the dream woke her up, its horror rushing through her. She lay there, with the dream slowly receding. It was almost dawn. The birds had started singing. A little later, she heard paper tearing—Emmett opening a packet of Tender Vittles and dropping them into the dish by his bed. She heard Moon Pie dancing on the vinyl floor, warbling sounds of pleasure. Moon Pie's life was so simple, Sam thought.

On *M*A*S*H* sometimes, things were too simple. She could see right through them. The night before, Dr. Sidney Freedman, the Army psychiatrist, arrived to treat Hawkeye's mysterious sneezing fits, and within ten minutes he had located the cause in a repressed childhood memory, evoked by an odor of stagnant water on a wounded soldier's clothing. Hawkeye stopped sneezing as soon as he realized the source, and his recognition gave him a crying fit. In the second episode, at six-thirty, a sniper was trying to kill Colonel Blake, so Trapper and Hawkeye sent him off on R & R in a chopper, flown by a strange cowboy, who turned out to be the sniper, a man who had a grudge against Colonel Blake for not sending him home so he could find out if his wife was cheating on him. The cowboy planned to push Colonel Blake out of the chopper, but back at the 4077th, Trapper and Hawkeye suddenly realized what was happening, and they got on the radio in time to talk the cowboy out of his plan. The cowboy mellowed out when they read him a sweet letter from his wife.

Emmett had been mellowing out for years, Sam thought. He had just been watching the wheels turn, like John Lennon in one of his last songs. As long as John Lennon was watching the wheels spin around, he was safe, but when he returned to the public eye, he got blasted. If Emmett got a job to repay the government, it could be like that for him, a terrible shock, like going back to the war.

It occurred to Sam how ironic it was that Colonel Blake eventually did fall out of the sky when he was on his way home from the war.

Something landed on the bed. It was Moon Pie, purring. He sat in the middle of the bed and washed his face. Sam wished she could be a cat. She would sneak into Tom's garage and spy on him. There were several people she would like to spy on. She would like to spy on Lonnie's mother, Martha, in her frilly pink bathroom with the little picket fence around the commode and the butterfly motif on the towels and shower curtain. Sam thought about Lonnie's parents' canopy bed. Martha had heart-shaped pillows, something she had styled after a picture she saw in the *Courier-Journal* of the bed John Y. Brown and Phyllis George had slept on when he was governor. Martha had a bedspread rack to hold the bedspread at night. Lonnie's parents didn't sleep under their bedspread, because it was so nice they probably didn't want to slobber on it.

Sam ate supper with Lonnie and his parents that evening. Martha had fried chicken, corn pudding, three-bean salad, and creamed cauliflower. On the wall by the table, Sam could see her face in the horse-collar mirror. The dining table was a round oak one Martha had found in an old man's barn. It had been covered with bat manure, but Martha had refinished it and found spindleback chairs in some other barn. Lonnie's house was full of fancy old furniture his mother had antiqued.

During supper, they talked about Lonnie's brother's wedding.

"They're not having a sit-down dinner," said Martha. "They're having finger foods."

"I hope we know how to act," Lonnie's dad said, chuckling. He was still in his work clothes. His shirt had his name, Bud, embroidered on the pocket.

"It's a theme wedding," Martha said. "Everybody's coming in

jeeps. Did you ever? Where are we going to get a jeep?" She laughed.

Sam took out more corn pudding and chicken. Bud teased her about getting fat, meaning that she was skinny. Lonnie teased his mother about drinking champagne at the wedding, but she got offended.

"Everybody gets drunk at weddings," Lonnie said, stripping a drumstick.

"They're sending Jim Shields' boy to AA," said Bud, shaking his head in disbelief. "It's not drugs so much as it is alcohol now that's the big problem."

"His mama and daddy are both big in the church too," said Martha. "It's a shame."

"How's that medicine working on Emmett?" Lonnie asked Sam.

"Can't tell yet."

"Is your uncle sick, Sam?" Martha asked, as she took a bowl of jello with fruit cocktail from the refrigerator. "I didn't have time to make a fancy dessert," she said apologetically.

"I think he's got Agent Orange," Sam said, almost inaudibly, as she sucked a thighbone.

"I can't really believe that," Lonnie said. Sam stared at him.

"The government will never give in on that," Bud said. "It'll cost too much money. And then every one of them will be saying they've got it."

"The government and the chemical companies should pay," Sam said. "I don't care how much it costs."

Bud said, "But you can't sue the government. It's the law."

"Doesn't Emmett get disability?" Martha asked. "I thought that was why he didn't work."

"No. He wasn't wounded." Sam ate some jello. It was embarrassing that Emmett didn't work, and that his sister sent him money. She said, "It's not that he couldn't work. Somebody offered him a job at the cookie factory just the other day, but he didn't take it."

"Why not?"

"He didn't need it. He's busy." Sam squirmed, and Lonnie's foot touched hers under the table.

"Is he independently wealthy? I wish I could get by like that." Martha laughed.

She and Bud told a story of how they had had to scrimp and save in the early years of their marriage, with Bud holding down two jobs and Martha working even after she was pregnant.

Sam didn't answer. It was so hard to keep defending Emmett. Her own mother had given up. Lonnie got up and found some Oreos in a cabinet.

Martha said, "Carolyn Crews, this girl I work with at the beauty shop, thinks Emmett's as cute as a bug's ear. It just kills her that he won't pay any attention to her. But he gave her a mess of vegetables from his garden once, and she was the proudest thing!"

"Emmett doesn't care anything about women," Lonnie said to his mother. "He hangs around with his Army buddies."

"He used to go with Anita Stevens," said Sam defensively.

Martha said to Lonnie, "If you don't get a job, you'll end up in the Army, and I'll worry myself sick."

"I'd go if I had to," Lonnie said.

Sam said, "And then you'd just get killed and that would be stupid."

"I can't bear to think about boys going off to war," Martha said. She jumped up from the table. "I've got to show you this spice rack I'm giving Jennifer for her shower," she said.

While Martha was out of the room, Sam ate an Oreo that Lonnie poked in her mouth.

"All we've heard for the last week is that spice rack," said Lonnie, grinning at his father, who grinned back knowingly.

"If there was a war, would you sign up?" Sam asked Lonnie.

"It depends. But if America needs defending, then I couldn't stand back, could I?"

"That was what Emmett thought."

Bud said, "I was lucky, I guess, to be between wars. But I never felt right about it. My daddy and his daddy both fought, and I felt like I missed out on something important." He licked the edge of his jello dish.

"I don't get it," Sam said. "If there wasn't a war for fifty years and two whole generations didn't have to fight, do you mean there should have been a war for them? Is that why we have wars—so guys won't miss out?"

"Now, Sam, don't go twisting my words," Bud said.

Martha returned with the spice rack. "It's not really a shower," she said. "It's a gift tea, and everybody brings their favorite spice and a recipe to go with it, and I give her the spice rack, as the hostess. I'm going to make banana-split cake with a cranberry-based punch. Doesn't that sound good? I'm proud of this spice rack. I just gave twenty dollars for it at that outlet in Paducah, and they're twenty-nine-ninety-five at Gift World out at the shopping center."

"It's neat," Sam said. If she married Lonnie, would anybody give her a spice rack? What would she do with a spice rack? She couldn't even name five spices. Marco Polo brought spices back from China. A picture flashed through her mind—Martha and Bud in their canopy bed, fucking.

Later that evening, Lonnie wanted to drive her home, but she said she would walk. She needed to burn off the calories, she said. Lonnie caught up with her in a moment, as she was crossing the street.

"What's the matter?" he said.

"I'm tired of taking up for Emmett. It's depressing."

"Don't take it personal. They don't know anything about Emmett."

"Nobody understands the vets," she said, almost crying. "They're different. People expect them to behave like everybody else, but they can't. If the Russians sprayed Agent Orange over here, it would be chemical warfare for sure, but the United States poisoned its own soldiers. I can't imagine why you'd want to defend a country that would do that."

"You've been talking to those veterans Emmett hangs around with, haven't you?"

"What makes you think that?"

"I hear things. I heard you went riding around with Tom Hudson."

"So what if I did?"

"I don't like the idea of you hanging around with a bunch of veterans."

"What are you talking about?"

"It doesn't look right."

"Well, I'll be! I thought you worshipped Emmett. You've got a Army jacket like his and everything."

"I like Emmett just fine, but what if he snapped and did something crazy? I started to worry about that the other day when we were at the Cracker Barrel. There was something about the way Emmett was talking that sounded funny. And then I thought back to that night at the pond."

"Why would you want to go in the Army?" Sam demanded.

"I told you if the country needed me, I'd go."

"That's what they told Emmett, and look what happened. And it's your idea that he's cracking up. Not mine." Sam wrenched her arm away from Lonnie.

"I'm going to the lake next week with the guys to stay in a cabin that belongs to Kevin's parents," Lonnie said. "Would you promise me you won't go riding around with Tom Hudson while I'm gone?"

"Good grief! He's got a *car* for sale and I'm thinking about buying it."

"I just felt jealous, I guess, at the thought of you riding around with somebody else. Come here, Sam."

He pulled her into his arms and kissed her, and she could taste Oreo cookies. He tugged on her earrings playfully. "Ouch! Those things are sharp!" He still held her, and he said, "Come on. Let's go fool around. We ain't fooled around in three days."

"Not tonight. I want to get up early tomorrow and run."

She had to get home, to see if Emmett was all right. She decided something about Lonnie. Lonnie had admired Emmett because he had been to war, not because he had become a hippie and turned against the war. Lonnie was just like all the other kids at school. In her history class last year, 90 percent voted in favor of the invasion of Grenada. They were afraid of the Russians. Sam ran the rest of the way home.

She bounded in the side door and saw Emmett playing *Space Invaders* in the darkened living room. Moon Pie was sitting right beside him, like a trusted assistant, as though Emmett were playing a game the cat truly understood. Emmett sat there, firing away, and for the first time Sam had a picture of him with an M-16, in a tropical jungle, firing at hidden faces in the banana leaves. And then sitting down for a meal of ham and motherfuckers.

13

Hopewell was having Flag Days, sidewalk sales around the courthouse square. The merchants were trying to save downtown from the attractions of the shopping center and the Paducah mall. Even the old Capitol Theatre shut down after the Cinema I–II opened at the shopping center.

All the flags flying from the stores that week made Sam preoccupied with the Vietcong flag Emmett had flown from the courthouse clock tower years before. She felt like flying a Vietcong flag herself. She was feeling the delayed stress of the Vietnam War. It was her inheritance. It was her version of Dawn's trouble. The pregnancy test had turned out positive—the test strip turned pale pink. Dawn was afraid to tell Ken.

The sidewalks were crowded with shoppers the afternoon Sam went to buy some new pom-pom socks. They were three for a dollar at a table in front of the trophy store. After buying socks with purple pom-poms, she wandered down the street, looking for bargains. She was considering some half-price hand lotion at a table of beauty aids in front of the drugstore when a fat woman in yellow shorts said to her, "My oldest girl used this bubble bath and she broke out." Sam wished she could think of something scandalous to do.

The sun was glaring. The square had come to life, even though several of the stores were dark and empty. The old variety store that used to be Sam's favorite was gone now, replaced by a crafts store, which was displaying dollhouse furniture and decoupage kits out front. Sam missed the old store. It sold toys and school supplies, and in the rear it had a mysterious shelf of books and magazines where she used to spend hours.

She bought a devil's-food cupcake from the fire-hall bake sale and ate it as she walked along. She waved at Allen Wilkins, who was busy selling a T-shirt to a woman in sunglasses. Then a man behind a table of children's running shoes called out to her.

"Hey, Sam, did Emmett find his bird yet?"

"No, not yet."

"What kind of bird's he looking for?" His name was George. She didn't know his last name. Emmett used to mow the man's yard.

"An egret."

"There's eagles not that far off. Over at Monkey's Eyebrow, where they have the wildlife refuge. Every Christmas you can go and see a whole flock of 'em, touching down on their way somewhere."

"An egret, not an eagle."

"You can see eagles down at Reelfoot Lake too."

"He's not looking for an eagle. He's seen eagles. He's looking for egrets. It's the state bird of Florida." She balled up the plastic wrap from the cupcake and threw it at a trash barrel beside a parking meter. Bull's eye.

Thoughtfully, the man said, "I must have seen those when I took the kids to Disney World, but what would a bird like that be doing up this way?"

"I don't know," Sam said. "Maybe it's just a notion in Emmett's head. You know how the vets get a notion in their heads. Like Agent Orange? There's some things they just can't stop thinking about."

The man gave her an odd look, and Sam practically ran across the street toward the bank. She had spotted Jim Holly at a table in front of old First Federal Bank. Now she realized Tom was there too. They were wearing camouflage fatigues.

"Hi, Sam," Tom said. In his camouflage outfit, he looked fashionable. Sam felt out of breath.

"Hi. What are you selling?"

"Anything you want," he said, grinning.

"I'd like a big orange, then," she said. "About a gallon of Agent Orange ought to do me."

"It's hot enough to drink Agent Orange, especially in my clown suit."

Tom and Jim were gathering signatures on a petition to the V.A. about Agent Orange. And they were collecting money for Buddy Mangrum's child, who needed an operation on her intestines, which were twisted.

"The vets' dance is Friday, Sam," said Jim. "Is Emmett coming?"

"He claims he can't dance."

"Anita's going," Tom said. "I saw her this morning and she said she'd come."

"Oh, good!" Sam was pleased. "I'll be there too," she said, looking at Tom.

"Do you still want that car, Sam?"

"Yeah. I've got to round up some cash, though."

"Well, let me know when you want it and I'll fix it up for you."

Tom looked handsome in his Army outfit, and there was no sign of grease except under his fingernails. With the strong sunlight behind him, the black-and-green camouflage pattern seemed all black. She wished he would ask her to the dance. Lonnie would be at the lake then. She liked riding around with Tom the other day. It gave people something to think about. It reminded them, maybe, of who she was. She felt proud. She wished she had camouflage pants like Tom's. They were in style.

There were about thirty names on the petition. Sam didn't recognize any of them except Anita Stevens. As Sam signed her name, she had an idea.

"Come with me to the courthouse," she said to Tom. "There's something I want to look for, and I need some help."

"Sure, Sam," said Tom, grinning. "If you can stand to be seen with me."

"Come on. It won't take long."

They entered the courthouse through the basement, which was at ground level on the north side. Smells of tobacco and urine assaulted them. The derelicts hung out in the basement. Sam saw an old man slumped over in a chair and rubbing his crotch. Another man, in dark gray work clothes, was sprawled out on a green vinyl couch. Some other men were playing checkers.

"They patrol down here to see that those guys don't bring any booze in," Tom said as they walked down the hall. "But they go drink behind the movie show and then come back here to sack out. Where are you taking me, Sam—to jail?" The entrance to the county jail was at the end of the hall.

"No. We're going up in the tower. I want to see where Emmett flew that Vietcong flag that time."

"Up in the clock tower?"

"Yeah. I just wanted to see what it was like."

"I remember the day he did that," Tom said with a smile. "Emmett was a lot wilder then."

Sam looked back at Tom, the way he was following her up the stairs. She wished she could keep on climbing up and up and up and see him following her that way, full of curiosity. On the third floor, the stairway ended, and they walked down the hall, passing men in short-sleeved pastel shirts and ties. A woman with old-fashioned bouffant hair and flashy red lips peeped out of a doorway and said, "Can I help y'all?"

"Where's the clock tower?" Sam asked. "We wanted to go up in it."

The woman seemed puzzled. "The clock tower? You've got me."

"Isn't it open to tourists?" asked Sam innocently, scooting her hands into her shorts pockets.

"I don't think I've ever been up in it," the woman said. "Try that stairway down past the prothonotary's office. I don't know where it goes."

"Much obliged," said Tom.

Tom led the way. The stairway was small and narrow. It turned and they climbed faster. Tom held his shoulders rigid, climbing with his leg muscles, without swinging his arms. A small window on the landing overlooked the courthouse square, and the door next to the window was padlocked.

"Shoot," Sam said, disappointed.

"I guess they don't want anybody flying any more V.C. flags," Tom said with a laugh.

"Did they really think Emmett would sneak back in with that flag?"

"You think a lot of Emmett, don't you?" Tom asked, turning toward her.

"Yeah." Tom's pants brushed Sam's knee and sent chill bumps over her.

"Emmett's probably not easy to live with," he said thoughtfully. "But he's a character."

"I'm used to him." She asked, "What does a Vietcong flag look like?"

"It's blue and red with a gold star in the middle. Didn't you ever see the one Emmett had?"

"I don't remember it. Emmett gave it to a neighbor a long time ago to put in her yard sale."

"Hey! That flag's probably in somebody's den, for decoration." Tom chuckled.

"Why do you think Emmett flew that flag?" Sam asked. "Was it treason, like some people say, or was it just a protest?"

"Why don't you ask him?"

"I'm afraid to. I don't want to set him off or anything."

"What are you afraid of, Sam?" Tom suddenly had her pinned against the wall. He wasn't touching her, but he had a hand on the wall on each side of her, and he was looking straight into her eyes.

"I don't want him to have a flashback."

"I have flashbacks. Didn't I tell you?"

"Yeah. But you made it sound like nice memories. Not scenes in a horror movie."

"You've been watching too much television, Sam. You're afraid he might freak out—and hurt somebody. Isn't that it?"

Sam squirmed uncomfortably. "I don't think that. My boyfriend thinks that. He thinks I'm in danger." She laughed nervously, regretting that she had brought up Lonnie.

"Are y'all getting married?"

"No."

"I heard you were getting married in September."

"It's not true."

He moved away from her and leaned on the opposite wall.

"Why don't *you* get married?" she asked. "Why don't any of the vets I know get along with women?"

"Ask Emmett," he said. He pulled out a cigarette and lit it. "That's not true of all of us," he said. "And I never said I didn't like women."

"Well, do you have a girlfriend?"

"No."

"Why not?"

"Maybe I'm too choosy."

Sam watched him smoke on his cigarette. The way he leaned against the wall favored his right shoulder. He even smoked with his left hand.

"It's so hard to find out anything," she said fretfully. "I want to know about that bird Emmett's looking for. And I want to know all this stuff about Agent Orange. It's so frustrating."

"Now you know how some of these guys feel after they've dealt with the V.A. for years. They're butting their heads up against a brick wall."

"I want to know what it was like over there. I can't really imagine it. Can you tell me what it was like?"

"Hot. I'll tell you that. Hotter than here."

"Did you see palm trees?"

"Yeah. They had palm trees over there. At least they did before we napalmed and defoliated everything."

"All I can see is a picture postcard. I see palm trees and rice fields. And that's it."

"Once I saw a palm tree disintegrate, if you can believe it. One minute it was a tree on a postcard, like you say, and the next minute it just exploded and disappeared. At first I thought it took off into outer space. It was like something out of science fiction."

He paused, reflecting. Then he said, "It was the most beautiful place you ever saw in your life, and we went in . . ." He stared out the window.

"Did you get around Agent Orange?"

"I didn't work with it. But I was probably around it. It was pretty widespread, and it got in the water. Once we came across this place that had been defoliated. And I remember thinking, This looks like winter, but winter doesn't come to the jungle. It's always green in the jungle, but here was this place all brown and dead. I didn't know it then, but I figured out later that must have been where they sprayed Agent Orange."

He mashed his cigarette under his black boot.

"Hell, we drank the water there. But I haven't had any of those symptoms yet. Knock on wood." He knuckled the woodwork on the window. "Except I was real sick at the time. And I had a headache for a year, and I was depressed. You know something else odd? Emmett talks about those birds all the time, but out in the jungle, around that time when we came up on that dead place, there weren't any birds. Maybe for miles, there weren't any birds."

"That bird Emmett's looking for was around the rice paddies."

"I don't know, though. Birds wasn't one of those things I would have known much about back then. Maybe there were birds. Are you ready to go? Did you haul me up here to give me the third degree?" He smiled nervously at her.

"How'd you get wounded?"

"Being in the wrong place at the wrong time." He started down the stairs and she followed. "Look, Sam. It's hard to talk about, and some people want to protect you, you know. They don't want to dump all this stuff on you. There are some vets who would take their sons to Canada before they'd let them be drafted. You shouldn't think about this stuff too much."

"I can't really see it," Sam said. "All I can see in my mind is picture postcards. It doesn't seem real. I can't believe it was really real."

"It was real, all right. You don't want to know how real it was."

He stopped on the stairway and reached up to touch Sam's waist. "I think you're cute," he said.

Sam didn't know what to say. Her knees trembled as they walked past the courtroom, its oak benches shining. On the second floor they passed the offices where the courthouse records were kept. Sam thought of all the documents on file there that were connected to her—her parents' wedding license, birth certificates, death certificates. She wished she had copies of all these official proofs that she was who she was, but it was a silly thought. Official documents were meant to be hidden away, on file, in a safe place—not in the house on display like a bowling trophy.

In the basement, the man slumped in the chair was asleep. A stooped white-haired man in a striped T-shirt pushed a dust mop forward, gathering cigarette butts. He spoke to Tom. "It's fairing up nice out there today." There were no windows and the only light came from the glass doors at the end of the corridor.

The man stared at Sam and said, "My daughter's in the hospital. She had a baby and run into trouble. It was a blue baby, and her husband wouldn't let the doctors do anything. He said the Lord would take care of it. And He did. The baby lived. It got its color!"

"Did you see it?" Sam asked curiously. She was aware that Tom had her hand, clasping it tightly, as if to protect her, even from this sad old man.

"Yeah, I seen it. Not when it was blue, though. It had already turned."

Another man, sitting at a table, spoke up. "Sometimes they're born yeller, lavender, peach, ever which of a color." He laughed in little throbs, with a hacking cough. "How do you reckon they know if a nigger's born a blue baby?" he said, choking on his laugh.

"Let's get out of here," Tom said to Sam, pulling her away, out into the sunlight.

14

Bruce Springsteen's new performance video, *Dancing in the Dark*, was on TV. His jeans were tight as rubber gloves, and he danced like a revved-up sports car about to take off.

"He's awful good," said Emmett.

"He turns me on *high*," said Sam, mesmerized.

"What do you mean?"

"It's something about the way his jeans fit," Sam said. "You wouldn't understand."

It made her sad. She kept thinking about what it would be like to dance with Tom. He had said she was cute. But he could never move with Bruce Springsteen's exuberant energy. She recalled Frankenstein and his monster dancing to "Puttin' on the Ritz" in an old Gene Wilder movie. The monster wore clubfoot shoes and clomped. It was pathetically funny. She hoped the veterans' dance wouldn't be like that. It would be too depressing.

"They call Bruce 'the Boss,'" Emmett said idly. Bruce was still dancing in the dark. Sam loved the part where he picked a girl in the audience to dance with. The girl was in shock that he chose her.

"Man, he can boss me around any old time he wants to," Sam said.

Moon Pie was asleep at the foot of Sam's bed with his paws curled around his nose. Sam and Lonnie were sprawled on the bed, eating Doritos, and *Abbey Road* was playing on the stereo. Lonnie had come over unexpectedly, to bring a caulking gun Emmett wanted to borrow.

"Are you still mad at me?" Lonnie asked when she didn't respond to his kiss.

"Well, I didn't like what you said about Emmett the other night."

"I didn't mean it."

"You have to take it back."

"I was just worried about you."

"What do you think Emmett might do, hold me hostage and make demands? He has less demands than anybody I know."

"I'm sorry," Lonnie said, rolling over to touch Sam's face. He rubbed the back of his hand across her cheek lovingly. His hands were rough from working with lumber. "Tomorrow's when I go to the lake for several days. While I'm gone, I want you to think about me."

"O.K." Sam was glad. Lonnie wouldn't have to know about the dance Friday night. She had so many secrets from Lonnie, but nothing as terrible as Dawn's secret from Ken. Lonnie's alligator-shaped birthmark, peeping under the edge of his T-shirt, seemed to wink at her.

Lonnie lit a cigarette, and Sam handed him the ashtray she kept in a drawer for him. He blew out his match and said, "You have to give me a token of affection, something to tell me you'll think about us."

"Do you want one of my earrings?"

"I like to nibble your ears," he teased. "But I don't want to choke on all that metal."

"You don't have to suck on my earrings!"

"They're having a stag party for John over there this weekend, and I have to bring some women's underwear? Will you let me have some of your panties? Those black ones I like?"

"Those are my best ones!"

"Well, I'll bring them back!"

"That's ridiculous."

"No, it's not, if you care about me."

Moon Pie woke up and drummed his chin. "Moon Pie's still got fleas," Sam said. "Emmett will have a fit. He sprayed him yesterday."

Outside, a car pulled into the driveway with a toot.

"Hey, Anita's here!" cried Sam, jumping off the bed.

"I've got to go pick up Daddy at the store," Lonnie said, glancing at his watch. "His battery's dead."

Emmett had spent all afternoon making lasagna. He seemed pleased that Sam had invited Anita, and he put tomato ketchup in the sauce to give it a little zing. Sam had helped him clean up the house, and he propped up the couch with a block of wood. All afternoon, they played Irene's old records and some old 45s Emmett had discovered at a yard sale—"Wooly Bully" by Sam the Sham and the Pharaohs and "Tutti Frutti" by Little Richard and "Maybellene" by Chuck Berry. Emmett danced around the kitchen, miming the words, and Sam collapsed in giggles. They were the funniest songs she had ever heard.

Anita had on a slinky pink dress and spike heels. She was smiling.

"You look like a flamingo," Emmett said.

"Why, thank you, Emmett—I guess." Anita handed Emmett a bottle of wine and a paper plate of her special brownies.

Sam put the wine in the refrigerator. It was a good thing Anita had brought wine. Emmett's bootlegger was sick, and they had only three cans of beer.

During supper, Anita and Emmett chattered nervously. Emmett wore his Pepsi cap at the table. He picked at his food. When the fire siren sounded, blocks away, Emmett jumped up and looked out the window. Anita said the lasagna was delicious and that Emmett's face looked great. She said the wine tasted better in brown mugs than it would in wineglasses. She even liked Emmett's skirt. He didn't wear it anymore, because he had washed it in hot water and it shrank, but Anita had heard about it and begged to see it. Her hands flew up in a good-natured whoop. Anita was cheerful about everything, even Emmett's pimples.

"But you should go to the V.A. and have that Agent Orange test, Emmett," she said.

"I'm thinking about it. Jim Holly's getting after me about it."

"Isn't it a shame about him and Sue Ann? Did you hear she left him and took their little girl to Lexington?"

"No kidding!" Emmett grabbed his head and held his temples. His forehead wrinkled. In a moment he said, "I just saw Jim yesterday at the grocery. He didn't say nothing about it."

"She just left yesterday. Her mother came down from Lexington, and they loaded up her station wagon with Pammy's things, just what they'll need for a while. A girl I work with told me."

"I saw him last night backing up his pickup to the community center," Sam said. "He has a tall cap on the back that looks like the Pope-mobile."

"That's so he can haul pianos," Emmett said. "He delivers pianos sometimes for his daddy at the Melody Mart."

"I was down at the community center a couple of nights ago," Anita said. "I helped them decorate for the dance. But he didn't let on anything was the matter."

"I thought Jim and Sue Ann were doing fine. They just built that house out in the Fairview subdivision." Emmett stopped eating and lit a Kent.

Anita said, "Personally, I think she's crazy about him and she'll be back. She just couldn't adjust to small-town life, after growing up in Lexington."

"Jim had everything going for him, though," Emmett insisted.

"I don't know what the real story is, but I bet Sue Ann was frustrated. She's a trained computer programmer and she couldn't get a job around here."

Emmett scooted his chair away from the table and got up. He dumped his lasagna into Moon Pie's bowl and raked his salad into the sack under the sink.

"Jim was out here the other day," Sam said, playing with the last of a flat noodle on her plate. "He said the vets used to have rap groups everywhere but here."

Emmett grunted. "Rat poops," he said.

"Emmett thought Jim said rat poops," Sam said to Anita.

"Emmett, you're always so funny," Anita said, smiling.

He drank some wine and flicked his cigarette ash into the sink.

"These are good brownies, Anita," Sam said.

"Why, thank you, Sam. Tell that to Betty Crocker." She chuckled, then laughed harder. "Emmett, that skirt is a *hoot!*"

Emmett's Indian skirt was draped over the back of a kitchen chair. He balled the skirt up and threw it. It sailed into the living room and landed on the couch. "How's your daddy?" he asked Anita.

"Better. He's home from the hospital now, and he has to walk a mile every day. He cusses every step of the way too!"

Emmett went to the bathroom, and Anita helped Sam clear away the dishes.

"I had to go and open my big mouth," Anita said sadly. "Now I've upset him. I knew this would be a mistake. Maybe I better go."

"No. Please don't," Sam begged. She covered the brownies with plastic wrap, then decided to have another one.

"He probably thinks I'm just chasing after him, and I don't want to go through what I went through before with him."

"But he needs you," Sam said. "He's just shy."

"Shy? Emmett?" Anita laughed.

"Well, he's afraid."

Anita nodded. "That's the story of my life. I scare off men."

"I don't think you're scary. I think you're nice."

Anita wiped the kitchen table off with a sponge. Her heels spiked across the floor. In this tacky house, she looked out of place—like a flamingo in a flock of chickens, Sam thought.

That evening on *M*A*S*H*, the surgeons were racing against the clock as they tried to patch a soldier's aorta. They had to wait for another soldier to die so they could get a graft, but that soldier took his time dying. He was brain-dead, but his heart wouldn't stop. Father Mulcahy hovered over him. If they didn't get the aorta fixed in twenty minutes, the wounded soldier might become paralyzed. There was a little clock in the corner of the screen, to heighten suspense. The brain-dead soldier's heart finally quit, and they finished the operation, but it went overtime. Hawkeye was furious when he learned the time, sensing the failure of their effort. Afterward, when the soldier was waking up from the anesthesia, B.J. and Hawkeye tickled his feet and shouted at him, "Wiggle your toes!"

"Watch this," Emmett said to Anita. He leaned forward apprehensively.

The soldier's toes bent forward slowly, then back, then forward. B.J. and Hawkeye and Hot Lips were shouting, "We did it! We did it!" Emmett was shouting with them.

"I knew he was going to wiggle his toes," Emmett said with a sigh of satisfaction.

They had seen this episode three times. It irritated Sam that Emmett didn't know what to do with Anita except watch TV. They should be dancing to "Wooly Bully." If Emmett had a VCR, he could tape his shows and not have to miss them. The color on the set needed adjusting. All the outfits were blue instead of army green, so that the characters appeared to be wearing blue denim, as though they had all traveled forward in a time machine. No one got up to fix the color. Sam's mind was somewhere else. She was on the courthouse stairs, necking with Tom.

When the second *M*A*S*H* began, Emmett started laughing at Frank Burns.

"Emmett says Frank Burns was just like his commander in the Army," Sam said to Anita.

"My C.O. had a stupid whine like that," Emmett said.

"Who was he?" Anita asked curiously.

"Nobody. He got fragged. Blown away."

It occurred to Sam for the first time that the phrase "blown away" had come from the war. Tom had said it the other day. She had read that sometimes the soldiers stepped on Bouncing Bettys, mines that leaped up chest high before they exploded. She had been told that something like that had happened to her father. His corpse in the body bag was probably like hamburger.

"Moon Pie's jealous," Emmett said when the cat jumped into his lap and began aggressively rubbing against Emmett.

"Oh, I love that big saucer face and those big eyes!" Anita said.

"Moon Pie's a good boy," Emmett crooned to the cat. "Yessir, Moon Pie's a *good* boy!" Moon Pie danced around in Emmett's lap and then settled down in a comfortable position. "I'm going to invent a video game for cats," Emmett said. "Mouse Invaders!"

Upstairs, Sam turned on Rock-95 and dialed Lonnie's phone number. Anita and Emmett were playing *Chopper Command.* Their laughter floated up the stairs, mingled with the bursts of electronic gunfire. They hollered like contestants on *Let's Make a Deal.*

"Get it!" Emmett cried. "Get it!"

"Do you think they'll make it?" Lonnie asked when Sam told him about Anita.

"I don't know, but she sure makes good brownies. And if he can't see how pretty she is, then he's blind."

"I know."

"I've been thinking," Sam said. "Before you leave, you can come over here and take those panties you like."

"Hey! All right. I'll sleep with them under my pillow."

Sam laughed. "Why don't you wear them on your head like a nightcap?"

She felt guilty. She knew she was going after Tom at that dance, but she thought if she gave Lonnie her panties, it would be a kind of bond, like a wedding ring, something to keep her from going too far. On the radio, the Boss was singing "Cover Me," in that strong, rocking, blues voice that sounded like something her mother would have loved once, before Lorenzo Jones started taking her out in his Ford Cobra, with his car radio set to the easy-listening station.

15

At the Burger Boy, Sam and Dawn sat out back on the parking lot railing. It was Dawn's break. Some guys drove by and honked. Sam used to hang out at the Burger Boy even before she started working there. Lonnie used to pick her up after work and they would drive around. It all seemed innocent then, but what it amounted to, Sam thought now, was having babies. This was the mating ground Emmett talked about. It made her feel sick. It was tragic that Dawn hadn't taken the pill. Sam thought about how it used to be that getting pregnant when you weren't married ruined your life because of the disgrace; now it just ruined your life, and nobody cared enough for it to be a disgrace. Lonnie had come over the night before, just as Anita was leaving, and he was so loving and apologetic about Emmett that Sam let him spend the night. When she popped her birth-control pill in her mouth at midnight, two hours after the usual time, she wondered what ninety-nine percent effective meant. Did it mean if you screwed a hundred times, you'd probably get pregnant? In bed, Lonnie labored over her, mashing her breasts, and in about thirty seconds a billion wiggle-tailed creatures with Lonnie Malone's name on them shot through her. Down the hall, Emmett belched. It was the tomato ketchup in the lasagna.

A Pontiac Firebird with a sunroof zoomed by the Burger Boy, then a Trans Am.

Dawn said, "You know Yvonne, that black girl that comes in at four-thirty? She let me do her corn rows!"

"What did her hair feel like?" asked Sam, impressed.

"It was weird. Did you know they have to put grease on their hair to keep from getting dandruff? Their hair's naturally dry!"

"I thought it was naturally greasy."

"No. They put grease on it. If we put grease on our hair, we get dandruff, but it's just the opposite with them."

"What did it feel like?"

"It's real soft. Like real soft pubic hair. And it's not really that curly till they put the grease on it. That was an experience. I felt privileged." Dawn rattled the change in her apron. Orange and brown weren't her best colors. "Yvonne's got a brother who's going to make a video," she said. "He's got a camera. I'm going to beg him to let us be in it."

"Really? Gah!"

"Yeah. I want to do something real wild. I feel mad at the world."

"We could wear black leather pants and sunglasses with bright pink rims."

"Yeah. If he lets us be in it, we could just prance around looking cool. We wouldn't have to sing. We'd just have to look tough. It could be really great. Everybody would know who we were." Dawn shifted her weight on the railing and the skirt of her uniform hiked up. "You know what we could do?"

"What?"

"We could dress up like that and have our picture taken, and then put an ad in the newspaper. We'll say we're a group from California and we'll be signing autographs at the shopping center and we'll go see who shows up." Dawn laughed and then Sam laughed. "You know what we could call ourselves? This is going to kill you. We'll call ourselves the Gay Deceivers. You'll never guess what it means."

"What?"

"It means falsies!" Dawn cupped her breasts underneath. "Get it? The Gay Deceivers. It's a real old term. I came across it in an old book of my mother's. Isn't that funny?"

Sam doubled over, laughing. "Falsies!"

"Does Emmett's girlfriend wear falsies?"

"I don't think so."

"She's got the biggest boobs I ever saw on somebody not fat."

"Hey, Dawn!" yelled a guy in a Dodge Dart. "I saw Ken down at Bob's Car Wash. He said tell you he has to work late and can't pick you up."

"How am I going to get home?" Dawn said to the street. The Dodge Dart was already gone. "Shit. I'll have to call my brother."

"I don't have a ride anywhere either, with Lonnie over at the lake with Kevin and them."

When Sam told Dawn about the stag party and the panties Lonnie took, Dawn said, "Ken went to a party like that and they stayed drunk three days. They had dirty movies! I'd like to be in a dirty movie. That's what I feel like doing." Dawn picked at her nail polish. Her polish was lavender, with gold flecks in it. She sighed. "God, I don't want to be pregnant."

"That test might be all wrong. It's still early."

"I'll take it again, if I can scrape together the money to buy another one of those dumb kits."

Sam said, "Why don't we just go away, like we said? You could have the baby in Florida and we could work at Disney World. Ken wouldn't even have to know about the baby." As soon as she said it, Sam regretted this idea. She didn't want to be tied down with a baby.

"I've always played mommy," Dawn said. "I'm sick of playing mommy. I want to play daddy. No, I want to play Las Vegas.

That's funny!" She checked her watch. "I have to get back in or Walt will come out here and drag me in. He's a mean boss. Do you want me to sneak you a free Coke or anything?"

"No, that's O.K. I don't want to get you in trouble."

A bunch of boys piled out of a Buick. They were tanned and sweating, and none of them was really cute.

"See you, Dawn," Sam called.

"Later."

16

The night before the dance, there was a thunderstorm. During the night, Sam heard Emmett shutting windows. The storm would test his work on the basement leak. Mrs. Biggs had informed him that all basements leaked and that he should just buy a sump pump from Sears, but Emmett told her he had a plan.

When they went outside the next morning in the drizzle to inspect the ditch, Emmett said worriedly, "I may have to dig a trench along the south wall too."

"A frog's in your ditch," said Sam. She could see the frog's eyes peeping at them through the muddy water.

"Get out of there, frog," yelled Emmett. It disappeared in the mud. "Water seeping under a house spawns all sorts of life," he said with a shudder. "Mosquitoes, tadpoles, water bugs, dry rot, funguses, all kinds of worms and snakes."

The house was damp and musty, and the humidity exaggerated ancient smells in the old walls. The wallpaper was coming unglued. It was many layers of gaudy flowers, like some repressed life that wanted to emerge. Emmett inspected the basement and found some dampness that he wasn't sure was a real leak. His face was moist too from the salve he used. He sometimes looked as though he had been crying. Sam remembered the time last year when they, along with most of the country, had watched the final episode of *M*A*S*H*. Irene had made a double popping of popcorn in advance and kept it warm in the oven, and they had sat riveted before the television set. Emmett was choked up the whole last half hour, during the farewells among the characters, when the war was over in Korea. Even Irene sobbed, but Sam wouldn't let herself cry. Later, she thought how odd that long, tearful ending would seem to someone who had not followed the series.

When he returned from McDonald's later that morning, Emmett said, "I saw Jim, and you can tell he's real tore up about his wife going off, but he won't admit it." Emmett unlaced his running shoes, which squished. He shook his head sadly.

"Anita said he's worked so hard on that dance," Sam said.

"Hell, yes. He's got music and food and decorations and everything. He worked his butt off. And then his wife ups and leaves him."

"How come she'd do that? Is it because he was so involved with the vets?"

"No, I don't think so."

"I bet it was. Maybe he drove her away. It seems to me like some vets I could name are afraid of women."

"Women weren't over there," Emmett snapped. "So they can't really understand."

"Well, Mom took care of you all those years, and you think she didn't understand?" Sam said angrily. "And what about me? I feel like there's a big conspiracy against me. Like something the CIA would be in on." Sam grabbed up one of her Vietnam books from the table and shook it at him. "But I know about stuff that went on."

"Don't throw that at me," Emmett said, wincing.

Sam thought he meant the book, but then she realized he meant what was in the book. He didn't want to be reminded. She said, "There were women in Vietnam too. Anita knows a nurse at the hospital who was over there. Anita could understand what you're talking about."

"Anita's too softhearted for her own good. She lets people take advantage of her." Emmett bent his head to peer in the refrigerator, and Sam touched his neck, turning his head toward her to look at his rash.

"It's going away," he said.

It was healing, and the crust made a little design on his neck. Sam thought of the mysterious brand "X" on the back of the mother's neck in a science fiction movie she couldn't recall the name of. The aliens had branded the woman like a cow, to control her mind.

Emmett took out ground chuck to thaw. "I've got an idea," he said. "After I get the foundation fixed, I'm going to work on insulating the house so it will be tighter. I'm going to see if I can find some used storm windows somewhere, or maybe tape Mylar inside to keep us warmer this winter."

"Taping plastic on the windows is what poor people do."

"I ain't proud."

"If you had a job, you could pay that money you owe and buy some storm windows. I'm tired of everything being so tacky." Sam felt suddenly that her whole life was rigged up as precariously as some of Emmett's contraptions.

He clunked the frozen meat into the sink. "You just show me a job worth doing. I could have had a job selling microwave ovens at that appliance store at the shopping center. But that may not even be moral. Lots of jobs ain't right, if you ask me. Microwaves cause cancer."

"Microwaves cause cancer and Agent Orange doesn't?" Sam asked sarcastically. "There are plenty of jobs worth doing. You could be a disc jockey."

"Ha ha."

"Or get into video machines. That's something you like. The guy that runs the arcade gets to play *Ms. Pac-Man* all day for free. He hogs *Ms. Pac-Man*."

"That's stupid."

"Jello wrestling," said Sam. "You could coach a team of women who wrestle in a ring full of jello. You could rake in the money. People are crazy about jello wrestling."

"Stop bugging me, Sam. I told Jim I'd go to that dance, and that's all I can manage right now."

"Hey, all right! That's fine. But you have to promise to dance with Anita."

"O.K."

"Especially if she wears that flamingo outfit."

"Oh, do you think Anita will wear her flamingo outfit?" Emmett asked, his face lighting up.

"She might."

17

On the day of the dance, Lonnie called from the lake. Kevin's father had taken them out the night before to eat steak. Lonnie told Sam he had slept with her panties under his pillow. "Were you expecting the tooth fairy?" Sam asked. She asked Lonnie a dozen questions about the cabin and the steak place. Lonnie wanted to know what she was going to buy his brother for a wedding present. Sam said she hadn't thought about it. She asked him about the birds at the wildlife refuge. "Be sure to remember what birds you see," she said. "Emmett will want to know." She didn't mention the dance.

Sam wore tight jeans with her studded belt and a turquoise tank top to the dance. It was at the community building, which had a gymnasium. Lonnie had given Sam his ring at a Halloween dance there last year. She wasn't wearing his ring now. It was in her sock drawer.

At the door, Allen Wilkins greeted Sam and Emmett. Allen looked different in his green fatigues. Sam was used to seeing him dressed up, behind the counter of his menswear store.

"You be good now, Sam," he said with a wink. "The law's liable to get after us for entertaining minors."

"Don't I belong here?" she said innocently. "My daddy was in the war."

"Sure thing, Sam. You sure do."

Jim Holly's loud voice boomed out, "Emmett, you old hound

dog! If you hadn't come, I was going to go out to your house and drag you here personally."

"I feel like a wallflower at the prom, with my face broke out like this," Emmett said, grinning and punching Jim's arm.

"We're taking you to Louisville to get that Agent Orange test," Jim said.

"My basement's flooded and my foundation's weak," Emmett said with a grin. "And my house might fall down while I'm here."

"Your house couldn't fall down like mine did," Jim said, shaking his head.

"Well, Sue Ann'll be sorry she went off," Emmett said.

"Yeah." Jim drank from his paper cup of beer. "She got a job offer up at this place where she used to work. She's just going to try it out. Maybe we'll be one of those long-distance marriages." He laughed. "We always tried to be modern."

Sam looked around for Tom. That morning, she had run past his shop, and she saw him working inside the dark cavern of his garage, his back held at that funny angle. The VW was still sitting there, with its patches of rust. She had the wishful thought that he was saving it for her.

The gym was decorated with red-white-and-blue crepe-paper streamers and balloons, like a birthday party. In a corner by the bleachers there was a green cardboard tank with a cannon sticking out. Under one of the basketball hoops was a refreshment table, with a keg of beer, soft drinks, and potato chips. Emmett had brought a pan of mini-pizzas and a couple of wives had furnished dips. Under the other basketball hoop was a set of loudspeakers and a turntable. Bob Dylan was twanging away. Sam got a paper cup of 7-Up and a handful of potato chips and went to look at the records. She flipped through a stack of albums—the Beatles, the Stones, the Who, a lot of familiar groups—and picked out a few to play.

Allen Wilkins joined her just as the Beatles started singing "All You Need Is Love." "I must have heard that song a hundred times when I was in country," he said with a wistful smile.

"Did you hear the Beatles in Vietnam?" Sam asked, surprised.

"Yeah. A guy in my outfit had a tape player and his girlfriend sent him all the latest stuff. And there was the Armed Forces Radio too." He paused and gazed dreamily at a balloon hanging from the basketball hoop. "When you're in country, there's so little connection to the World, but those songs—that was as close as we came to a real connection."

"Did you listen to music out in the jungle?" Sam asked.

"Yeah. Of course most of the time you had to be quiet, but now and then when you had a secure place you could let loose." Allen smiled. "My favorite song was 'White Rabbit.'"

Sam tried to imagine Grace Slick bellowing out at the enemy. With that kind of music, why didn't the North Vietnamese just lay down their weapons and get stoned? If they had understood English, maybe the music would have won the war. But now, listening to "All You Need Is Love," she realized how naive the words were. Love didn't even solve things for two people, much less the whole world, she thought. But it wasn't only the words. Sometimes the music was full of energy and hope and the words were just the opposite. Emmett had said rock-and-roll was happy music about sad stuff.

Sam overheard two guys discussing Buddy Mangrum. One said, "Ain't it a shame Buddy couldn't come? He just didn't feel up to it. That poor guy's had every symptom in the book, and the V.A. just laughs in his face. Nausea, the runs, jaundice, chloracne. His muscles twitch and he can't sleep and he's lost weight. He can't even drink one beer. It makes him drunker'n a hoot owl."

"That sounds like Agent Orange, all right. I heard he peed blood."

"Yeah. His kid's being operated on down in Memphis. They're going to reroute her intestines somehow to keep 'em from twisting so bad."

Just then Sam noticed Pete Simms come in with his wife, Cindy, who looked older than Pete. She had brought a cheese log.

Admiring Sam's earrings, she said, "Girl, I wouldn't have the nerve to put that many holes in my ears."

Sam had on the horseshoe nails Dawn had given her and the heart studs. The new holes had almost healed.

Later, Pete said to Sam, "Don't tell my wife I showed you my tattoo."

"What will she do to me?"

"That's not the question. It's what she'll do to *me.*" He laughed and patted Sam on the rear. His hand was large and searching. That hand had fired guns, she thought as she twisted away from him.

Drinking her 7-Up, Sam studied the display of snapshots on the bulletin board. Grinning soldiers in fatigues and jungle boots stood in front of tents and hooches. There was no background or landscape, just flat dirt patches, some wooden huts, a jeep. The boys posed for the camera, with their hands on their hips, trying to look tough. They were just boys, like Lonnie, not like the aging men in this room. Sam noticed sandbags, a spotted dog, some oil drums. Hopewell had sent dozens of boys to the war. One class had three killed in just two months. Sam didn't find her father's name on the list of the dead, written on lined notebook paper and tacked up beside a set of dog tags. He wasn't from Hopewell. He was from a small community far out on the edge of the county.

Sam found Emmett and a man she didn't recognize examining a table covered with plastic toys—M-16s and M-60s, tanks, mortars, choppers, fighters. "They're like the models we used to make, Sam," Emmett said, holding up a Phantom II. There was some other gear from the war—a regulation mess kit, a flak jacket, a rain poncho, even a helmet. The helmet looked incredibly small and fragile.

"Remember this, Earl?" said Emmett, holding up the poncho.

"Too well," the man said. He lifted his paper cup of beer and drank. He was overweight and short.

Emmett said, "See, Sam, this is how it would be. You'd take your poncho and make a tent out of it, and sleep under it. And you'd use your helmet to wash and shave in. And this here's a C-rats kit. That's where you'd have your ham and mother-fuckers."

Earl said, "I'll never eat those again. I can't go near ham and beans—of any kind."

"Me neither." Emmett laughed and thumped the cardboard tank. "I never thought I'd see anything like this again." Jim was standing there, and Emmett said, "Goddamn, Jimbo, that machine gun looks like an elephant's peter."

"Anita helped make it," Jim said. "That gal's really artistic. Where *is* Anita? She should be here by now."

"These old things look like antiques," Emmett said, fingering the battered old C-ration kit.

Cindy appeared, holding a drink and one of Emmett's little pizzas. "Y'all did a good job, Jim," she said.

"I wish more people would come," Jim said worriedly. "This isn't a good turnout at all."

"Those weapons look real," Cindy said, finishing the pizza.

Earl said to Jim, "On TV, they make us all out to be psychos and killers. But most of us have adjusted just fine. I haven't had any problems. I've got a good job."

"That's fine, Earl. We're proud of you."

"I don't go around stirring up trouble. Sure, I've got memories, but I've learned responsibility. I've come to terms with what I did. You never forget it, but you go on living. You have to. You have to think of the future. Your kids. You have to make sure they don't get sucked into a war they can't win, like we did."

"Correction," said Pete. "A war they wouldn't *let* us win. We could have won it and you know it."

"But the point is you can't live in the past. This is sickening." Earl gestured at the room. "Balloons. Toys." He kicked at the tank. "Why have reminders like this? This is stupid."

"Stupid, huh?" said Pete. "It just so happens I drove a tank just like this and I'm mighty proud of it."

Earl made Sam nervous. She was standing by the toys, listening. She was afraid Earl was drunk.

"Don't pay any attention to this," Emmett said, nudging her elbow. "Earl gets on his high-horse, and Pete likes to bug him."

Jim was caught in the middle. Pete was defending Jim, and

Earl wouldn't stop. He glared at Pete and Jim. He said, "You can't live in the past, and you can't drown yourself in memories. The question is, what are you going to do *now*. I didn't have any trouble coming back because you know why? I didn't whine. That's why. I did my job and I'd do it again." He sloshed his beer at Jim. "You self-pitying people make me sick."

"If Earl doesn't watch it, Pete's going to flatten him," Emmett said as he maneuvered Sam across the gym floor. Two couples were dancing. "Hey, there's Anita! Would you look at her! Hey."

Anita had on tight jeans and high heels and a bright red top with string straps. Her large breasts filled out the top.

"She's not a flamingo tonight," Sam said.

"No. She's a redbird. A Kentucky redbird."

"Emmett—well, how in the hell are you!" cried Anita, giving him a hug. He squirmed and turned red. "Hi, Sam! You look darling! I *love* your earrings!"

Anita hugged Sam. She smelled nice, like a store at the mall that had a perfume blower in the doorway. She had large brass disks hooked on her ears, and she was laughing.

Sam left Anita and Emmett, laughing together, and went to get some chips and dip. She ate three of Emmett's mini-pizzas and stood around for a while watching the people. It was depressing that so few vets had come. Pete and Cindy were dancing. Sam tried to imagine Cindy ordering around a guy who was brandishing a shotgun, as Emmett had said. The cheese log she had brought had blue cheese in it. Blue cheese smelled like dirty feet. It made Sam gag.

Now Anita and Emmett were actually dancing. Anita danced with low-key, subtle rhythms, the way the black kids danced, and her bushy hair and her red top were flamboyant. Emmett, moving with self-conscious jerks, gazed at her the way he watched birds.

Sam was looking through the records, wishing she could find a Doors album—the one that had "The End," from *Apocalypse Now*—when Anita joined her.

"I'm so smashed," Anita said, wobbling on her high heels. "I was so nervous over seeing Emmett I got tanked up. Can you tell?"

"You look nice," Sam said.

"Emmett's gone to the little-boys' room. Oh, he's so cute," Anita said with a sigh. "He'll say something that just makes me speechless. You know what he said just now? He said, 'I ain't got nothing but hard times and bubble gum and I'm fresh out of bubble gum.' I thought that was so funny. He makes me laugh. I like a man who makes me laugh."

"I like to hear y'all laugh."

"I used to see Emmett walking everywhere, and I used to offer him rides. I had a Mustang, bright red, and I thought I was hot stuff. Not just hot *stuff*. I thought I was hot *shit!*" She laughed. She had a hearty, warm laugh, like poppin'-fresh dough from the oven, Sam thought. "That's how I got to know Emmett, giving him rides," Anita said. She was drinking something the color of plywood. She said, "I guess you've heard about Vietnam all your life, haven't you, Sam?"

"In a way."

"I'll tell you my Vietnam story," Anita said. Her eyes kept watching for Emmett, and Sam kept glancing around for Tom. They were two desperate females looking for men. What made them think earrings would do it? Sam felt shabby, compared to Anita. Anita said, "When Vietnam was going on, I was in a fog. My marriage had busted up, and in 1967 I went to nursing school and I was working hard and didn't think about the war. I didn't know anybody who went over there, and it just seemed too far away. But one spring weekend in 1969 I was on a bus to Bowling Green going to see my aunt, and some boys got on at Fort Campbell. They were in soldier uniforms, with those baggy green pants and black boots like Pete's got on. One of them sat across from me and talked with me. I was reading a book of poetry. This boy tried to read it over my shoulder, and he told me he liked poetry. Well, that really impressed me, because how many guys will read a poem? He wasn't just saying it to flirt, either. He told me about some poems he had read. And then he told me that he was shipping out to Vietnam the next day. All of them were. And that really got me. I thought—why, he could go over there and *die!* It just really bothered me. I never knew who he was or if he came back alive. But you know, for years, I didn't know anybody who died over there. The boys in my class were a little older and missed it. I'm thirty-nine. Did you know that? But for years I thought—that was *my* Vietnam experience. It always sounded silly to tell it, but I think it affected me more than hearing about the war on the news. Because it was *real* and I was right there, on that bus with all those boys. I just know some of them didn't come back."

"Wow," said Sam. She didn't know what to say.

Anita said, "What I tell myself is if this affects me that much, then just think how much somebody would be affected if they had a boyfriend over there and he didn't come back. Or if they had a husband over there and he came back and had been through that hell. And then after I got involved with Emmett, I thought I knew. Do you know what I'm saying? Oh, I hate to be drunk. I feel so stupid. Do you know what I'm saying?"

"Yeah."

"I'm saying I can appreciate your situation, Sam. I really can. I try. I try so hard." She tugged at the strap of her top. "There's Emmett. I'm going to make him dance with me again." She floated off, her bright laughter flooding the room.

Finally, Tom appeared. Sam felt her face turn red. He walked in, with a paper sack, wearing jeans and a blue T-shirt. He looked comfortable with himself. That was what made a guy sexy, Sam realized, as she sped across the floor, spilling a little 7-Up as she went.

"Hi, Sam." He grinned and reached for a cigarette. "Where's Emmett?"

"He's here. I got him to come."

"I would have asked you to come with me, but I didn't think you would go out with me," said Tom in a teasing tone.

"I would have come with you."

"What about your boyfriend, Sam? Is he here?"

"What boyfriend?" Sam said.

Tom nodded, then looked away from her. "Well, then," he said. "Do you want something to drink?"

"Sure. Let's get some Cokes." She led him toward the refreshment table.

"I mean do you want something in it?"

"If you say so."

"I'll spike it just a little. Just to give you a little kick," he said.

The paper cup of Coke foamed slightly. It tasted bitter and strong. The whiskey was Jim Beam, and Sam thought of Lorenzo Jones' collection of Jim Beam bottles. Her eyes fell on the toy tanks and airplanes on the table under the basketball backboard.

"Hey, look at that," Tom said. "Emmett's dancing with Anita."

"I think they're getting something started again," Sam said. "I hope so. I like her. She came over the other day and watched TV with us."

Sam hadn't realized Tom was so tall until they danced. He was tall like Colonel Blake. His movements were smoother than she had expected, as though he had been limbering up, practicing. Only a few couples were dancing. Anita and Emmett were sitting down now, and Anita had her hand on Emmett's shoulder, talking to him. She touched his face with concern. Emmett, embarrassed, was eyeing the basketball hoop across the gym, as though he were about to shoot a basket. Sam saw Jim talking to Allen and Betty Wilkins. He was gesturing dramatically. Tom handed Sam a balloon and she wrapped the string around her finger and let the balloon bob above them as they danced. In a corner, barely visible, flashing in the strobe light Jim had rigged up, was the cardboard model of the tank, like a lurking monster. When a slow song by the Mamas and the Papas started, Sam and Tom danced close together, and Sam let the balloon go.

"You dance good," Tom said in her ear.

"You do too." She couldn't identify his aftershave. It smelled something like peaches.

The end of the song deposited them beside the table of toy weapons. Tom caressed an M-16.

"This is littler than the real thing," he said, picking it up. "But the M-16 is plastic, so it's real light and easy to maneuver. Except it had a habit of jamming on you."

"Emmett used to build models like this," Sam said. "I used to help. Here's my favorite one. The C-141 StarLifter. It's so big. Emmett used to tell me how big it was. But he'd exaggerate. He'd say it was as big as the Astrodome."

"This really hurts Jim," said Tom, setting down the rifle and surveying the handful of people there. "He expected a whole lot bigger crowd. Let's go talk to him."

"I don't see why Sue Ann couldn't have waited till after the dance to go to Lexington," Jim said to Tom. "This is embarrassing." He worked at a piece of crepe paper in his hand, balling it and pulling it to bits.

"Oh, everybody understands, Jim."

"I don't think she thought it through. She always jumps into something feet first."

"She's probably excited about that new job."

"Yeah. She'll be making twice what they paid her before. I can't argue with that."

Sam was getting smashed. Tom gave her some more whiskey. She was getting used to the taste, and she liked the way it made her feel. Several vets came up and said things to Sam. "Nice to see you here, Sam. What do you want to hang around a bunch of crazy old soldiers for?" Or "Watch out for Tom. He's got a reputation." It was all teasing. It was the way people communicated for the most part, she thought. She saw Pete by the refreshment table, arguing with Earl again. Their paper cups flew at each other in emphatic gestures.

A vet Sam didn't know said to her, "I went to school with your daddy, Sam. He was a senior when I was a sophomore. He was going with Irene then, and they made a good-looking couple."

"Oh, tell me what you remember! What else?"

"Him and her would go to Paducah on weekends and mess around. He wasn't wild. He was a good boy."

"What was he like?"

"He was the quiet type. He didn't have a lot to say."

"What else?" It was maddening that no one knew anything but

the obvious. Even Emmett had little to tell her. He hadn't known Dwayne that well.

"Let me tell you this, Sam. Dwayne was lucky. He was damn lucky. He never knew what hit him."

"Lucky? Isn't it better to be alive, no matter what?"

The man wouldn't answer. He made fists, opening and closing his hands.

"I wonder if he was around Agent Orange," Sam said.

"If he was, then he's twice as lucky he died."

Tom steered her by the waist across the floor. "Don't believe that, Sam," he said. "Your daddy wasn't lucky at all. He never got to know you."

He was still trying to protect her. But now she felt grateful. And she thought he had just given her a big compliment. She felt light-headed. Tom was staring at her, as if about to speak.

"What are you thinking about?" she said.

"You."

"Oh."

Emmett and Anita interrupted them, laughing hysterically. "Oh, no, I've spilled my drink all over my good top!" Anita cried.

"That *is* a good top, Anita," said Emmett, staring straight at her breasts. "You said a mouthful." His pimples didn't even show in this light. He looked happy.

Sam handed Anita a Kleenex from her shoulder bag. She happened to have it because she had taken a handful from Martha's bathroom the last time she was over there. It seemed like years ago. The Kleenex were pink, matching the dainty bathroom. Sam thought of Martha's gift tea, the jeep wedding. Sam was supposed to buy a fancy wedding present. Maybe she could buy a model kit of a C-141 StarLifter or a Huey Cobra instead. They could hang it from the ceiling.

Tom squeezed her hand and said, "I'll be right back."

Sam sat down in a folding chair to wait for Tom. Against the wall, a couple of veterans she didn't know were aiming the toy M-16s playfully at each other. Cindy walked by. She looked bored. Maybe she was embarrassed about her cheese log. She was tough, with a clenched jaw, like a lady truck driver. Jim was drinking a lot, and Earl, the guy who had started the argument, seemed to be arguing with someone else now. The entwined red and white and blue streamers flowed in the breeze from the air conditioner. Buddy Mangrum's kid's intestines were twisted like that.

The newspaper account of Martha's gift tea had said she decorated her house with hurricane posts wrapped in satin, with crepe-paper streamers. Sam thought of the guy who encircled those islands near Florida in pink plastic. Emmett had been furious, because of the ecology—all the dead birds, he groaned. But Sam had admired what the artist did, because he seemed to mock the idea of fancy wrapping. You could work hard wrapping a package and buy some pretty paper and a nice ribbon and a name tag, but the person would just rip it all up to see what was inside. Packaging was supposed to deceive, Sam thought, but it never really did.

Her father came back from the war in a plastic bag. Attractive and efficient. A good disguise. The body bags should have been red, white, and blue, with stars all over, like the stars she used to get on her sheet music when she took piano lessons. Her grandmother Hughes was a Gold Star Mother. Sam got a gold star for mastering "Für Elise," a Beethoven tune, but she quit piano after a year because she wanted to play the Liverpool sound. The music teacher had never heard of the Kinks or the Beatles and wanted her to play exercise pieces with no tune to them. "Imagine," Sam said aloud, "not ever hearing the Beatles." *Imagine there's no heaven . . . Nothing to kill or die for.*

The gymnasium blinked under the strobe light, and in the corners it was dark, like a foxhole where an infantryman would lie crouched for the night, under his poncho, spread above. The place would be damp and dirty. What was the dirt like in Vietnam? *In country,* they said. Was it clay like Emmett's trench, or red like the dirt in Georgia she had seen pictures of? She didn't know. The rats and spiders would creep in and get active as the night wore on, and above there would be flashing lights, the tracers beaming across the sky, identifying the crisscross path of a distant firefight. The strobe light was like that. The pain in Emmett's head. Sam couldn't understand why this scene in the gym wasn't causing the veterans to have a collective flashback. The toys blinked in the strobe light. Sam could look at the table of toys through squinted eyes and imagine she was seeing real transport planes and tanks from a distance, through a fog, through a strafing, through mortar shells exploding in the night, making wild colors. The models she had made with Emmett gathered dust, and when their decals flaked off, Irene threw them away. Sam thought about snipers hidden in the tropical foliage. Soldiers said they sensed when snipers were watching them. The cardboard of the tank was hollow. The red, white, and blue were dead colors.

"I had to see a man about a dog," Tom said with a smile as he sat down beside her. He touched her hand again, and Sam realized the music on the loudspeaker was "The House of the Rising Sun" by the Animals. Emmett had told her that song was about a whorehouse. She spotted Allen and his wife dancing. They were the only couple on the floor, and they were moving slowly, close together.

Sam said to Tom, "Did you have a girlfriend back home that you wrote to when you were over there—in country?"

"Yeah. But she got fed up with me. I wrote her letters, but she got tired of waiting."

"Did she marry somebody else?"

"Yeah. But it was O.K. She couldn't have coped with me when I got back. She wanted everything normal, a family and a ranch house with a two-car garage. She wouldn't have been able to fit in my story. So she married the first do-good good old boy that came down the pike. But you know what, Sam?"

"What?"

He touched her earrings. "Those earrings are something else," he said.

They heard shouts. Pete and Earl were at it again. They were on the other side of the gym, and Sam could not hear what they were saying, but all of a sudden she saw Pete crash into the cardboard tank. Earl had slugged him.

"Oh, Pete will never stand for that!" cried Tom, rushing forward.

Pete and Earl were locked in a wrestling grip. They fell on the tank and smashed it.

"Oh, all my hard work," Jim moaned. "And all that expensive spray paint."

It was Emmett who stopped the fight. Sam didn't know how he did it, but both men seemed to respect Emmett. Sam was surprised. She saw Earl leave, and Pete had a big grin on his face. He wasn't hurt. "I had to defend the tank," he said, "but looks like I ruined it in the process." He laughed and drained his beer. "He was looking to get his ass and head rearranged. You talk about somebody with problems. Even the V.A. would know he's got problems."

Sam ran into Cindy later in the restroom. She was putting on her lipstick.

"It never fails but what I have to be humiliated," she said. "But this time Pete was right. Earl was just spoiling for a fight."

"I think he's drunk," Sam said.

"He can't hold his liquor," Cindy said, blotting her lipstick with yellow tissue. "Isn't it a shame about Buddy Mangrum's little girl?"

"Yeah."

"I heard Emmett's got liver trouble, Sam. Is that true?"

"No. I don't think so. I hope not."

"I saw he was drinking beer, and I thought if he had liver trouble he couldn't be drinking."

"He's got a lot of trouble, but not liver trouble." A wave of panic struck Sam. She hadn't thought of liver trouble.

"Buddy can't even drink one beer." Cindy plucked at her tight, curly hair with a plastic pick. "Emmett's face doesn't look so bad now."

"He's got some salve." Cindy was so nosy. Sam hated the way everybody knew everybody else's business in Hopewell.

"He sure seems to be having a good time with Anita," Cindy said.

"Yeah. She's nice."

"That woman's been after him for years. Did you know that?"

When Sam started combing her hair, Cindy said, "I wouldn't have the nerve to wear all those earrings. How do you do it?"

"It's not hard. My friend Dawn's got four holes in each ear. She's got fifty pairs of earrings."

"It reminds me of what some of those guys did over there."

"What?"

Cindy shuddered and yanked at her hair. "You're probably too young to know this, but some of them cut off the ears of the enemy for souvenirs. It was awful. They brought them home and showed them off. Pete brought some home and I didn't think anything about it for a long time. He was proud that he served his country, and I was proud too. And it was years before those ears got to me. I can't wear earrings anymore. I think about them ears. They're so sweet-looking. And brown. Like button mushrooms. Little mouse ears. Oooh! For years, I've wanted to get rid of them, but what would I do with them?"

Sam didn't want to hear about ear collections. She didn't believe Cindy. She hurried away. Cindy wasn't somebody who loved to laugh, like Anita. In the gym, Donovan was singing "Sunshine Superman." "I know a beach where, baby, it never ends." It was a song full of mystery. Sam longed for the sixties.

She wished she could go to Tom's garage apartment and watch him work on a dirt bike. She wanted to see his scars. Maybe he needed a little physical therapy in a whirlpool bath. Or a hot tub. Tom looked even better in jeans than he did in the baggy fatigues. He had strong legs and a flat ass. When she danced with Tom, he was stiff like a mannequin above the waist, but it gave him a certain flair. She liked it.

She found Tom with Jim and Allen. Jim was crying. "People don't really care. Why didn't more come? Why didn't they dance? People don't really care about people, Sam. I've been fooling myself. It's disappointing."

Allen tried to reassure Jim, but Jim filled his cup again from the keg. He was getting louder and weepier. He said, "I thought when you went through something like war together it meant something."

"But it does, Jim," said Tom.

"Is that what Emmett feels, Sam?"

"I imagine so."

"He lost a lot of buddies over there. A *lot* of buddies." Jim drank some beer and said, "People don't always understand how Nam was different, though. Take my daddy. He thinks I should have been just like him fighting in the Pacific in the second big one. But he was out on a ship, and he could see the Japanese coming. He knew who the enemy was. He knew what he was fighting for. You can't tell him Vietnam was any different. He's hardheaded."

Jim made Sam uncomfortable, and she was glad when Tom squeezed her hand and asked her if she wanted to leave.

"Can you get home O.K., Jim?" Tom asked.

"Yeah. I'm going to clean up awhile and go on down to McDonald's and get some coffee."

"I'll drive," said Allen, touching Jim's elbow.

Sam realized that Anita and Emmett had left. She followed Tom out to his car. His hand was behind him and she held on as they crossed the parking lot. She felt she was doing something intensely daring, like following the soldier on point. A pool of orange light from a mercury lamp was the color of napalm. A napalm bomb frozen in time, she thought. Palm trees under the light. Nay-palm. No palms.

At first she thought she had a rabbit in her lap, but it was Tom's hand. It was a long, thin, strong hand, a bird with slender claws. She found the grease under his nails. Tom's lips were so different from Lonnie's. Lonnie's were hard and wrinkled, and Tom's were broad and soft, enveloping her.

"What are you doing to me?" he said at last. "I'd better get you home. I'm afraid I let you have a little too much to drink."

"No, I don't have to go home. I don't have a curfew."

"Where do you think we ought to go?" He sat waiting—for her to make the decision, as though he didn't want to be responsible.

"I don't have to go home. Emmett won't be there. He won't know if I don't come home. He's going home with Anita."

"That tickles me that he got together with Anita," Tom said, turning the key. He sat there for a moment, waiting, before pulling out.

Sam turned on the radio and twisted the dial to Rock-95. Rock-95 was playing that Beatles song again. She would recognize the Beatles anywhere. John was singing the lead. "You better leave my kitten all alone," he sang. "I told you, big fat bulldog, you better leave her alone." Sam had to find that record. She wanted to play it for everyone she loved. It was a fresh message from the past, something to go on.

18

"It really *was* a new record by the Beatles," Sam said, climbing the outside stairs to Tom's apartment. He was following her, his keys jangling. She was walking point now.

"I didn't know they were still singing."

"It's not exactly new, but it just now came out. My mother used to be crazy about them. She had all their old records, but she didn't have that one."

Tom had left his outside light on. He unlocked the door and snapped on the kitchen light. His kitchen had an old single-unit porcelain sink-drainboard littered with dirty dishes. The table, a card table covered with oilcloth, had goo and crumbs on it. Tom scooped up a pile of clothes from the floor.

"If I'd known I was going to have company, I would have straightened up," he said apologetically.

He took the clothes into the bathroom, and when he came out, Sam went in. It seemed that no time had passed, but he had flushed the commode, and the water was still whirling down, counterclockwise. At the South Pole, if you flushed the commode, it flowed clockwise. How did they know? How many commodes were at the South Pole? It would have taken someone very observant to notice that. Maybe some explorers had taken along some Rent-A-Jons. In the jungle, toilet paper was included in C-ration kits. Sam's head was whirling—clockwise or counterclockwise? She splashed water on her face. She dried her face on a damp, smelly towel and pushed her hair back behind her ears, exposing her earrings. She was aware that something was about to happen, like a familiar scene in a movie, the slow-motion sequence with the couple rolling in the sheets and time passing. She hoped there wouldn't be jump cuts. She didn't want to miss anything.

Tom was slapping a quilt across the bed. Grandma Smith had a quilt something like it. It was pleasant to think of a guy like Tom with a quilt. She wondered if his grandmother had made it, but it seemed inappropriate to ask. In the jungle, they had military regulation ponchos to keep out the rain. They slept in muddy ditches.

Tom had pulled off his shirt. He wasn't very hairy. His posture wasn't so bad. And she didn't see any scars. Now she remembered standing in the doorway of the bedroom a couple of minutes before, when he was in the bathroom. She had stood there, staring at his unmade bed, with the quilt crumpled at the foot. She was on rewind. Start again.

"Come here," he said. "I want to get to know you."

His shoulders were strong and stiff. She put her arms around him slowly, and gently she explored his back. His muscles were as tight as drapery cords. She didn't want to hurt him. She was afraid he would be in pain if he thrashed around in bed, twisting his shoulders in a way they didn't want to go.

The light from the bathroom was the only light, and she couldn't quite see his face, but she could feel tiny bumps on his back.

"Shrapnel," he said. "It ain't nothing."

He held her breasts, lifting up on them, very slowly, not the way Lonnie did, so rough and fast, as though he were squeezing red rubber balls.

The radio was playing, she realized after a while. Rock-95. Pat Benatar was screaming "Hell Is for Children!"

"Are you all right?" Tom said.

Sam nodded. She was trying very hard to concentrate. The

strip of bright light under the bathroom door was like a yellow marker pen highlighting the major themes of her life. She was afraid she would throw up. She was aware of the slow-motion moves, the jump cuts, but they seemed to go nowhere. After a while, he pulled away from her and sat up against the pillow. Herpes, Sam thought. He has herpes.

"This is embarrassing," he said, lying back with his hands across his eyes. Her hand felt below his waist. She felt a pile of kittens. He didn't even have an erection. Sam remembered being at one of those Halloween parties where you feel weird things in the dark. Maybe he was too drunk. Maybe he was too old to do it.

"You're such a nice girl," he said. "Promise me you won't laugh."

"What do you mean?"

He reached for a cigarette in his clothes on the floor. He tapped it against his palm and struck a match. In the flame, the pockmarks on his shoulders stood out. "I shouldn't have brought you here. This is awful."

"What's the matter?"

"Here I'm on fire, but there ain't nothing I can do about it. You're driving me crazy I want you so bad."

Sam nestled her head on his shoulder, but he didn't move toward her. He smoked his cigarette. The radio was playing a new-wave song she couldn't name by a group she didn't know. They sat there for a while and Sam's mind slowly cleared.

"You can't call this corruption of a minor," he said bitterly. "I thought maybe I could do it, because you turned me on so much."

He reached across Sam and tapped ashes in the ashtray by the bed. Sam took the ashtray and held it for him. She hadn't even minded the tobacco on his breath.

"Did you get hurt down there too?" she asked. "Is that what's wrong?"

"No. It's just in my head. Like a brick wall. The Great Wall of China. I butt up against it."

"I never heard of anything like that. Did you get hit in the head?"

"No. There ain't nothing wrong with me. It's just my head. You've heard of mind over matter?"

"Yeah."

"Well, my mind gets in the way. It takes me where I don't want to go. I thought it would be different with you, but it's not." He dragged on his cigarette and then put his arm around her. "I don't mean that as an insult. It's just me."

Sam laid her head against him, trying to get closer. She had never felt anything so terrible. She didn't understand what he was talking about. She felt nauseated. The light from the bathroom cast a sick glow over the room. They lay there, not moving, until he finished his cigarette.

"It's nothing unusual," he said. "A lot of people have the same problem." He put out his cigarette and pulled the quilt around their shoulders. His air conditioning was cold. He said, "I saw this program on television where you can get an operation. They put a thing inside you that you can pump up when you touch a button. It's the amazingest thing. You touch this button and it fills up with salt water that's stored inside a little sac, and it'll stay hard from now till Christmas if you want it to. There's a release button to make it go down. I saw that and I thought hell, that's for damn sure what I need. It'd be like getting a jump start when your car's cold on a winter morning."

"Oh, wow. You've got to get one."

"Ha! They only cost ten thousand dollars. Where am I going to get ten thousand dollars?"

"Do they do that operation at the V.A.?"

"I'd be liable to end up with something amputated there, the way they go at things."

Sam imagined his penis expanding and growing, like Pinocchio's nose. Modern technology could do anything, she thought. If you had the money.

"They give them to the paraplegics so they can get a hard-on to please their women," Tom said. "But they're numb. Don't misunderstand, Sam. I'm not numb. I can feel, and it's driving me crazy."

"Do you get disability for this?"

"What do you think?"

"Have you been to the V.A.?" This was really depressing. Her whole life centered on two men at the mercy of the V.A.

"Yeah. They gave me Valium and sent me to a therapy group, but I stopped going when I moved back down here from St. Louis. They can't do anything." He turned over on his side, away from her.

Sam didn't know what to say. She almost felt like giggling, but she didn't want him to take it the wrong way. The whole thing was absurd. She stroked his face. It felt like crushed vinyl, and his beard was sprouting.

"Nobody knows about this," Tom said. "If the guys knew, they'd tease me about getting one of those prick pumps. I shouldn't have let you come here. You're too nice a girl."

"What makes you think I'm such a nice girl? I'm a dope fiend and now I'm smashed and my uncle's crazy. Are you afraid I'll tell Emmett about this?"

"No." He sat up and reached for another cigarette. Before he could light it, Sam put her arms around him and snuggled closer, trying to get really close to him. Since he couldn't get inside her, she wanted to enclose him with her arms.

"Hold me," he said. "Just stay real close." He buried his head in her hair.

"My God, Sam," he said, coming up for air. "I've never felt muscles on a girl like you've got."

That was a compliment, she thought. When she woke up a couple of hours later, her head spinning in the dark, he was still clinging to her in his sleep.

19

The next morning, her head hurt and her mouth tasted like rust. Earlier in the morning, they had turned toward each other and she smelled his sour breath. She fell asleep again, and when she awoke he was gone. The sheets smelled. She found a Coke in his refrigerator, and she was so thirsty she drank half of it chug-a-lug. The Coke made her feel dizzy and sick.

She found Tom downstairs tinkering with a dirt bike. He was already dirty from his work. He asked her if she wanted some eggs and she said yes, thinking he would come back upstairs with her, but he told her where the bread and eggs were and told her to help herself. He was drinking a Coke and smoking. She said maybe she would run instead. She would walk home and change into shorts.

"Let me know if you want to buy that Volkswagen, Sam," he said. "I've been working on it some."

He nodded at the car, which was still sitting where it had been all summer, with the rusty splotches resembling a fungus that had grown on it.

She walked home in the dazzling sun, the night replaying in her head. She realized he had been so embarrassed that in the daylight he couldn't look at her. He was too ashamed. She didn't know what to say. It made her furious that she never knew the right things to say. Last night she had been too smashed, and now she let his embarrassment intimidate her.

As she spotted the Golden Arches, she thought of Emmett. And then it occurred to her that Emmett might have the same problem as Tom. It seemed so obvious now. That was why he didn't have any girlfriends. Maybe Emmett even had an actual wound, nerve damage of some kind. Tom said he didn't have a wound, but maybe he did. Emmett didn't want a job because men had jobs to support families, and if they couldn't have families, then why bother? It seemed a simple explanation. Women wanted jobs to prove a point, but men had jobs because of women.

Tom *had* to get one of those pumps, she thought. And maybe Emmett needed one too. She wondered what had happened between him and Anita last night. She'd had such a pleasant picture in her mind of them together, in Anita's apartment. But now she wasn't sure.

She realized a song was playing in her head.

You can't start a fire without a spark
This gun's for hire
Even if we're just dancing in the dark

Emmett wasn't home. Moon Pie was still inside, and Sam fed him and let him out. She didn't feel like running. She hadn't swabbed her ears with alcohol since yesterday morning, and they were crusty from the pressure of the new earrings she had worn. After cleaning her ears, she ate a bowl of Total and then lay on the couch watching MTV until she fell asleep.

That afternoon, she went to the shopping center. She intended to look for a present for Lonnie's brother's wedding, but it occurred to her that if she broke up with Lonnie, she wouldn't have to go to the wedding. Appropriate wedding presents were too expensive. At Penney's, Sam zipped past lamps, luggage, typewriters. She looked at silver, china, fake flowers. Martha had mentioned Jennifer's china pattern several times, but Sam couldn't remember the name of it, and the bridal registry was in a store downtown. Place mats cost four dollars. One place mat wouldn't do. As she looked at the sheets and pillows, she was reminded of Lonnie's mother's bed. One night when Sam and Lonnie were there alone, she was tempted to lie down on his parents' canopy bed, but Lonnie didn't dare do it. Instead, they got between Lonnie's Superman sheets and Sam imagined herself as Lois Lane, flying away in Superman's arms, something like a ride on a hang glider might be.

She didn't feel any desire for Lonnie now. She had lost it, the same way she got tired of chocolate-covered cherries one Christmas. Now she throbbed with desire for Tom. She had to figure out a way to make it work with him. She should have been sexier, more grown-up, more understanding. The thrill of being with an older man had been too overwhelming. She hadn't known how to handle it. She had so much to tell Dawn later.

She left Penney's and went to the K Mart, at the other end of the shopping center. Sheets were cheaper there. The place mats looked cruddy. In the sportswear department, she looked at tops, but they were all cheap-looking, not sexy like Anita's. After meandering around in the store for a while, Sam had a sudden urge to buy a bright red ceramic cat with a big grin on its face and a slit in its back for coins. The cat was round and fat, the size of a watermelon. Its round, wide face reminded her of Moon Pie. It was exactly right for her mother. It was kooky and personal, very expressive, she thought. Irene would get a kick out of it. She would laugh. Sam wanted to hear her mother laugh.

"Everybody's buying these cats to set by their fireplaces," the cashier said.

"It's the spitting image of our cat at home," Sam said. "Except he's black."

She paid for the cat, and the cashier said, "Thank you for shopping at K Mart."

In the doorway, Sam ran into Pete Simms.

"Well, I'll be," he said. "Hi, Sambo."

"Hi."

"Did Emmett get home all right?"

"I haven't seen him today. Are you O.K. after that guy beat you up?" she asked, teasing.

"Hell. That guy was cruisin' for a bruisin.' What you got in your box?"

"A present for my mom."

Sam didn't want to talk to Pete. She was feeling hung over, and she wanted to go home, but she didn't want to ask Pete for a ride.

"What did you get her?"

"Just something silly," she said, embarrassed. "It's a statue of a cat. People are setting them by their fireplaces now. It's the latest fashion."

"Oh." He didn't seem impressed.

"It's also a piggy bank, if you want to know. But you're just trying to aggravate me."

"I like to aggravate. My wife can't stand the way I aggravate her."

"I don't blame her." Sam winced, remembering what Cindy had told her in the restroom the night before. It seemed unreal.

Pete laughed. "My wife, she gets on her high-horse and says,

'Stop it!'" He imitated her in a funny falsetto voice, like Mick Jagger imitating the Bee Gees on "Emotional Rescue."

Pete reached over and grabbed Sam's elbow, zinging her funny bone. "Hey, you want to go down to the Bottom with me? It's early and there's a good long Saturday night coming up."

"Nope. Can't. Got other fish to fry." Pete hadn't shaved and he had a rim of toothpaste, or maybe Maalox, on his upper lip. He wore his jeans so low down on his hips they seemed about to fall off.

"You've got a thing for Tom, haven't you?" he said, staring at her. "I saw you making eyes at Tom. I saw the way y'all were dancing."

Sam didn't answer.

He said, "Let me buy you a Coke, then, if you won't go to the Bottom with me."

"Well, O.K." She was thirsty and would appreciate a free Coke. At least he couldn't try anything funny in the K Mart.

At a booth in the rear of the K Mart, Sam and Pete drank Cokes and talked about Tom's VW.

"My mom used to have a VW and I like the way they drive." Sam twirled her straw. "I'm tired of walking everywhere."

"Emmett don't care if he walks everywhere, does he?"

"No, he likes it. He doesn't have anyplace special to go. When he wants to go to the Bottom, he can ride with you or Tom or somebody."

"Did he go home with Anita last night?"

"I guess so. I haven't seen him."

"I saw Anita's car at the Sunoco this morning. She was having her tires checked. Emmett wasn't with her."

"That's funny." Sam was puzzled. Maybe Anita and Emmett were going to take a trip and she was getting her car checked.

"Emmett takes the cake," Pete said, laughing and shaking his head as though he had seen it all.

"Emmett told me you really missed Vietnam," Sam said cautiously. "He told me you'd rather be there. Is that true?"

Pete examined his knuckles and flexed his fingers and then

scrubbed the table with his elbow. "It was O.K. there," he said, nodding slowly. "It was the best life I ever knew, in a way. It was really something."

"Emmett never said anything like that. He said it was horrible."

"Well, a lot of it was. But there was things you got out of it that you just couldn't get any other way."

"Like what?"

"Oh, I don't know. It's hard to explain. It was just the intensity of it, what you went through together. That meant something."

He drank some Coke and said, "Hell, yeah, I admit it. I enjoyed it. I felt good over there. I knew what I was doing. I knew certain things. There was a dividing line. Life and death. But it was frustrating. The war would have been fine if they'd let us win it."

"What do you mean by that?"

He sucked on his straw. "Hey, they'd send us in to do a job, and then they'd take us out, and then we'd have to do it over again, or maybe we'd just let it go. We'd always get ambushed, and we didn't capture any territory. We shouldn't get in another war unless we're in it to *win*. You know how I've been working on this crew making that bypass to I-24? Man, we just laid that road right down, bulldozed it right out and cut through them little hills and laid that sucker smack down pretty as you please, and now you can get all the way to Paducah from here on I-24. If we'd had a road project like that over there, we could have won the war. If we'd done anything with that kind of commitment." He laughed. "We should have paved the Ho Chi Minh Trail and made a four-lane interstate out of it. We could have seen where Charlie was hiding and we would have been ready for him. With an interstate, you always know where you're going."

"The green signs tell you," Sam said.

"I had visions of plowing that place under, like turning topsoil in the spring." He laughed. "I don't know, though. The weather was our big problem. The tanks just mired up. But all that firepower we had—we could have blown 'em up ten times over if we'd been allowed to. The strategies were all wrong. We had the technology to win that war. No question but we *had* the technology. We just fought that war all wrong. We didn't use our *real* technology. We just used enough for those little boogers to figure out and mess up somehow. They'd learn the traffic patterns, the routines. They knew when the shells were coming, where the helicopters would be. If you destroyed one supply depot, they'd just have another one in an unexpected place. They had backup systems. They were sneaky, the sneakiest little bastards you ever saw." He slammed his fist on the table. "There's nothing as devious as the Oriental mind. You know what it was like? Over near Nashville there's this little zoo and it's got a prairie dog town? You look over this concrete rim and you see all these holes in the bare ground, and the prairie dogs have made an underground network. They run around inside them tunnels and the only way you could get them out would be to bomb or smoke 'em out. The enemy was like that. I bet they had tunnels running all the way from Hanoi to Saigon. It would have taken a lot of bombs, but we could have done it. At least it would have been something constructive."

"How would blowing them up have been constructive?"

Pete didn't answer that. He said, "At least your daddy was there doing his job before morale got fucked up. Excuse my French, honey. He probably had a sense of purpose. Later on, soldiers lost their drive. They wouldn't fight, and they'd get stoned and it made it hard on everybody."

"Were you scared over there?"

"Yeah, but looking back, that's not what you think about."

"What do you think about?"

"Oh, lots of things." Pete laughed—the way Frank Burns laughed the time he drove a tank into the women's shower. When Burns ran over Colonel Potter's jeep, the Colonel took out his pistol and shot the jeep. He had been in the cavalry in World War I.

Sam said, "My mom always said the war messed up Emmett's head. Didn't it mess up your head?"

"I didn't get my legs blown off, so I don't have anything to complain about. I can't get steady work, but hell, who *can* around here is the way I look at it." He jabbed his straw in his Coke and whirled the ice around. "Stop thinking about Vietnam, Sambo. You don't know how it was, and you never will. There is no way you can ever understand. So just forget it. Unless you've been humping the boonies, you don't know."

"What's humping the boonies?"

"That means going out in some godforsaken wilderness and doing what you have to do to survive. But I survived and I ain't going to waste it now." He laughed. "Now, if they want to get my wife in one of those counseling groups and beat some sense in her head, that would be all right with me. I wish they'd straighten her out."

He was teasing about his wife. Sam was sure he was just shooting off his mouth. He stood up and crammed his Coke cup into an orange trash barrel. "I gotta go. Sure you don't want to go with me?"

"Nope. I'm not through shopping."

"Well, take care, Sambo. Don't let that uncle of yours watch too many dirty movies on cable."

Sam waved at him as he plunged down an aisle of housewares. Pete was sentimental, she thought. Anybody who would tattoo a map on his chest showing the location of his car was sentimental, no matter how tough he talked about women. He was covering up his feelings, she thought.

"You go tell Tom you want that little VW," he called to her. "That'll be a classic car before you know it."

"O.K. When I start work."

"Bye now, Sambo."

"Hey, don't call me Sambo," she said.

Pete's a space cadet, she thought. A real space cadet.

20

At Kroger's, Sam, on a wild impulse, blew some of the grocery money on strange food from the gourmet section—cocktail hot dogs, smoked baby oysters, odd-shaped crackers, even a can of smoked octopus. Then she bought cat food and two boxes of small moon pies called Granny Cakes, made by the local factory.

By the time she arrived at home, she was sweating and her arms were aching from carrying the ceramic cat and the grocery sack. Emmett still wasn't home. She called for Moon Pie, but he didn't come. She took a shower and put on clean shorts and a Wildcats T-shirt. She dabbed alcohol on her ears.

In Emmett's room, the sheets were a wad in the center of the bed. She wondered if they smelled like Tom's sheets. Maybe Tom would call her and apologize for last night. But it wasn't his fault. Maybe he would feel that it was. He would suggest that they get together again. She would say the right things this time. She had been so smashed.

She found a joint Emmett had hidden in the can of cocoa mix. Getting high was different from getting smashed. It didn't make her feel bad afterward, and somebody had said pot was good for a hangover. The joint tasted nice, like chocolate. She had an idea. She went into Irene's old room and rooted around in her jewelry box. Some of the jewelry had belonged to their great-aunt, Bessie, who used to own the house. Sam took the box to the kitchen and poked through imitation pearls, colored beads, appleseed hippie beads, rhinestone necklaces and brooches (stars and sunbursts), cluster earrings with clamps, and Irene's high school ring with her initials inside it. Sam fastened on a pair of the earrings and looked in the small mirror next to the refrigerator. They pinched. She imagined two bloated ticks sucking on her ears. She pulled them off.

She cleared away some dirty dishes and wiped the oilcloth with a dishrag. Then she set the red ceramic cat in the center of the table and regarded it admiringly while she finished the joint. The cat grinned at her. She pushed the roach inside the slit on the cat's back. She was pleased with the cat, and she was glad she hadn't shown it to Pete Simms. She wasn't going to show it to Lonnie either. He would give her hell for not buying a fancy piece of china to impress his brother. What Lonnie really needed was a girl like Jennifer, his brother's fiancée. One of those girls with shiny hair and skin and an artificial smile, a girl who wouldn't embarrass him by doing something strange. Like all the strange things Sam did last night. Or the holes in her ears. Or having a Coke with Pete. She didn't want to think about Pete.

She turned the radio on, hoping to hear Bruce Springsteen. Somehow there was a secret knowledge in his songs, as though he knew exactly what she was feeling. Some dumb song by the Thompson Twins was playing. She dumped the jewelry on the table. The cat was surrounded by beautiful splashy colors. She thought of a movie she had seen long ago, *King Solomon's Mines*, with Deborah Kerr. She seemed to remember a cave filled with fabulous jewels, sparkling and colorful, but she knew she must have seen the movie on their old black-and-white television. When people saw *Psycho*, they swore they saw the red blood in the shower, although the movie was not in color. It was strange how some memories stood out. She wished they would hold still, like photographs.

After searching through several shelves of junk, Sam found some Elmer's glue. The container had a picture of a cow on it. The glue was like rich milk, condensed to a syrup. She wondered if mother's milk was thick and syrupy. Irene talked proudly about breast-feeding her new baby, but when Sam was growing up, she bragged about Sam being a bottle baby. Sam thought if she had a baby she would breast-feed it because that would be sexier. Lonnie was rough with her breasts, but Tom did something else, something unbelievably subtle and stirring. She wished desperately that he would call her up. She imagined him driving up now. "I came over to play with your breasts," he might say. Now Billy Joel was singing. She thought about how distant and businesslike he was in that video where he wore garage mechanic's coveralls. She wished Tom would drive the VW over from his garage. "I came to give you this car and while I'm at it I want to hold your breasts again."

Sam draped several necklaces around the red cat's neck. She laughed. She wished Moon Pie would come in so she could put some necklaces on him. She felt the way Emmett must feel when he watched birds. It was as though the most ordinary thing had opened up into a thousand meanings. Emmett had told her of a Zen exercise for controlling the mind. It was a way of grabbing it and bringing it back every time it started to wander. She hadn't been interested at the time, but maybe, she thought now, when Emmett watched birds he was trying to keep his mind from wandering. That was like an old song, the Beatles singing "I'm fixing a hole where the rain gets in/And stops my mind from wandering." That was what Emmett was doing with his hole, trying to stop the rain. If he concentrated on something fascinating and thrilling, like birds soaring, the pain of his memories wouldn't come through. His mind would be full of birds. Just birds and no memories. Flight.

The Saturday oldies show was on. The Doors were pounding away on "Light My Fire." She turned the volume up. When it ended, the D.J. said, "We play kick-ass rock-and-roll." The D.J.s on Rock-95 were college students and when they read the news they often broke down in giggles. A news item came on about a lost cat. Moon Pie was missing. But Moon Pie occasionally went off on little trips. Emmett was missing too. Sam watched an ant crawl into a hole in an electrical receptacle. A moment later, it crawled back out.

After the news, the D.J. told a joke. "What does a walrus have in common with Tupperware? Give up? They both like a tight seal! Now here's the immortal 'Ubangi Stomp.' Remember this?" Sam hated the sick jokes on Rock-95—especially the quadriplegic jokes and the dead-baby jokes. The D.J.s were morons.

With some toenail scissors, Sam clipped the thread of a pearl necklace, and the pearls slid off with a satisfying snap of release. They rolled across the table, and some of them spilled on the kitchen floor. She cut some more strings and heaped the beads in a dish. She cut the appleseed necklace and pulled the seeds off the brittle thread. Then she decorated the cat. She glued on rows of beads, pearls, and rhinestones, making tiger stripes. She fastened a rhinestone necklace around the cat's throat and shortened it to fit. She worked methodically and patiently. The radio played several sixties songs, and she listened to all the words, trying not to lose any. Words were important. She and Emmett had concentrated like this together on their stamp collection, long ago.

Upstairs, Sam found an old formal her mother had worn to a dentists' dinner dance—the Molar Ball, Emmett called it. Molar Derby, Sam thought. She took the formal downstairs and snipped off the sequins. They were purple. She liked that. Purple on a red cat would look royal. She outlined the cat's eyes with purple sequins, and she put lines of them on its face for whiskers. He looked like a punk maharajah. The cat was smiling—more of a smirk than a smile. She set rhinestones on the front toes. This little piggy.

She switched on MTV. Cyndi Lauper and her fat face. On Channel 7, *The Dogs of War* was ending. It occurred to Sam that being a mercenary soldier in Africa would be more exciting than anything she could think of doing around Hopewell. She switched back to MTV, hoping the Springsteen video would come on. Tom's smile was like Bruce's. Tom was the only exciting thing in Hopewell. The only reason to stay there was so she could work at the Burger Boy and wait on Tom if he came in. The sadness of his affliction hit her then like a truck. She thought of all the lives wasted by the war. She wanted to cry, but then she wanted to yell and scream and kick. She could imagine fighting, but only against war. All the boys getting killed, on both sides. And boys getting mutilated. And then not being allowed to grow up. That was it—they didn't get to grow up and become regular people. They had to stand outside, playing games, fooling around, acting like kids who couldn't get girlfriends. It was absurd. She thought she was crashing.

She fastened a sequin on the cat's cheek. A cat like this could be used for smuggling dope. Or for a terrorist's bomb. It had a mysterious slit in its back. Hubert Humphrey had a slit in his abdomen for a piss-bag. So did Mr. Watterson, the civics teacher at school. Some boys claimed to have seen it. They had sneaked into the faculty restroom and watched from a stall when he emptied it in a urinal. Sam didn't believe they had done that.

Hubert Humphrey died when she was in junior high. At school, they had watched the funeral on TV. Some kids cried and some giggled. Sam didn't cry. She wasn't sentimental. Pete was sentimental.

She picked a marigold from the yard and stuck it in the cat's slit. He looked like a king, fat from all the tax money he collected. He was psychedelic. She liked the way cats did what they pleased, without thinking about public opinion. Dawn said cats were *funk*adelic. She knew a lot of jive talk from Yvonne. Moon Pie wasn't there. Usually he was at the door by five. And there was no sign of Emmett.

On TV, *Blow Out* was starting. Lonnie had used the word "blow-out" for the stag party. She punched through thirty-one channels—a rerun of *Mayberry R.F.D.*, baseball, CNN news, preaching. She turned back to MTV and watched a video by Queen.

She was hungry. Her stomach made a noise exactly like the door of the electric oven whirring when it locked into the Clean position. Once she had left a pan of leftover chicken in the oven when she turned the oven on Clean. Later, she found the tiny gray-and-black bones in the pan, and she would not let Emmett see, because she thought he would have had a fit at the thought that it might be the cat.

She called up Dawn.

"I tried to call you this afternoon," Dawn said anxiously. "I bought another one of those kits and tried it again. And it's positive again. What am I going to do? My stomach feels weird all the time, like all the blood's rushing to it."

"Wait and see what the doctor says," Sam said, with an odd feeling of detachment. "It's still so early. It's even too early to get an abortion."

"I'll pretend I didn't hear that word," Dawn said. "I haven't said a word to Ken. He thinks I'm acting funny, but I'm not going to tell him until I know for sure."

"Come over and watch television with me this evening," Sam said. "Emmett's not here and I'm sort of wrecked."

"You got hold of some good stuff, huh?"

Sam giggled. "Emmett calls it his sweet stuff. It tastes like chocolate. I've got a lot to tell about the dance last night. So come on over."

"I can't because I promised my brother I'd help him paint his basement, and he's going to pay me. He's putting a bar in his rec room."

"It's so spooky here. Emmett's been gone since last night. I think he went home with Anita."

"Hey! All right!"

"I really like Anita. I wish they'd get back together. When are you going to see Ken?"

"Tomorrow. We're going to Paducah after church. If I tell him I'm pregnant, he'll say I planned it this way. I hate it when guys think you're always scheming something."

After talking to Dawn, Sam impulsively dialed Anita's number, but no one answered. Dawn was going to have a baby. The news still seemed unreal. Now Dawn would never get to go to Disney World. She would live and die in Hopewell. Sam would have to encourage Dawn to breast-feed the baby.

She shaved hot-pepper cheese into three taco shells and set them in the oven. She ate them out on the porch with a Pepsi. Next door, Mrs. Biggs drove up in her puke-yellow Plymouth and hauled out her groceries.

"I got to the grocery and forgot my billfold," she called to Sam. "But they let me charge my groceries. I'd forget my head if it wasn't screwed on."

"Have you seen Emmett?" Sam asked. Her head was buzzing. The light outside was shimmering, and Mrs. Biggs looked like an enormous bumpy toad frog.

"Not since he mowed my yard the other day. He mowed under my forsythia bush for me. I just can't reach under all those limbs, they've got so bad."

"You didn't see him here this morning?"

"I left here about ten to go to my daughter's. My daughter's off work this week and she's putting up blackberry jelly. What a mess! Her whole kitchen's purple."

Sam watched the news. The President was in California. An Amtrak train had derailed in Vermont. Sam realized that Ronald Reagan looked exactly like Dagwood Bumstead. She thought she heard Lonnie's van, but it was a neighbor's car backfiring. On TV, a flood in the Northeast had stranded a lot of people. A flood like that couldn't happen in western Kentucky because of the man-made TVA lakes, which cut the region off from the rest of the state. It was like being stranded on an island, far away from civilization. If she were really stranded on a desert island, she would want to have plenty of cold drinks. She had to write a theme once on what book she'd want to have with her if she were stranded on a desert island. It was a dumb question. It was highly unlikely that anyone in the class would be stranded on a desert island. Miss Castle had wanted them to choose a Shakespeare play or the Bible, but Sam had perversely chosen the dictionary. Sam thought that going around with your favorite book in case you got stranded on a desert island sounded paranoid. By the time it happened, you'd be sick of the book. With a dictionary, she could make up any book she wanted to. She ate two Granny Cakes and debated about whether to call Tom. She could ask him if he had seen Emmett.

Instead, she telephoned Jim Holly, but no one answered. *Blow Out* was half over. John Travolta was wiggling his dimple. The red cat seemed to take on a new personality, more contented with his new appearance than smirky. Carefully, she set the cat in a drawer she cleared out in her room.

Later, when it cooled off, she went running. She ran through the new Tennis Club subdivision, where Emmett had been going recently to watch a new house being built. She remembered the time she and her mother found him drunk under a bush at the high school. It had been so long since he had done something like that. She thought their TV routines had saved him from being an alcoholic. Emmett was not used to changing his routines, and she hoped Anita knew what to do.

She liked to look at the new houses. They were so imaginative.

No two were alike. The old houses in town were all similar white wood or brick houses. But the new houses were large and stylish and as varied as women's fashions. They had Tudor beams, bay windows, Cape Cod eagles. She ran up Golf Club Lane toward Tennis Club Court. Then she ran down Country Crescent. Crossing Paradise Way, she passed a little girl on a plastic tricycle constructed like a racing car. The child had a sucker in her mouth and was pedaling furiously. Sam did not see a soul in the whole subdivision, other than the kid on the tricycle, but the smell from the charcoal grills was intoxicating. She remembered the time Moon Pie had brought home a barbecued split broiler from someone's grill. She and Emmett had giggled until they were sick. She wished she knew where Emmett was, but if he was with Anita, it was O.K. He should stay with Anita forever. They should get married, not Dawn.

21

On Sunday, Emmett had not returned, and Moon Pie was missing too. Sam dialed Anita's number, but there was no answer. She went running in the mid-morning heat. When she ran, her head was clear, and everything seemed new, the way it did after a storm. *Eddie and the Cruisers*, a movie she had watched on HBO the night before, kept going through her mind. Eddie and the Cruisers were ahead of their time—a rock group in a time warp. Eddie had disappeared, like Emmett.

Emmett wasn't at McDonald's—just the church crowd in their Sunday clothes. Sam left and ran on down to the Burger Boy. The Baptists from the church across the street were gathered there on their break between Sunday school and church.

Walt, the new manager who had hired her for the fall, said, "Hey, Sam! You're not going to work here dressed like that, are you?"

"No. Have you seen my uncle?"

"No. Is he lost?"

"No. I'm just looking for him. I thought he might be here."

Walt was an overweight man in a thin white shirt and a tie, with blue pants. When he hired her, he had said he needed some T and A to brighten the place up. He had said that to Dawn too.

"Bye, Walt," Sam said.

Grandma Smith came by the house at noon and took Sam home with her to eat Sunday dinner. She had been to church. She was a tall woman with frizzy gray hair and a bright tan face wrinkled like a squeezed-out string mop. She had on a baby-blue pants suit, but normally she wore blue jeans and tennis shoes. On the drive, she chattered about Florida. Sam didn't say she was looking for Emmett, but evidently Grandma hadn't seen him, or she would have mentioned it.

"I'm so worked up," Grandma said as they left town. "George doesn't want to shell out the money for the trip—it's an excursion fare and it includes your hotel and meals—and he had me so bumfuzzled I forgot what day it was yesterday and I missed this special I wanted to watch. And then I ate cucumbers, which I shouldn't have. But I think I'll get to Florida somehow. I intend to go, even if it harelips me. That's an old saying you probably never heard."

Sam's grandparents' house, five miles south of town on the main highway, had fake brick siding and a new kitchen and a den and a brick fireplace. The porch had decorative wrought-iron railings and green indoor-outdoor carpeting. When Grandma pulled into the driveway, Sam suddenly imagined Emmett returning from the war. Although she couldn't remember it, she had a clear image of him in her mind—the spacey look in his eyes, his silence, his edginess. She had heard how Grandma cooked him country ham and field peas and chess pie, but he didn't seem to enjoy them. He would get up early and flip a Pepsi and go walking out through the pastures. When he came back, he was drenched with dew, like a cat prowling at dawn. Later, he went out west, and when he returned, he had those hippies with him.

"Is Emmett done with his digging?" Granddad asked Sam when they arrived. He never went to church.

"Just about. He still has to put on another coat of waterproofing and fill in that trench." Sam slammed the car door and petted the shepherd, Buster.

"He's always got to be piddling with something," Grandma said with a chuckle. "I call it playing paper dolls."

"What happened to Rusty?" Sam asked. Rusty was the nervous fice.

"Oh, I traded him off," Granddad said. "He wasn't any 'count." He started laughing.

"What's so funny?"

He shook his head and laughed so hard he couldn't answer.

"He's laughing about them Jehovah's Witnesses that come here yesterday," Grandma said. "That's the second time they've been out here and they ought to know they're not going to get anything out of old tightwad here."

"I ain't a tightwad!"

"He don't want to turn loose of that dollar," Grandma said to Sam. "I have to pay a deposit on that trip to Florida at the end of the month, and I'm not going to have any more luck getting any money out of him than the Jehovah's Witnesses did."

Granddad snickered. "Them crazy fools! They come here and I was out there working on my mower, and the driver rolled down his window and said, 'Hey, call your dog off so we can get out. I want to talk to you.' I recognized who they was, and Buster was barking up a storm. And you know what I said? I said, 'If you got faith, you won't be scared of that dog.' That shut 'em up! They got mad and left!"

Granddad continued to laugh, holding his side.

Grandma said, "And I just know one of them in that car was somebody at the feed mill he has to do business with. I'm so embarrassed."

"If they'd had faith, they wouldn't have been scared of Buster," Granddad said, petting the dog. The dog's ears went back self-consciously.

"Faith's what I need," Sam said. "If I had enough faith, could I get a good job and a car?" Would faith get Tom one of those pumps? she wondered.

"Be serious, Sam," said Grandma. "Young people are losing their faith, and there ain't nobody but old people at church."

"Maybe I should be a Jehovah's Witness," said Sam. "They get to ride around a lot and see the world."

"I wonder why they always pack a whole carload in when they go out," Granddad said. "There must have been six grown people and two or three littluns in that car."

"I don't know," Sam said. "To save gas?"

"Y'all stop making fun and come on in and eat dinner," said Grandma. "We'll eat as soon as I change into my everyday clothes. We're still eating on that smoked picnic I got at Sureway last week for seventy-nine cents a pound. Sam, do you want ice-tea or sweet-milk?"

At dinner, which included Grandma's special Waldorf salad with miniature marshmallows, Sam asked Granddad about the hippies Emmett had brought to Hopewell years before. "Is it true you run them off?" she asked.

"Hell, I've still got a bone to pick with them eejits."

"Your language, George," said Grandma.

"Oh, she hears 'hell' on television."

Granddad stood up and pointed out the window to a bush at the side of the house, where the driveway turned. "See that mock orange out there? There used to be a rose bed there, and one day those kids got stuck trying to turn around, and they plowed into the rose bed. They made two big gullies in the yard trying to turn around in that painted-up Volkswagen truck they had. I had to get out the tractor and pull them out. They never said they was sorry nor nothing, and them gullies stayed there till I filled them in. What on earth did they have to try and turn around on the grass on a muddy day for?"

"That was about the time I thought everything started to change," Grandma said sadly. "Hopewell used to be the best place to bring up kids, but now it's not. Young folks don't appreciate the value of a dollar. They think they've got to have it all, right now." She chomped on a raw onion. Granddad sat down again and plunged into another piece of ham.

Later, he smoked a cigarette and leaned on the porch railing, looking out over his soybeans. The cookie factory in the industrial park behind his fields had extended its sewer line across his property. They hadn't paid Granddad anything for the disruption they caused when they dug the trenches for the pipes, but they had promised that he could hook on to the pipes if he ever developed the land. That would be never, Granddad told them. With a spirit of resignation, he had signed a permission paper.

He finished his cigarette and came back inside, where Sam and Grandma were loading the dishwasher. Sam asked her grandparents if they remembered the time Irene took Sam to Lexington when Sam was a small child.

"Lord, yes, honey," Grandma said. "That was when she took up with that wild hyena Emmett brought back. He had the rattiest hair I ever saw."

"I remember him a little. He had funny blue eyes."

"And now Irene's in Lexington again!" cried Grandma. "This time with a different baby. There's something about that girl that just wants to wag a baby off to Lexington."

"I wasn't exactly a baby then," said Sam.

Grandma said, "Irene was too old to have that baby. But when she had you, she was too young. She had a hard time both times."

"Irene never would do things the normal way," Granddad said.

"She's lucky neither one of us had birth defects," Sam said. "Did you ever think that if my daddy had come back from Vietnam, she might have had a baby with birth defects? The Army sprayed all kinds of chemicals over there. If they had waited to have me, I might have been born without a spine, or maybe I'd have flippers."

"Sam, don't think that way." Grandma pinched Sam's cheek and said, "I'd love you even if you did have flippers."

"Mom always said the war messed Emmett's head up," Sam said.

"I'll mess his *butt* up," Granddad muttered.

"That war nearly killed him!" Sam cried. "He might even have cancer. Not to mention his nerves and his bad dreams."

"Shush, Sam," Grandma said. "Your granddad knows about all that."

"He was raring to go over there and fight," said Granddad.

"You were all for him going!" Grandma cried angrily. "You said the Army would make a man out of him. But look what it done."

"It's not too late," Granddad said. "It's not too late to pull himself up and be proud."

He went outside to check on his calves, and while Sam helped Grandma with the dishes, she asked her if anything could have happened to Emmett in the war so that he couldn't be with women. It was a delicate question, and she phrased it in a roundabout way. "Aren't there some men that just can't get married because of what happened to them in the war?" she asked.

Grandma said, "It wasn't the war. I always thought it was the mumps."

"The mumps?"

"He was about eleven and he had the mumps. Mumps are real dangerous at that age. He couldn't hardly get out of bed, but he got up and opened his door, and the mumps fell on him then. He never should have opened that door."

"What does that mean?"

"He was too weak to get out of bed, but he did anyway, and he opened that door, and then he laid back in bed so weak he couldn't move a finger. It broke my heart. I just knew the mumps fell on him."

"What kind of talk is that?" Grandma said a lot of strange things, things she expected you to know.

"Don't you know what mumps falling means? They affect boys in their—balls—and when they grow up they can't have children." Grandma whispered the word "balls." "Sometimes they fall on one side and sometimes on the other. But sometimes they fall on both. If they fall on one side, you can't have girls, and on the other you can't have boys. I can't remember which is which. Estelle Williams had a brother and they fell on him, and she said one of his got as big as a gallon bucket!"

"Wait a minute," Sam said, trying not to grin. It was weird to be talking to Grandma about balls. Grandma would die if she knew what Sam had done with Tom Hudson. Sam said, "If you've got the mumps, your glands on your neck swell up and then they work down through your body?"

"No, they don't do that. It's just if one gets big or you can't walk, they say the mumps fell. My lord, youngun, this ain't fit talk for girls! But I've heard it can happen to girls too."

"How?"

"Well, it hurts their insides and they can't have babies."

"Have I ever had the mumps?"

"No. You had a shot." Grandma dried her hands on the dish towel and then ran her fingers through her hair. "Sam, don't you go telling this. It's not nice to talk about."

"Do you think that's why Emmett doesn't get married?"

"Your granddad thinks this whole idea's crazy, but I don't know. Sometimes I think if I hadn't gone on so about the mumps, then maybe he wouldn't know the difference and at least he would have married."

"Mom always blamed everything on the war. Do you think he could have had a wound—you know where?"

Grandma shook her head. "I never heard tell about it."

"Maybe he wouldn't tell."

"What are you girls talking about?" said Granddad teasingly. He had suddenly come into the kitchen with a calf bucket. The bucket had a big rubber tit sticking out the side, for a calf to suck.

"It's girl talk," Grandma said, swatting her dish towel at him.

22

The next day, Sam slept until nearly noon. She wandered through the house, but there was no sign that Emmett had been there. She had left the side door unlocked in case he came back. Moon Pie was still gone, but she was less worried about him than she was about Emmett. Sam had stayed up late the night before listening to a talk show on Rock-95. Between records, college students called in their opinions on world issues. Several of them called up in favor of the Ku Klux Klan, denying it was violent. "They have a right to their opinion," most of the callers insisted. After midnight, Sam watched *Jesse James Meets Frankenstein's Daughter*, but it was disappointing.

It was still too early to call the police. A person had to be missing for three days, according to the cop shows. In her room, her father's picture stared at her accusingly from the frame of the mirror.

She ate some Total and then dialed Dawn's number.

"Come over," she said to Dawn.

"I can't. I got called in to work early."

"Did you see Ken yesterday?"

"Yeah. We went over to eat with his mama and daddy and then we cruised over to Paducah."

"What did you wear?"

"That hot-pink top and the print skirt with the ruffle."

"And about two dozen earrings."

"Yeah." Dawn giggled. "Guess what."

"What?"

"Ken's got a chance to rent an apartment over Jones' Furniture Store downtown real cheap. So he's talking about getting married. Can you believe it! And I haven't told him a thing. At least he's in the mood for the news."

"You don't sound so depressed now."

"Well, it might work out O.K., you know? I was thinking how much I like my little nieces, and I'm looking for an excuse to get out of this house."

Sam still intended to talk Dawn into getting an abortion, but she couldn't think straight. First she had to find Emmett.

Dawn said, "Wish me luck, kid."

"Luck. I'll see you later."

"Later."

"Bye."

Sam found the flashlight and went down into the basement. She hadn't wanted to look there last night.

Even though the basement had dried up after Emmett repaired the leaks, it still smelled damp and moldy. It was full of junk and crud. In one corner were years' worth of the *Hopewell Citizen.* They had saved them for the Boy Scouts, but they hadn't gotten around to bundling them up. Next to them were stacks of old *Reader's Digest* magazines. They were swollen and mushy. Aunt Bessie's *Upper Rooms* were tied in neat packages on a shelf, and her tubs of dirt still squatted in a musty corner. Irene had neglected to set them outside the spring after Bessie died and they moved there. Sam remembered when the plants would stubbornly send up green shoots in the spring, in the dark basement, but finally all the plants had given up seeking the light. She didn't remember what year they died. The dead stalks in the tubs made her cringe. They were oppressive, something useless and ridiculous that she had had to look at all her life. Like the trash can filled with liquor bottles that had always been there. They had belonged to Bessie's husband. She hadn't thrown the bottles away because she didn't want people to see liquor bottles in her trash.

In another corner was a tangle of spindleback chairs, with peeling pink enamel, and odds and ends of beadboard, lumber, and scraps of Formica and vinyl left over from when they had had the kitchen remodeled. Sam flashed the light behind the furnace. Nothing was there. She opened a large cabinet big enough to hold a murder victim. Inside were rusted paint cans and smells of mildew, dirt, and machine oil. She hurried up the stairs.

Outside, Emmett's ditch had dried out. He had filled in most of it, but there was still a sizable hole in front of the crawl space under the kitchen. The piece of plywood that Emmett kept propped in front of the hole had fallen down. Sam flashed her light into the space and called "Kitty, kitty." A chill went over her at the thought that Emmett might be under there, with a heart attack.

A horn blared in the driveway. The car was a red Trans Am. Irene jumped out, arms spread, crying "Surprise!"

Sam almost fell in the hole.

Her mother had on high-heeled sandals and pink shorts. She had a new curly permanent, which made her hair look something like Mrs. Biggs' spread-eagled forsythia. She had on a white scoop-necked T-shirt, and her freckles drifted down her pale skin and splattered between her breasts. When she hugged Sam, her lavender-rimmed sunglasses clashed against the horseshoe nails in Sam's ears. Irene stood back, holding Sam by the shoulders.

"I just want to look at you," she said. She fingered Sam's earrings, then nodded at the car. "Guess who I've got."

Sam didn't have to guess. In the back seat of the car was the baby, a sticky bundle in a disposable diaper, smacking her lips in a dream. And in the front, hunched up, with his head on a pillow, was Emmett, fast asleep, just like the baby. His shirttail was coming out, and the top button of his jeans gaped open. His complexion was rough and blotchy.

"Guess who shows up at my doorstep in the middle of the night—so drunk he's about to pass out?"

"Why didn't you call me?" cried Sam angrily. "Grandma would have called if he'd gone there. She'd have known I was worried."

"Mama worries just to have something to do. That's her profession."

When Irene hauled the baby out, Emmett stirred. "Get down," he said, boxing the air in his sleep.

"I've put up with this since we left Lexington," Irene said with a sigh.

"Well, I've been wandering around like a dork looking for him," Sam said.

They left Emmett sleeping in the front seat and went inside with the baby. Sam carried a diaper bag and a blue tote bag. Irene told Sam she had made the trip from Lexington in four and a half hours, stopping only once to change the baby and buy gas. Emmett had stared out the window. Around Elizabethtown, he had fallen asleep. She said a guy in a pickup truck had dropped him off in Lexington.

"He said he was stranded," Irene said. "Larry was in bed and I was up watching the late show—have you seen *The Invasion of the Body Snatchers?* The new one, not the old one. It was real strange. Anyway, the doorbell rang and there was Emmett. I didn't get to see how the *Body Snatchers* turned out."

"They all got snatched," said Sam.

"I thought it was headed that way, but that didn't seem right." The baby, on the couch, cried then, and Irene shushed it with cooing sounds. The baby had a pie face. Sam was depressed by this family trait. Moon Pie was still missing, and she was afraid to tell Emmett.

"Have you seen *Ghostbusters* yet?" Irene asked.

"No."

"It's really funny. Anyway, Emmett just leaned there against this big bush. It's such a heavy, strong bush it supported him, so he just leaned against it with a funny smile on his face like he had been up to some meanness. Just a sheepish little look—that real cute look he gets when he's been up to something? And so I said, 'Come on in, Emmett, and take a load off that bush.' He staggers in, like one of those clowns in the circus, all exaggerated features and pretending they can't talk? Well, he *couldn't*, he was so drunk. At first, I thought he'd flipped out again, but then he grinned that silly grin. He just likes to show out."

"Why did you bring him back?" Sam asked.

"Well, I couldn't send him on the bus. The bus takes sixteen hours. It stops at every little pig path."

Emmett stumbled through the kitchen door then. He had the sheepish look, but it wasn't really cute.

"Y'all are telling stories on me," he said.

"Hey, Emmett," said Sam.

He grabbed a quart of Pepsi from the refrigerator and twisted off the cap. The Pepsi hissed. He poured the Pepsi into a glass and drank it without ice.

Irene stuck her lavender sunglasses in a pocket on the side of her tote bag, then rummaged inside and plucked out a Kleenex, like a magician finding a white dove in an unlikely nest. She said, "Sam, are you sure all the bodies got snatched in that show? That doesn't seem right. Usually there's some redeeming feature in a movie like that—the hero saves the girl and they escape somehow."

"Nobody got saved." Sam studied Emmett. He had fastened his pants. His clothes were dirty. He was wearing what he wore to the dance, even his Army boots. "Where did you go all weekend, Emmett? I was worried."

"It's hard to explain," he said. He looked tired and scared. His hands trembled.

Irene drew herself a glass of water from the sink. She had set the baby on the floor in a plastic carrier, and the baby was wiggling her legs and gooing. Sam wondered if the carrier would curve the baby's spine. She used to get tiny naked rubber dolls with crooked spines from the gum machine at the shopping center.

"Show your toofie, Heather," Irene said. The baby crowed and spit.

"Ain't she too little to have teeth?" asked Emmett, pointing with his glass.

"She's precocious."

"Does she bite your titty?"

"No. She's careful."

"I've heard of babies born with teeth," said Sam. "And tails too. One in a hundred thousand babies is born with a tail. Does that baby have a tail?"

"The very idea, Sam! Where'd you hear that?"

Sam went to the bathroom. Her digestion was screwed up and seeing the baby made her nervous. Dawn was going to have a baby like that, and she'd have to take it everywhere with her. It was depressing. It was as though Dawn had been captured by body snatchers.

When Sam returned to the kitchen, Emmett was eating cold split-pea soup from the can and Irene was searching the cabinets.

"Campbell's soup is full of salt," she said. She took jars of baby food out of one of her bags. Blueberry buckle, strained liver, strained carrots.

"Can I have some of that blueberry buckle?" Sam asked. "I love that stuff."

"Sam, I swear! I need it for Heather." Irene twisted open the jar of liver and stuck a spoon in it. "At home she eats natural foods that I fix in the food processor."

"What's Lorenzo Jones up to?"

"Larry's gone to Hazard to see his brother. Ron was supposed to come up and work on our roof, but he's in the hospital with a slipped disk."

"I'm going to work on this roof next year," Emmett said. He set his soup can on the newspaper that Sam had put under the ceramic cat two days before. He brushed a pearl off onto the floor and Irene swooped it up. "Heather might get ahold of that," she said.

"How's the pain in your head, Emmett?" Sam asked.

"It comes and goes," he said.

Irene fed the baby. Heather slurped the liver, and Irene wiped the baby's mouth with a wet paper towel. Irene said, "Sam, is Mama really going to talk Daddy into going to Florida? I called her last week and it was all she could talk about."

Sam explained the situation. "Granddad's got her worked up because he hasn't said he'll go yet."

"He likes to aggravate her," Irene said. "They just want to torment each other. I bet he won't go. Some people just don't want to take a chance. Why, some people here would rather order their gravestone right now than get on the parkway! Thank God I got out of this place."

Irene was holding a spoonful of carrots poised over the baby's mouth while she talked, and the baby had her mouth open like a baby bird waiting for the mother bird to vomit food into its gullet. When Irene saw the baby waiting, salivating, she giggled and apologized in baby talk.

"Didn't you want to come back and see us?" Sam asked.

"Yeah, but I want you to come up there! I'm sick of this place. This house is a dump, and I'd be happy if I never saw Hopewell again in my life." The baby gurgled and Irene shouldered her and patted her back until she belched, drooling liver and carrots on Irene's neck.

"Ooh, messy baby," she said. She got up and ran her free hand under water in the sink and rinsed off her bare shoulder. She wiped the baby's lips and kissed them.

Sam picked at a hangnail. "Are you going to explain yourself or not, Emmett?" she asked. "Did Anita take you to Lexington?"

He shook his head no. He yawned and flexed his muscles like Popeye. Emmett could never have Popeye's energy because spinach gave him gas. "Well sir," he said thoughtfully, moving his glass around and making a wet spot on the newspaper. Sam thought of the soggy magazines in the basement and was angry with Emmett for making her have to go down there. He said, "I believe my body was entered by aliens and I was transported." He raised his eyebrows. "It was no coincidence that Irene was watching that body-snatching movie. I was overtaken by a pod. It was growing in the crawl space and—"

"I looked for you in the crawl space," said Sam. "I thought you might have had a heart attack and died under the house."

"You mean you were beamed up to Lexington, like on *Star Trek?*" Irene asked. She had spread the baby out on the couch in the living room and was removing her diaper. "Stinky baby!" she said to the baby.

"I arrived at Irene's doorstep at the climax of her movie," Emmett said to Sam. "I was the end of her movie. She rescued me, so it wasn't such an unhappy ending."

"That's not the first time you've pulled that trick," said Irene, reaching into her diaper bag for a diaper. The baby's legs bicycled.

"I don't know what come over me," said Emmett. He fingered his temple.

Sam thought of a man on the other side of town who drove away in his pickup truck two years before and hadn't been seen since. He simply drove away.

"I wish you'd tell a straight story," she said. "I thought you were with Anita."

"Anita Stevens?" Irene asked. "Is she on the loose again?" She picked up the baby and jiggled her and kissed her. "See her toofie!" The baby grinned, her tooth shining like the ivory inset on the pendant Irene was wearing.

Sam asked about the pendant, and Irene said defensively, "I had it made. It's ivory, but I didn't have to kill an elephant to get it. It's recycled piano keys."

"I didn't think you killed an elephant," Sam said.

"A girl in my crafts group made it. Correction. A woman, not a girl. We're supposed to say 'women' now. *Not* 'the girls in the office.'" She laughed and put the dirty diaper in the garbage under the sink.

"Where's Moon Pie?" Emmett asked.

"Out somewhere. He was just here," Sam lied.

"This couch is crawling with fleas!" he said.

"Emmett's paranoid about fleas," Sam said to her mother.

"It used to be ticks," Irene said calmly. "Emmett, you ought to get one of those flea bombs and fumigate the house."

Emmett switched on the TV and punched through the buttons. On MTV, Chrissie Hynde, with the Pretenders, was singing "Back on the Chain Gang." She was standing with her legs apart, looking tough. Men were swinging pickaxes.

"Do you know this song?" Sam asked her mother apprehensively.

"No." Irene glanced at the TV, then busied herself with the baby.

Chrissie Hynde had a baby, and the father was in the Kinks, one of the old British groups Irene used to love. But Sam realized her mother would probably not be interested in this information.

When the song finished, Emmett began playing *Pac-Man*, and Irene said she was going to take a nap with Heather. Outside, it was starting to drizzle. Sam went upstairs and played a Kinks album, hoping her mother would hear it and remember the old days. It would be O.K. to have a baby if you were a big rock star, Sam thought, even though it would be inconvenient, but Dawn wouldn't have a chance. Maybe it was just as well that Tom couldn't make it with Sam. Sex ruined people's lives. But she wanted him so badly, she didn't really care. While the album played, Sam stood at the window. It was starting to rain. She could tell this was a gentle, slow, thunderless rain, the kind that made her feel a thrilling melancholy. She watched a mourning dove bathing itself in the rain on an electric line. It was lifting its wing and letting the rain shower its wingpit. It leaned far over to one side to expose the pit. Then it switched wings and leaned the other way. Sam saw Moon Pie streaking through the rain across the yard toward the porch. Everyone was home now.

23

Sam's mother insisted on taking them out to eat at a place in Paducah she was crazy about. It was one of those places Lorenzo Jones used to take her to. Everything had changed so much since those Saturday nights when they used to watch all the comedy shows. Now Irene had a baby, and a bushel of hair, and a husband with money, and a Trans Am. Emmett had Agent Orange and a sinister pain in his head. Dawn was having a baby. As they rushed up I-24 in the drizzling rain, Sam had the feeling that everyone was shooting off in different directions. Lonnie was still at the lake. Grandma was supposedly going to Florida. Even Emmett had been to Lexington on a whim. Sam wondered where she would go if she had her own car. Irene wouldn't let Sam drive the Trans Am. She said Larry would have a fit if it got a dent.

At the restaurant, they had to get a special seat on suction cups for Heather. She beat her tray like a drum and threw a fork on the floor.

"Would you just look at these gorgeous antique chairs?" Irene said.

"They're just like those crappy old chairs in the basement," Sam said. "You painted them pink once."

Emmett had showered and shaved and put on his striped T-shirt and clean jeans. His pimples made him look younger than his age. Irene had dismissed Sam's talk about Agent Orange, saying plenty of people got acne when they were older. She said it was a delayed reaction to growing up. She went on and on about it when Emmett was in the shower, but Sam grew bored and edgy. Her mother had an explanation for everything, now that she was taking psychology.

Emmett and Irene ordered beer, which came in fruit jars.

"I feel goofy drinking out of a fruit jar," Emmett said.

"They have the best barbecued ribs here," Irene kept insisting.

"I like pit barbecue better," said Sam. "I thought you liked pit barbecue."

"Well, I do, but this place is famous for ribs. I don't usually eat anything this fatty, though, and I don't fry anymore."

Emmett ordered the large rib platter with slaw and baked beans, and Sam and Irene ordered the medium size. The waitress brought a pile of napkins with the food. The ribs made their faces greasy. The baby threw a fistful of beans across the table.

"Say something, Emmett," said Irene. "Don't just sit there and feed your face."

"I'm busy," said Emmett, jerking a strip of meat off a rib.

"Tell us about your big adventure in Lexington, Emmett," said Sam. "Who'd you ride to Lexington with? Did Anita go?"

"And don't give us that stuff about aliens," Irene said. "Hush, Heather."

"Me and Jim Holly," Emmett said, still working on the rib. "I went to the lake with him, and he was aiming to fish, and I was going to look for some little blue herons. But he got on the parkway and failed to get off at the right exit and we just kept going. I just said what the hell. We had a couple of six-packs and a piece of a bottle of Jim Beam and so we just went. That's all there was to it."

"And he dumped you at my house," Irene said.

"I didn't know he was aiming to stay a week! His wife and little girl are there, and he was dying to see Pammy. Sue Ann wants him to move up to Lexington, but I don't know if he can leave his business now."

"That's not a very dramatic story," Irene said, jabbing a rib bone in sauce. "Why didn't you tell that in the first place? Do you want my beans, Sam?"

"No, I've got beans." Sam said to Emmett, "I thought Sue Ann dumped him."

"No. It's more complicated than that. Things ain't just black and white, Sam." Emmett hoisted his fruit jar and looked around for the waitress.

"I should have let you walk back home, Emmett," Irene said.

"You wanted to come back down here," he said. "Admit it."

"Where did you go after the dance, Emmett?" Sam asked.

He shrugged. "Jim and Allen and his wife met up with me and Anita at McDonald's, and we messed around."

The waitress brought Emmett another fruit jar of beer. Irene said, "Let me tell you what we're going to do. We're going to all order chocolate-pecan pie because this place has the best chocolate-pecan pie in Paducah."

"That's what you said about the ribs," said Emmett.

"Weren't they good?"

"I like pit barbecue better. But they were all right."

"Well, O.K. then. Sam, eat those ribs." Irene ordered three pieces of pie. "If we don't want it all, we'll take it home."

"Grandma makes the best pecan pie in Kentucky," Sam said. Irene hadn't even called Grandma to say hi.

"Sam, what's got into you?" asked Irene. "I haven't seen you in two months, and I come down by surprise and you act all sulled up. And y'all wonder why I wanted to leave home."

"We wanted you to come back," said Emmett.

"We're taking those ribs home," Irene said to the waitress, who was removing Sam's plate.

"Sam's been hard to live with all summer," Emmett said. "Lonnie quit his job and she was unhappy, and she doesn't have anything to do till she starts her job next month."

Sam stuck her tongue out at Emmett. She said, "I'd talk if I's you. Talk about hard to live with. The next time you go wandering off, you could leave a note or use the telephone."

Irene said to Emmett with a knowing smile, "She's going to be a worrier just like Mama. But she's got Daddy's stubbornness."

The baby squealed and whirred her lips.

"Well, who pulled your string?" cried Irene, delighted.

Irene drove her Trans Am through Paducah like a goddess driving a chariot. She whipped across railroad tracks. She made left turns at busy intersections without hesitation. Sam sat in the cramped back seat with the sleeping baby and wished she could drive the car. Maybe Irene would let her drive it tomorrow. She could drive Emmett to McDonald's and let everybody admire it. If Irene stayed till Lonnie got home, Sam would drive to his house and pretend the car was hers, to see what he would say. Heather's fist clung to Sam's finger. The baby's hand was like a naked little bird. Sam was glad her mother hadn't embarrassed her by nursing the baby in the restaurant.

The baby gave off a sour smell. The pods in the body-snatchers movie were about the size of a baby. It was a strange thought. A baby was more like a vegetable than a human—with its odd sick smell and pulsation, like a watermelon growing fast in the night. On TV one morning that week Sam had seen a watermelon that weighed 148 pounds. At eight cents a pound, it would cost—Sam tried to figure it out in her head, but the numbers disappeared just as soon as she fixed them in her mind.

"I'm taking the back roads because there's something I want you to see," Irene said.

Emmett turned to Sam and said, "Ain't she something? Your mother is full of the joy of life." He grinned and slapped Irene's shoulder.

"Here it is," Irene said a few minutes later, as she rounded a curve on a small hill. She pulled into a dirt lane and stopped. "Look," she said, opening her car door.

The rain had quit and the sun glinted through the clouds. It was still daylight, but it was growing dimmer, like ink dissolving in a vast amount of water. Irene had to explain that what she wanted them to see was the landscape, some fields and trees along a hillside. The last-minute sun was casting broken yellow light over everything. There were bushes and clumps of weeds in the fields, making round shadows.

"I always thought this place was so pretty," Irene said. "With those hedgerows and all the bushes scattered around.

And see those piles of rocks? And look at the Holsteins over there."

"I don't see any cowbirds," Sam said.

"They're not around much anymore," said Emmett.

The fields were cluttered. Sam's grandfather's fields were as clean and clear as bed sheets. There wasn't a tree or a stray sapling or a clump of weeds in Granddad's fields, but these were like rooms scattered with furniture.

"The reason I like this so much," Irene went on, "is that it's just like England. I've seen pictures of England that look like this."

"England?" Sam said, her voice catching.

"That's a place I always wanted to go, but I don't guess I'll ever get the chance."

They piled back into the car. Sam stuck her finger in the baby's fist again, and the baby tugged at it as they drove home in the gathering darkness. Irene turned on her headlights, and they glided on, twisting on the back roads, past old farms with remodeled houses. All the houses were near the road, and the barns were leaning, and the silhouetted farm equipment was standing silent and still, looking like outwitted dinosaurs caught dead in their tracks by some asteroids. None of the other farms looked like England.

24

Sam had helped Emmett clear out her mother's old room while Irene watched *Between Friends* on TV. The bed was loaded with empty Purex jugs, old magazines, stacks of grocery sacks, and boxes of clothes. Emmett took some of the junk to the basement, and Sam made up the bed with two fitted bottom sheets. She couldn't find any clean top sheets. Most of their sheets were ragged, but Grandma had promised to get them new sheets for Christmas.

Sam realized how much of her mother was still in the room. On a built-in shelf near the window were her old paperbacks and 45s. All her albums were in Sam's room. The closets and drawers were still filled with Irene's old clothes, and on the wall were pictures she had painted when she went through her artistic period. She had copied them from a book. They were abstract forms, much like some photographs of magnified V.D. germs Sam had seen in a health pamphlet at a doctor's office.

Irene had insisted on sleeping with Heather. She laughed when Sam asked her if she was afraid of rolling over on the baby. Pandas usually suffocated their babies that way, Sam told her mother. Then they argued about Sam's future, and Irene said Sam would be stupid not to get out of Hopewell and go to a large university. Irene said she was studying psychology because human nature fascinated her.

During the night, Sam heard the baby crying. Moon Pie, who seemed preoccupied and jumpy, as though he had had an unnerving adventure during his absence, had been sleeping at the foot of Sam's bed, but he bounded out when he heard Irene going downstairs to the kitchen. Outside, rain was falling softly, and a delicate wind was pushing the willow tree against the side of the house. The baby was like a growth that had come loose, Sam thought—like a scab or a wart—and Irene carried it around with her in fascination, unable to part with it. Monkeys carried dead babies around like that. A friend of Emmett's knew a lot of dead-baby jokes, but Sam couldn't remember any she had heard. In Vietnam, mothers had carried their dead babies around with them until they began to rot. As she grew more fully awake, she began to wonder how she knew that. She could picture it vividly, although it seemed like something she had made up. In the final episode of *M*A*S*H*, Hawkeye had cracked up after seeing a woman smother her own baby to keep it from crying. He had seen so many soldiers die, but he fell apart when he saw a baby die. It seemed appropriate that Hawkeye should crack up at the end of the series. That way, you knew everything didn't turn out happily. That was too easy.

Sam lay awake and listened to Irene humming to the baby, but she could not identify the tune. The noises of the rain and the willow tree obscured the melody. And Emmett was snoring down the hall. He had had a hard time getting to sleep because the barbecue gave him gas. Sam heard him belching for a long time after she went to bed. A car swished by, its headlights flashing on the wall. Sam could see the arms of the willow tree shadowed on the wall, and she thought of the creepy jungle vines in Vietnam. She wondered if they were anything like kudzu vines. Kudzu enveloped everything, even cars and abandoned buildings. It stopped trains. Sam remembered *The Thing*, on the late show. She hadn't seen the new version, which was supposed to be a lot scarier. The Thing was a vegetable man from outer space. For a long time after she saw that movie, Sam couldn't go outside in the dark because she thought the trees and the bushes were deceiving her.

She wondered why horror movies had to be remade—maybe because the world was getting scarier all the time.

Sam padded downstairs, feeling like a ghost in the glow from the living room lamp. Irene was in the kitchen poking blueberry buckle into the baby's mouth. The baby's face was blue, like the blue baby the man at the courthouse had told about. Sam could smell the dirty diapers under the sink and the cigarette butts in the ashtray on the kitchen table.

"Sam, are you up? We probably woke up the neighborhood. Heather was squalling for something to eat." Irene said to the baby, "That baby was hungry—yes!"

"I was thirsty." Sam poured from a partial quart of Pepsi and drank it without ice. She turned on the TV and recognized a Twisted Sister video she had seen several times. She turned the TV off.

"I put the cat out," Irene said.

"Oh, Emmett will have a fit!" Sam rushed to the door and saw Moon Pie sitting under the Trans Am. She dashed outside and brought him in. His fur was beaded with rain. She told her mother, "Emmett's afraid he'll get hit by a car at night. Cats get blinded by the lights."

"You should have stayed up to see the rest of *Between Friends*,"

Irene said, wiping the baby's mouth with a wet paper towel. "It was really good."

"I just like funny movies. Emmett and me won't watch tear-jerkers."

"You don't have to do everything Emmett does."

"What makes you think I do?"

"I just do." Irene, with the baby on one hip, swooped down to pick something up from the floor. "Where are all these seeds coming from? That looks like that old appleseed necklace I got in Lexington at that head shop. God, I wouldn't have thought of that for five dollars." Her face screwed up in distaste.

Sam searched for something to eat. Moon Pie was rubbing against her legs. The doggie bag of ribs was the highlight of the refrigerator. She gave Moon Pie a barbecued rib to gnaw on and found a bag of potato chips for herself. Moon Pie turned up his nose and strutted over to the couch.

"You're going to ruin your health with all that junk," Irene said.

"So what?"

"Honestly!" Irene set the baby in her carrier and then rinsed out the baby-food jar with an expert twirl of her forefinger. Sam's mother was always quick and efficient. When she washed plates, she rinsed only the tops, not the bottoms, to save time.

"If you want to worry about somebody's health, worry about Emmett," Sam said, crunching potato chips.

"His face doesn't look so bad. He said it was clearing up."

"It's not just his face. He still has that weird pain in his head. He won't mention it, but he has it all the time. About every two minutes he has it."

"That sounds like what he used to have when he flipped out that time."

"Well, that's what I'm saying, but you won't listen. He scares me. And that Agent Orange can cause every symptom in the book. Buddy Mangrum can't even drink a beer without getting sick, and his little girl's got a bunch of birth defects."

Irene shot ice cubes into a glass and poured some Pepsi. She said, "The trouble is, I carried Emmett around on a pillow all those years when I should have made him take more responsibility, and now you're trying to do the same thing I did. Well, if we leave him alone, he just might have to go to work and pay that money he owes, for instance."

"That's too scary."

"I don't like to see you stuck with him. You can go to school. You don't have to get a job. Uncle Sam will pay for everything."

Sam wondered if her mother had named her after Uncle Sam because she was a burden on Uncle Sam, or maybe a consolation prize from Uncle Sam.

"Do you still go out dancing?" Sam asked her mother.

"No. I can't dance like I used to now that my bladder's dropped. I carried Heather too low when I was pregnant. Aren't you seeing that Lonnie boy anymore? I haven't heard you mention him."

"He's off at the lake." Sam wondered if he was still partying, at this hour. He would be back Wednesday.

The baby was crying. Irene sat down on the couch and rocked her gently against her breast. She had on a nightshirt with pinstripes on it like a baseball uniform. Then she opened her shirt and gave the baby her breast. Her breast was pale and oval, and the nipple looked like the end of a Tootsie Roll. Sam wondered if that was where Tootsie Rolls got their name.

"You *have* to go to college, Sam. Women can do anything they want to now, just about."

"You just want me to get out of Hopewell and forget about Emmett, the same way you want me to forget about my daddy," Sam blurted out. "You want to pretend the whole Vietnam War never existed, like you want to protect me from something. I'm not a baby." She glanced at the baby, who was tugging away obliviously.

A flash of pain hit her mother's face, and Sam regretted her outburst. Irene said slowly, "I've told you about all there is to tell, Sam. I was married to him for one month before he left, and I never saw him again." She picked at her chin. "I hardly even remember him," she said.

"Where did you get married?"

Irene smiled. "At a justice of the peace out in the country. He was a chicken farmer, and we got married on his porch. When we left, a bunch of chickens got loose and feathers were flying everywhere. They were Barred Rocks, I believe."

"What did you do with the flag on his casket?"

"Emmett made a cape out of it. Oh, God, I'd forgot that! That was when Emmett's crazy friends were here. I was so mad at him. It hurt me that he did that, but I guess I didn't feel any special reverence for the U.S. Army, so it didn't matter." She hugged the baby to her breast. She said, "Why don't you go see Mamaw and Pap? You never go see them. They can tell you more about Dwayne than I can. I think they've got some stuff of his they'd let you have."

"They don't like me."

"Yes, they do. They just don't know you anymore."

"They didn't come to my graduation or even send me a present."

"Oh, you know how country folks are. They're standoffish. It's *me* they don't approve of, Sam. I used to take you there, out of duty, even though they never made me feel that welcome. But they always loved you. They always *made* over you."

"I don't have a car. I can't go see them."

"I think they've got a notebook Dwayne kept over there. They'd let you see that, I bet."

The baby stopped nursing and her head swiveled around. She looked at Sam curiously. "I guess she's not hungry," Irene said, flopping her breast back in her nightshirt. She burped the baby. Sam thought of the Tupperware joke about the walrus. Irene said, "Just look at her. I was nineteen, not much older than you. Imagine yourself with this little baby. How would you handle it? But I can't live in the past. It was all such a stupid waste. There's nothing to remember."

"Did he know you were going to have me?"

"Oh, sure. We wrote back and forth. He knew."

"Emmett said it was my daddy's idea to name me Samantha."

"He liked the name. I can't remember exactly how it came up. It might have been his idea."

"I still don't see why you never told me."

"I didn't think it mattered."

"Yes, it did."

Sam's mother sat there in her baseball shirt, smiling oddly, like the Mona Lisa, and holding on to the baby as if it were a piece of baggage fastened to her person with Velcro. Sam remembered where she had seen the Vietnamese woman carrying a dead baby. It was a vivid picture in her mind. It was the cover of a *Newsweek* magazine. It had arrived in the mail one day and Sam saw it first. When Irene saw it, she snatched it out of Sam's hands and ripped the cover off and burned it.

"Do you still have those letters he wrote you?" Sam asked.

"I saved them, but I don't know where they are now."

"Didn't you take them with you?"

"I don't think so. I threw away a lot of stuff. But they might still be in my room somewhere. Sam, I wish y'all would clear that room out—the whole house out—and have a yard sale. This house is going to fall apart from the weight of all the junk in it."

"Emmett's working on the foundation," Sam said.

"Come to Lexington with me tomorrow, Sam," said Irene, reaching for Sam's face and caressing it lightly, brushing Sam's hair away from her forehead. "I'll take you out to the Horse Park and we'll drive down to Natural Bridge. Maybe we can go to that Mike Fink riverboat restaurant on the river across from Cincinnati and have some seafood."

"I can eat catfish right here."

"Oh, Sam!" Irene stood up, carefully set the baby down, and went into the kitchen. She poured more Pepsi. "I shouldn't drink this," she said.

"There's something I want to ask you about Emmett," Sam said when her mother sat down again.

"What?"

"Did he get wounded in the war?"

"No, why?"

"I thought maybe some reason like that was why he never had any girlfriends."

Irene laughed. "No, it wasn't that. And he's not gay either, so don't think that." She rattled the ice in her glass and regarded the dim living room. "God, it took me years to get out of this place!"

"How come you didn't stay in Lexington that time when I was little?"

"Well, why do you think? Mama and Daddy made me feel like I'd committed a *crime*. And Emmett pitched such a fit. He was in real bad shape then."

"Who was that guy Bob who went to Lexington with us?"

Irene gazed at her glass. "Just somebody. I thought I cared about him at the time. He camped out in the back yard."

"I remember that," Sam said. "He let me play his flute in his tent out in the yard."

"It was a recorder," said Irene. "An alto recorder."

"Whatever happened to him?"

"The last I heard of him he was married and he named his kid Nuclear Ragtime. Can you imagine what that kid's life is like?"

"Probably they've told him some lie about why they named him that," said Sam.

"Maybe." Irene sucked on a piece of ice.

"Who were all those people, anyway? What were they doing here?"

"Oh, it was all so crazy. But when we were in Lexington, it was even crazier. I remember one time we went to this dinner and everybody had to bring something white. Everybody had to wear white, and all the food was white. I won the prize for the whitest outfit. I had on a long white dress with white tennis shoes. Can you believe it?"

"What did you have to eat?" Sam asked.

"Chicken breast, milk gravy and biscuits, angel food cake, white wine. I remember bringing white bread with the crust trimmed and spread with cream cheese. The whole thing was disgusting, but it was funny. I think it was supposed to mean something, but I can't remember what."

"What was the prize you won?"

"A pound of divinity fudge. I hate divinity, too."

"Were you in love with that guy Bob?"

"Yeah. But I came back here because we had the house and they still wanted me at my old job, and everybody was mad at me. And I felt guilty because I felt I owed something to Emmett because he'd gone over there for my sake."

"Was that true?"

"I don't know. I don't think Emmett knew beans when he went into the Army. He thought it would be just like killing squirrels, I guess. Why, he barely knew how to wipe his butt when he went over there. He was just a country boy."

"Granddad went to war," said Sam.

"World War II was a whole different situation."

"The Japanese were little, like the Vietnamese," Sam said. "They're not so little anymore, though, since they're eating beef." She wondered if Americans would get smaller from eating tofu and vegetable plates.

Irene finished her Pepsi. "Listen," she said. "Larry knows a guy in Lexington who's got a good job in public relations. He was in Vietnam and he killed a whole *family* of people in a hut: a mother, a father, three children, and some uncles and aunts and a grandmother. He killed every one of them, and he said it was two years before it hit him what he did. He was a dope addict and everything. But he finally got it worked out in his head and he figured the only thing he could do was try to live his life in some productive way. He's married and got kids now, and he even joined the church. And I thought, if that guy could do all that, then Emmett can do it."

"Emmett would vote for Reagan before he'd join the church," Sam said skeptically. "Did Emmett ever kill people?"

"I have no idea. He never talked about that."

"Did my daddy kill people?"

"I don't know that either. But look, Sam, it wouldn't be unusual if they did. That's what they were sent over there for. Hey, hand me my tote bag over there by your chair. I brought you a present."

Sam handed her the bag, stuffed with diapers and magazines. Irene pulled out a green T-shirt and handed it to Sam. It was a "M*A*S*H 4077th" T-shirt.

"I almost forgot to give it to you," Irene said. "But I remember how much you always liked that show."

"Gah!" said Sam. "Now I can look like Hot Lips!"

"Your boobs aren't that big."

"Yours are."

"Yeah, while I'm nursing. I feel like Jayne Mansfield."

"Who's Jayne Mansfield?"

"An old movie star. She had big jugs."

Sam put the T-shirt on over her pajama top and admired it in the mirror. She smiled, and in the mirror, Irene was smiling behind her.

Sam said, "Mom, do you remember that Kinks album you used to like so much?"

"Yeah. The one with 'Lola' on it?"

Sam nodded. "It's great. I've been listening to it."

"Yeah. I always liked it." Irene stood up and stretched. "I need to get an early start in the morning. But you think about what I said. You can go with me if you want to."

"Buy me a car and I'll move to Lexington," Sam said.

25

Sam felt like an idiot. She had been joking about moving to Lexington, but she did want a car. So the next morning when Irene handed Sam a check for six hundred dollars and said, "Here, go buy that car you were talking about," Sam felt embarrassed, as though she hadn't loved her mother enough. But she did love her mother. That was why it bothered her so much that Irene went away with that jerk who got her pregnant. Irene told Sam, "You don't have to move to Lexington if you don't want to, but you need a car and you can at least come and see me." Sam felt like giving her mother the cat bank right then, because she wanted to show her that she cared, but it occurred to her suddenly that it was the wrong present. Her mother didn't want a ridiculous cat with beads on it. The baby might choke on the beads.

"I'm going by and see Mama and Daddy for a minute," Irene said. Her head was in the refrigerator. "I guess Larry won't kill me if I'm late. But Mama would, if she heard I was here and didn't go see her. Don't you have anything I can take to eat on the road?" She closed the refrigerator door and said, "Why am I the one who always has to come down here? Why doesn't anybody come to see *me?*"

"I came to see you, didn't I?" said Emmett, who had just entered the kitchen, wearing jeans and no shirt. He was sleepy-eyed.

Irene shook a bottle of ketchup at him. "And I had to bring you back, you good-for-nothing, you."

Sam explained to Emmett about the car and he looked pleased.

"Well," he said happily. Then he opened the refrigerator and said, "We're out of milk."

"Will you sign for me, Emmett?" Sam asked.

"Sure. If you have a wreck, though, they can't get much out of me."

"I won't have a wreck."

Irene touched the bumps on Emmett's neck. She sighed. "Did you try that brewer's yeast like I said?"

"No. But I used Mama's burn plant."

Irene frowned at the bag of potato chips on the counter. Then she said, "Emmett, the next time you decide to get beamed up to Lexington, let me know you're coming and I'll bake a cake."

"There won't be time to bake a cake. Not if I'm traveling at the speed of light."

"See my T-shirt?" Sam said to Emmett. "Mom brought it."

Emmett grinned. "See, she understands you."

"He told me to get it for you," Irene said.

"Here, Mom," said Sam, pulling open a cabinet door. "Take some Granny Cakes. They're real good."

On the telephone, Sam told Lonnie she would have a surprise for him when he came home Wednesday. She meant the new car, but the real surprise, she thought, was that she wouldn't be driving it with Lonnie to that wedding in Bowling Green. She didn't care what he said about that. He couldn't force her to go.

Lonnie was eating raw steak for breakfast because somebody said it was good for a hangover.

"I think raw steak's for black eyes, not hangovers," Sam told him. "How was the stag party?"

"I'll tell you about it later," he said. "The parts I can remember."

"What did you do with my panties?"

"We decorated. It was like New Year's Eve." Lonnie giggled like a kid. Sam realized she preferred older men.

After buying the car and paying for insurance and a temporary registration, Sam had two hundred dollars left in her bank account. She was relieved that she hadn't forgotten how to drive. Irene's old VW buck-jumped, but this one drove smoothly. She was happy about the car, but not happy about Tom. When she picked up the car at his garage, Tom refused to go riding in it with her. He had washed and lubed it and he had given it a test drive, but he still kept his distance, the way he had on Saturday morning.

"Are you sure you know what you're doing?" he asked her.

"Don't you want to sell me this car?"

"I don't want you buying it for the wrong reasons."

"Are you sorry I was here the other night?"

"Let's just say some things ought to be forgotten."

"I didn't tell anybody, if that's what you're afraid of," Sam said.

"That's not what I mean. It shouldn't have happened."

He was polishing the car with a pair of ragged Jockey shorts. His jeans rode low on his hips, and he had on a black Budweiser T-shirt. The car looked great. He had filled in the rusted spots with patching compound.

"Go riding with me," she said.

"Your boyfriend might see us."

"I told you he wasn't my boyfriend anymore."

She got in the car and scooted the seat forward. It worked without getting stuck. Sam was amazed. In her experience, most things like that failed to work. "Why are you giving me such a hard time?" she said. "I had a good time that night. Why don't you come over to my house? We could watch television together. Or you could play with Emmett's Atari." She felt like Anita, frantic for Emmett's company, and she was embarrassed.

Tom said, "You don't want to mess with me, Sam. You'll just be sorry."

"No, I won't."

"I shouldn't have taken advantage of you like that."

"Isn't it a matter of my opinion whether you took advantage of me?" Sam was about to cry.

"Look, Sam. You'll be better off with somebody your own age. Now go off in your new car and enjoy yourself. And be careful."

"I could get into dirt bikes," she said.

Tom just smiled and waved her off. But Sam sobbed all the way home. At last she had a car, and it made her cry. It didn't make sense. What bothered her the most was the shame Tom was trying to cover up. She knew he felt humiliated by what she knew about him, and she didn't know how to tell him it was O.K. He seemed to have his mind made up. She had to figure out a way, though, to get through to him. She pictured herself suddenly famous. He would see her on TV and realize he loved her. If she got a lot of money, she could buy him that pump. She imagined herself in a wreck, because of faulty brakes or steering. And he would feel responsible and spend his life making it up to her. It felt strange driving her own new car at last, with tears running down her face. Grandma always said, "The more you get, the more you want." It meant that people were never satisfied. New cars didn't make them happy after all.

She had told Tom one lie. Dawn knew everything. But Dawn had promised not to tell. Besides, Dawn was preoccupied with her own problems.

That afternoon, Sam picked Dawn up at the Burger Boy and took her riding in the new car. Dawn was depressed, and Sam didn't tell her about the latest encounter with Tom. It hurt too much, the way he had said to find someone her own age. He thought she was just a kid, which was true in some ways, but not completely true.

Dawn had told Ken about the baby. "I think he likes the idea," she said. "He seemed real shocked, but then his face lit up in a big grin." As they rode around, Dawn kept talking about renting that apartment over the furniture store. Ken knew the guy who owned the building and he could get a special deal. "We wouldn't need much furniture," she said. "But I might go nuts living over a furniture store and seeing all that nice furniture that I couldn't afford."

"Maybe you could sneak down at night and sleep on a nice big king-sized bed," Sam said. She beeped her horn at an old woman in a Mercury who turned without signaling.

"That's a good way to get killed!" Sam shouted. Owning a car gave her power. She liked the way the car handled. It could turn on a dime.

"I really love Ken," Dawn said. "And I can't think of anybody I'd rather wake up with in the morning. But let me tell you this. Yesterday I bought a chicken at the grocery? And when I got home and pulled out those parts inside, all wrapped in paper, I had the sickening thought that the chicken was giving birth to a creature, but it was all in parts, so they had to be stuffed in a little bag." She shuddered.

"Good grief. That sounds like something I'd dream up."

"I know. I think that's how come I thought of it. When I pulled the package of parts out, I thought about you, and I knew what you'd think. Our minds must be that close." She smiled faintly.

"I kept thinking about you when my little half-sister was here," Sam said. "She's real cute, but I couldn't imagine having a baby."

"It might be O.K. to have a baby. You get attached to them. I'm crazy about my brother's kids."

Sam headed for the shopping center. Dawn wanted to buy some burgundy nail polish. She still had some money left from Friday's paycheck.

Sam said, "Look, Dawn, you're always wanting to do something wild. Get an abortion—for your own good."

"But having a baby would be as wild as anything I can think of. And besides, I think Ken will have some say-so in it."

"No!" cried Sam, banging the steering wheel. "Having kids is what everybody does. It doesn't take any special talent." The traffic threaded onto the road to the shopping center. Sam inched along, shifting gears carefully.

Dawn said, "I could do a lot of crazy stuff, but not that. I'm just too chicken to do that."

"But it's still early. It wouldn't be much different than popping a pimple. They start out so teeny they're not even real hardly."

Dawn shook her head. "No. I think about my mother and what she went through to have me. She had enough kids already when she had me. She could have decided not to have me. And she should have, for her own sake, I guess. But she didn't, for mine. That's what I'm thinking about."

"Well," Sam said. The traffic was crazy. She had never really noticed how many cars—big, long cars—were in town before. The plants were changing shifts. And people were headed for the shopping center. And others were going home from the shopping center. Everything was happening at once.

Dawn said, "I'm so glad you got a car, Sam. I really am. It's real neat."

After she drove Dawn home, Sam drove Emmett around town. Emmett looked at the scenery and waved at people. Sam realized that with the money she had spent on the car, she could have paid off the money he owed. But that wasn't really her problem. She was through worrying about his debt. Emmett's legs doubled up in the car like a spider lurking in its tunnel. She let him out at Sureway and drove around the parking lot while he went in for groceries. For once, he wouldn't have to wag home a clumsy carton of drinks. Inside the store, Emmett got involved in a conversation with a woman in charge of a pancake breakfast at the fire hall, and Sam drove 2.3 miles around the parking lot while waiting for him.

"You'll wear out your clutch that way," he said when he got in.

Maybe she was going nuts. It wasn't just Tom. Or just Emmett. Or Lonnie. Or Dawn's predicament. It was her. She was at the center of all these impossible dramas, and somehow she was feeling that it was all up to her. But she didn't really know where she was, or who she would be if all those people left town and walked into the sunset to live happily ever after. If she got all of them straightened out, what would she do?

It helped, having a car. Now that she had one, she could think of many places to go: Mammoth Cave, the Grand Ole Opry, Six Flags over Mid-America. She could drive Grandma to Florida. She felt a strange exhilaration, as if she were free to do anything she wanted to. She felt she had a point to prove, but she didn't know who to prove it to.

"I think Mom's right," Sam told Emmett on the way home. "You've got to get off your ass." Emmett just grunted.

At home, Sam explored her mother's room, looking for her father's letters. She found a fondue pot, a hot-curls set, two old hair dryers, a Dutch oven, a pair of framed pictures of chickens, some plastic kitchen curtains, an apple corer, an unused box of canning jar lids, a basket of bread that had been preserved with acrylic spray—enough junk to have a profitable yard sale. There was a crepe-maker Irene had gotten for Christmas the year they were so popular. Irene had used it only once. Sam flipped through a stack of pictures—framed dime-store prints of ducks, paint-by-numbers sunsets and lakes, a seascape in an ornate gold frame. In the chest of drawers, she found piles of old underwear, half-slips and strapless bras and panties with torn lace and stockings and black lacy garter belts. They smelled of talcum and age.

The letters weren't in Irene's dresser, although that seemed a likely place. The dresser was filled with tangled hair ribbons and rusted clips and blue brush-rollers. The closet was stuffed with old clothes. Sam felt sad looking at the tent-style coat, the mini-skirts, the good knit suits. Irene had kept them because they were too good to throw away. She would have given them to the Salvation Army, but she had said it depressed her to think of poor people walking around in clothes that were out of style.

On a closet shelf Sam found some small stationery boxes tied with strings of selvage. They were full of snapshots of old schoolmates and souvenirs from high school dances. Irene had saved labels from liquor bottles and plastic swizzle sticks that said "Stacey's" and "La Flame" and "The Embers." She had gone on her senior class trip to Mammoth Cave, and there were maps and a place mat from a restaurant with a map of the caves on it.

The letters were in a box on the top shelf. They were in one slim bundle, with a rubber band that broke when she removed it. Sam went downstairs and got some Doritos and bean dip and a cold Pepsi and a glass of ice and went up to her room to read the letters. She arranged everything around her, the Pepsi on the nightstand, the Doritos and bean dip on the bed in a cleared spot. Emmett was outside, mowing.

Sam arranged the letters chronologically. There was no telegram, telling how it ended. Grandma told Sam once that an Army officer had come to the house with the news. Irene was still at work, and after telling Grandma and Granddad, the man waited in his car for Irene to come home. He was a tall man with an inflexible face and a monotone, someone whose job was to travel around the state and tell families their boys had been killed. Eventually, there were over a thousand Kentucky boys who were killed, and Sam had imagined the same man visiting a thousand families with his grim news, and she wondered whether he had developed a stock technique for delivering his news. She pictured him stopping off at the Dairy Bar on his way home, ordering a hot-dog-on-a-stick and a milk shake.

Dwayne had a childish handwriting, with big circles and loops. He wrote with a pencil on lined tablet paper. He didn't leave margins.

Dear Irene,

I can't tell you how I miss you. I can't even try. All I can do is try to get by without you and do my job the best I can.

It's different here. It's not what I imagined, but I guess I'll get by. You never know what's going to happen. Sometimes they wake you up in the middle of the night for inspection and they don't even tell you why. We're sleeping in a big long tent barricks and it's okay but it's hot. The mosquitos are eating me alive! But that's the worst so far. I reckon I'll make it.

Everybody says this operation's a snap. We'll be out of here by fall. Everything's going good and we've got the best guys here you ever would want to meet. I can't tell you how lucky I am to be with the 109th—what a bunch. When I get back, I've invited this old boy I met from over in Trigg County to go fishing with me. He says he caught a 15-lb. bass at Ky. Lake once. I tell him when we get back, just watch me. We've got a bet on, whoever catches the most fish has to dress them and cook them for a big fish fry—his whole family and mine. (Don't I sound crazy? You get a lot of big ideas over here, just thinking about home.)

I've got your picture right inside my pocket next to my heart, so I can take a quick look at it anytime. It's the one with you standing by the Nash Rambler, in those red shorts. It's black and white but I see those red shorts.

Honey, I don't want you to worry about me over here. I want you to be proud of me. When we get back we'll make up for lost time like you've never seen. I'm proud to serve my country and I'm doing the best job I can. With your prayers, I know we'll succeed. I just feel it in my bones.

I love you forever and ever—enough bushels of love to make a path from Hopewell to Quang Ngai.

Sam dropped a Dorito fragment on the letter and she picked it up with a moistened finger. Atoms from the letter mixed with atoms of her saliva, across time. Lonnie had never written her a letter. She was disappointed that her father didn't say what Vietnam was like. His mind was on the fish in Kentucky Lake, not on the birds and fish over there.

The next two letters were much the same. He said he was going out on patrols, just in the daytime. He said not to worry because he had been well-trained. He didn't say whether he felt lonely or if he was having a good time or if he was miserable. He seemed to be excessively cheerful.

The next letter was one she was looking for.

> Your news surprised me! You could of knocked me over with a feather! Just to think I could be a daddy. I was so happy I danced a jig and guys poured beer on me (don't worry, I'm not drinking it!) Sometimes we get beer here, but I won't drink it. I can see why they drink it, though, the water's not fit to drink and you have to put a pill in it to kill the germs. Be thankful you're an American. Everybody's as happy as me. Bob from Trigg County says he's going to personally deliver a present from his daddy's store. His daddy works in a drug store and can get baby powder and things like that on discount. I'm floating on air. We have to sleep on the ground but last night I didn't feel it, I swear.
>
> I wish you didn't have to go through this by yourself. I wish I was there to watch you grow. You are going to be the prettiest mama in Kentucky, I swear.

He went on like that for several letters, without saying anything about Vietnam. He sounded like a preacher. He wrote about God and His blessings. He wrote, "I pray daily for the little babe." It made Sam feel funny.

> You asked me to tell you what it was like here. No, I haven't seen any tigers or gorillas. Let's just say it's not a place where you'd want to go for a Sunday drive. It's hot, even hotter than Kentucky Lake in August—and the rainy season is coming up. They say it rains for 6 solid months. Can you feature that? At home, everything would drown if it rained 6 months. That would be worse than Noah's Flood. But we need rain bad. Right now it's dusty. I can't hardly keep my rifle clean and we don't always get a bath but things are looking up. Our bunch went out on a successful mission this week. Every time we go out we push back the enemy a little further. We must be doing something right! You asked about the people here, they're real little and don't know English. One little girl comes and cleans up for us and washes our clothes and polishes our boots. I never had it so good! (Ha!) I say little girl but she's

probably 30. You can't tell their ages. Don't be jealous. She's too old for me!

The scenery is okay, but that rocky little beach right below the dam, give me that any day.

Sam skimmed several of the letters, from April through July. They gushed about how he missed Irene, and he wrote hopefully about the job he was doing (another successful strike against the enemy). The letters were full of silly things and little lectures telling Irene to be good. They sounded strangely frivolous, as if he were on a vacation, writing back wish-you-were-here postcards. Then she read the next-to-last letter.

I was thinking about what you wanted to name the baby and I really don't want to name it Darrell. That was the name of a guy in my outfit who isn't with us anymore. I'd feel too unlucky naming my baby Darrell. Your idea of Melinda Sue reminds me too much of that ugly girl I had to sit by one summer in Vacation Bible School. And Bill and Bob are too ordinary. But here's my favorite name: Samuel. It's from the Bible. If it's a girl, name it Samantha. That sounds like something in a prayer, doesn't it? I think it's a name in Chronicles. I've been reading the Bible every night.

P.S. If that guy at the Dairy Queen bothers you again, tell him I'll fix him when I get home.

The last letter said that work was getting tough and he wasn't sleeping much. He wrote about the pleasures of getting Irene's letters and the way he missed her. But he never said what he really meant. Miss Castle in English always said to be specific. He told Irene not to worry. He made marching through the jungle seem like a rare privilege. He didn't say he was scared. He didn't mention any more guys dying.

Sam felt cheated. He was counting on a boy. Samantha was an afterthought. Her father must have been very brave, but she thought he was just trying to protect Irene—and by extension, years later, her. The dead took their secrets with them. She wondered how far to go in honoring the dead if the dead offer you nothing except a little mindless protection, by keeping their secrets from you. The picture was there in the mirror frame, his eyes on her as she munched Doritos and read the old letters, and it almost seemed that he was playing a joke on her, a guessing game, as if he were saying, "Know me if you can."

The last paragraph of the last letter said, "When I get home, the first thing I'm going to do is take you out for a hamburger at the Dairy Queen and do all the same things we did on our first date. It'll be you and me and the little squirt—Sam. I hope you've still got that dress. Ha ha! You probably won't fit in it now."

Sam found a Bible on the bookshelf in Irene's room. Her mother had not even taken her Bible to Lexington. She found the Book of Chronicles and scanned it. Chronicles was full of "begats." She had heard that when her mother was in high school, Irene used to choose a chapter of begats from Genesis to read aloud in homeroom, just for fun. That was in the old days, when they used to pray in school.

There was no Samantha in either the first or the second book of Chronicles. Sam finished the Doritos. All the ice in her Pepsi had melted.

26

Lonnie wasn't impressed with Sam's car. He kicked the tires and thumped the hood, as though he were testing a watermelon for ripeness.

"You're just jealous 'cause I bought it from Tom," she said. Her cheeks burned at the intimate sound of the word "Tom."

Lonnie's suntan had deepened. He and his buddies had fished from a pontoon boat and roasted wienies at a campfire. It sounded like Boy Scouts. In Vietnam, her father ate ham and beans from a can and slept in a hole in the ground.

Lonnie said that at the stag party the guys had brought joke presents from the adult bookstore in McCracken County—purple pasties with tassels, a coffee mug shaped like a breast, some bizarre French rubbers, and a dozen sex books, with titles like *Marcelle's Primrose* and *Tough Titty.* At one time, Sam would have been curious and amused, but now his report seemed absurd. When he said they hung all the women's underwear on a clothesline, at eye level, Sam wondered if they blew up rubbers for party balloons, but she didn't bother to ask. On *M*A*S*H,* the doctors blew up surgical gloves. The gloves looked like cows' sacs.

When boys got together, they got drunk and bragged about sex. Girls talked about boys and clothes. When women got together, they talked about diseases and recipes. Sam didn't know what grown men talked about. Men were a total mystery.

Lonnie had forgotten to bring her panties. He came over after supper and played *Chopper Command* with Emmett. He was full of stories about fish and beer. Later, Sam went riding around with him in his van. She knew he was still sexed up from the stag party and would park on a country road eventually, and she dreaded that. She couldn't get the letters out of her head, and everything Lonnie said made her think of something her father had written to her mother. She had given the letters to Emmett to read that evening.

The jungle was closing in, and even the maple trees on Maple Street seemed as though they might be hiding snipers. Lonnie wouldn't know how to behave in the jungle. His world was Hopewell. Since Dawn got pregnant, Sam had been feeling that if she didn't watch her step, her whole life could be ruined by some mischance, some stupid surprise, like sniper fire.

Lonnie drove his van hard, jerking to a halt at stop signs, and squealing around corners with a serious intent. The van had developed new rattles since last week. He drove past the shopping center, toward the Burger Boy. The street lights were coming on.

He said, "I've got a great idea for what to do with my life. Do you want to hear it?"

"What? Are you going to join the Army?"

"Ha ha. No. Maybe I'll join the Navy. The Navy's not a bad deal. Those big aircraft carriers have got video games and everything. They say it's like being on a cruise ship."

"Would you rather go to Lebanon or Nicaragua on your cruise ship?"

"Be serious. Here's the deal: I'm going to take this correspondence course in camera repair. There's an ad in a magazine Mama gets. I've been giving it some thought, and I've realized there's not a place anywhere around where you can get a camera fixed. My aunt had to send hers to Memphis. If I fixed cameras, I could have my business at home, and I could set my own hours. They give you a camera to work on. And then you get a certificate when you finish."

"I didn't know you were interested in photography."

"It sounds like a good deal. See, you have to scout the market. A business succeeds when there's a need for it. You walk in anybody's house in Hopewell, and what have they got? Family pictures on the wall. And scrapbooks of pictures."

"They get a lot of them taken at a studio, or at Olin Mills, when they come through town and have special deals."

"But where do those studios get their cameras fixed? They probably have to send their cameras to Memphis. I could fix 'em right here. I bet there's thousands of cameras in Hopewell."

"Oh, yeah," Sam said breezily. "That's sort of like what Emmett does, fixing toasters and hair dryers. He must make at least fifty dollars a month!"

"Oh, come on, Sam. What's wrong with you?" He pulled into the Burger Boy and stopped at a parking place in the back. He turned the key off, and the post-ignition shut-off jet throbbed for a few moments. "Do you want to go see *Ghostbusters* tomorrow night?"

"No."

"What's going on in that stubborn head of yours?" he said, tousling her hair.

"It's hard to describe. You sort of have to *be* there."

"I'm sorry I said that stuff about Emmett." He clasped her hand, but it was dead weight. He removed his hand and lit a cigarette. "You've been reading too many of them Vietnam books," he said.

"I'm put out with Emmett," she said. "My mom says he has to stand on his own two feet, and I think maybe she's right. I think I see now why she left." She opened the door and fanned it a couple of times to let the smoke out. Some kids in a Chevy next to them were drinking beer. She said, "I was wondering if something could have happened to Emmett in the war, like a wound or something, that means he can't have girlfriends."

"You mean could he have had his balls shot off?"

"That's one way to put it."

Lonnie drew on his cigarette and looked thoughtful, as though he were some expert she had consulted for a professional opinion. "I doubt if that happened," he said. "But you know what Kevin said? He said his daddy said Agent Orange can affect you that way. It can settle there and practically turn you into a woman."

"Are you joking?"

"No. That's what Kevin said."

"I thought you didn't believe in Agent Orange."

"I'm just telling you what Kevin said."

"Grandma said the mumps fell on Emmett when he was eleven years old."

"What?"

Sam explained, but without amusement. It didn't seem at all funny. She took Lonnie's high school ring out of the zippered pocket in her purse and handed it to him.

"Here," she said.

"What?"

"You should have it back."

"What does this mean?"

"I don't know. It means I'm confused. And I don't want to go to that wedding."

"What have you got against weddings?"

"I've got too much on my mind," she said. "Would you drive up to the window? I want a cheeseburger. I didn't eat much supper."

"Get a double cheeseburger. You're too skinny."

As Sam ate her cheeseburger, Lonnie twiddled the ring in his fingers. "I can't believe you're serious," he said. "If you're wondering why I'm not throwing a fit, it's because I don't really believe you. You're just acting crazy."

Sam swallowed a hunk of cheeseburger. It was delicious, and it felt inappropriate to be enjoying her food so much right now. She didn't know what to say.

"Emmett's making you crazy," Lonnie said.

"No, he's not. Here's what it is. O.K.? It's Dawn. Dawn's pregnant." That wasn't even half of it, but she couldn't begin to explain. It would take hours.

Lonnie smiled. "Hey! I knew she'd marry Ken somehow. She's crazy about him."

"I think it's cruddy," Sam said. "She'll be like my mother, stuck in this town, raising a kid. That's not what I want to do with my life."

"You're weird."

"You don't know how weird I am. I try to tell you, and you don't believe me. You think I can be like everybody else, everybody in this shitty town."

"Your whole family's weird."

"That's what I'm trying to tell you."

Lonnie started the van and let the engine run a little. The radio came on, but he turned it off and sat there tugging on his cigarette, like Irene's little baby nursing. He said quietly, "Mama and Daddy will both be disappointed. They had accepted you into the family."

"I doubt that."

"Mama was wanting to take you to the mall. She said she'd help you pick out a dress to wear to John's wedding."

"I don't want a dress." Sam suddenly saw herself in black leather pants. And a lot of metal.

Lonnie said, "The trouble with you is you read all those war books and you watch all that television."

"What's wrong with that?"

"All that stuff on TV you and Emmett watch—it's just fantasy. It's not real. It doesn't have anything to do with here. It's all exaggerated. It's not how it is here."

"I don't care how it is here. I don't want to stay here."

Lonnie stared straight ahead. It was growing dark and the kids in the Chevy pulled out of the parking lot, screeching rubber. Sam felt as though something had loosened, like a knot that she had untangled. And she was drifting away, like an astronaut on a space walk. Astronauts had jet packs. Now she had a VW.

Lonnie stroked her leg and twisted her kneecap. "Sam—if you'd just explain what I did wrong. Did I say something to hurt you? Did I take you for granted—or what?"

"No."

"What is it, then?"

"It hasn't got anything to do with you." She couldn't tell him about the letters. She could show him the letters, but he wouldn't understand.

Lonnie said, "You know what I'm going to do with this ring? I'm going to throw it in the lake. That's what I mean to you—a little rock in the ocean."

"It's up to you," she said. "It's your ring, and you paid good money for it."

Sam shoved her waste paper in the trash barrel outside and got back in the van.

Lonnie asked, "Do you want me to take you home or are you still training for the Olympics?"

"You can take me home if you don't hate me. I don't hate you."

"I don't think you know who you care about." He pulled on his cigarette grimly. "You don't know your ass from your elbow, if you want my opinion."

"I'm sorry." She touched his leg gently, but he wouldn't look at her.

"Well, you can forget about them panties," he said. "You're not getting them back."

Lonnie dropped Sam off at the house, without kissing her goodbye. He gunned his motor down the street. Sam slammed the kitchen door. It burned her up about those panties.

Emmett was smoking and watching TV, with Moon Pie curled in his lap.

When Sam told Emmett what happened, he said, "That was awful mean to give him back his ring. Lonnie hurts easy."

"He doesn't know how mean I can be. I'm so mean, no telling what I'm liable to do next."

"I thought you were happy about your car."

"I am, and I just might take off in it for parts unknown." Sam turned the TV sound down. "He said I watched too much TV."

"You missed that *M*A*S*H* where Hot Lips kicks that door down."

"I'm liable to kick a door down." It was only since her mother moved to Lexington that Sam had grown so mean. Emmett was a bad influence.

"Don't kick the basement door," Emmett said. "It's half off its hinges as it is."

"I might kick somebody's butt," Sam said. "And I might start with yours. So don't mess with me."

Emmett scratched under his armpit. "Fleas! This house is occupied by fleas. I've got enough fleas here to start a circus."

"Did they have fleas in Vietnam?"

"The fleas over there were the size of puppy-dogs."

"Oh, I don't believe that. Did you read those letters?"

"Yeah."

"What did you think?"

"They didn't say much, did they?"

"No. Nobody will tell what it was really like. I want to know what it was really like. What was in that jungle?"

"Bugs. Bushes."

"What else?"

"It was too miserable to tell. It's something you just want to forget."

"Seems to me like you don't want to forget it at all." She scooted Emmett's feet over and sat down beside him on the couch, overcome by a sudden realization. She said, "You know what you're doing? You're just digging yourself a foxhole to hide in. Like the enemy was all around us. But it's not. There's a whole wide world out there. There's plenty of things to do and places to go. Don't you know that?"

"You could go to Lexington," Emmett said.

"If I did, could you get by?"

Emmett mumbled. He glanced at the TV and scratched Moon Pie's neck. Moon Pie rolled over on his back and stuck all four feet straight up.

"You could go to Lexington too," Sam said. "You could go to Flagstaff, Arizona, if you wanted to. Or Japan. What's keeping you here? Or you could stay here and do something besides watch TV."

Emmett grunted. "The TV goes everywhere," he said. "It saves a lot of fuel. I don't have to go to St. Louis to see the Cards. I can watch right here, and see better too."

"That's not the same as seeing something for yourself."

Emmett clutched his head. The pain again. "I saw for myself, Sam. I saw as much as I wanted to see." He held his head until the pain passed. Sam was tongue-tied. But she wasn't letting him off the hook yet. Something had to change. There was so much she had to find out before she took off the way her mother had. Her mother had gotten rid of her memories. She found someone else to love. First that hippie, and then Lorenzo Jones. Sam was worn out with worrying that Emmett was going to die. Maybe it was better not to care. Sam could drive her VW to Disney World and get a job there and make all new friends. One day soon, as soon as she could think straight and get some business taken care of, she'd do that. And somewhere, out there on the road, in some big city, she would find a Bruce Springsteen concert. And he would pull her out of the front row and dance with her in the dark.

27

Sam was driving her new car on the back roads toward her other grandparents' farm. They had invited her to spend the night, and she had told Emmett not to expect her back until the next day. Mamaw and Pap Hughes lived far out in the country and she had not seen them in almost two years. She felt uneasy, but she loved having a car. Tom had advised her to record the mileage and get gas every two hundred miles. He said he had worked with the gas gauge, but it was a subtle mechanism, harder to repair than something obvious, like a carburetor or a muffler.

All the men she knew fiddled with gadgets. They were always fixing something.

She passed the place her mother said looked like England. She was far out in the country, and soon she turned off on a smaller road. She passed old farms that looked unchanged since the time her father had lived out here. Irene had said Emmett was a country boy when he went to the war, but Dwayne was even more of a country boy. He rode a school bus to the county school fifteen miles from his house. He had met Irene at a basketball game. Irene and Emmett attended the city school, but they had to pay tuition because they lived outside the city limits. Now a consolidated county school was being built. Grandma Smith always said Irene had felt inferior in the city school because she was self-conscious about being from the country and so she did rebellious things to get attention, like read the chapter with the boring list of begats as her Bible passage in homeroom. But Sam was proud that her mother had been so wild.

Sam had wanted to care about her father, but she didn't know enough about him. She wasn't even sure how her mother had felt about him, if she had really loved him. If Irene had begun to see the war was wrong, would she have started to blame him after he died? Sam didn't know. She didn't know how she felt about him either. She thought of Tom, and how she had wanted Dwayne to be like him. But Tom was old, and in his letters Dwayne was just a kid. Dwayne and Irene, a teen-age romance. Sam had wanted to believe there was something magic between them that had created her and validated their love. But teen-age romances weren't very significant, she realized now. Sam and Lonnie. Dawn and Ken. Sam had been told so often what a miracle it was that she came along to compensate for the loss of Dwayne. She knew she had been making too much out of the brief time her parents were married before he went overseas. During that month, she had originated. She didn't know why the moment of origin mattered. Scientists were trying to locate the moment of origin of the universe. They wanted to know exactly when it happened, and how, and whether it happened with a big bang or some other way. Maybe the universe originated quietly, without fireworks, the way human life started, with two people who were simply having a good time in bed, or in the back seat of a car. Making a baby had nothing to do with love, or anything mystical, or what they said in church. It was just fucking.

The road meandered past an overgrown graveyard. Some new house trailers perched on blocks in bare fields. She passed through an abandoned settlement, with an old feed mill and a boarded-up store with a rusted Orange Crush sign. The Methodist church was whitewashed and had a newly graveled parking lot and a marquee on wheels that said KEEP THE CHRIST IN CHRISTMAS.

Mamaw and Pap lived up a narrow lane, which turned off a graveled road, with a new green sign, "Bob James Rd." She remembered that Bob James was one of the neighbors, a prosperous farmer with eleven children and several hundred acres. She wondered if having a road named after him meant he had died.

As Sam drove up, a speckled chicken skidded across the driveway in front of the car. She parked behind a green Cutlass. On the turnaround were a blue pickup, a battered black pickup, and a Pontiac. A brown hound in a pen roared.

They were expecting her, and Mamaw had dinner ready. Mamaw's daughter, Donna, was there with a baby in a blue romper suit. Somehow Sam never could think of Donna as her aunt. Mamaw's hair was pinned on top of her head, and she had on a dress with a design similar to the pattern of the chicken. She smelled like sweat and furniture polish.

"Are those chickens Barred Rocks?" Sam asked.

"No. They're Domineckers," said Mamaw, leading Sam through the back porch. The porch sagged, and it was cluttered with buckets and seeds and canning jars.

Pap lifted Sam up by her waist, the way he did when she was little. "I just wanted to see if I could still do it," he said, laughing. "My old bones is give out. I screek so."

"He's been down in his back," Mamaw said disapprovingly.

"But Sam's a beanpole," Donna said, regarding Sam with a curious air of disdain. "I could lift her with one finger."

They were filled with questions about Irene's new baby—her teeth, her hair, her weight—and they supplied comparisons to Donna's little boy. Donna wanted to know why Sam didn't go with her mother to Lexington.

"You mean you're still living with your crazy uncle?" she said.

"Leave the child alone," said Mamaw. "If she went up there, look how she might turn out. I think it's fine when children want to stay where they was brought up. Bill Holsum's boy over yonder has to pay three hundred dollars just to fly home every Christmas. It's a shame. Bill never gets to see his grandchildren."

"Fred Turner's boy's in the Air Force and he's stationed in Rome, Italy," said Pap. "Talk about a fur piece from home."

"I saw on *That's Incredible* this miracle in Italy?" said Donna. "This nun had saved a saint's blood? The saint had been beheaded. And in a ceremony every year the dried blood turns to liquid. The scientists have checked it out and there's no way dried blood can liquefy, so it's a miracle. The one year it wouldn't liquefy was the year of all those earthquakes—1980."

"Law, I'd hate to live over there—with all those miracles they have," said Mamaw.

"They're Catholics," said Donna.

Mamaw set a platter of fried rabbit on the table. "This is swamp rabbit," she said.

"I shot it down in Cole's Bottom," said Pap. "It was the biggest one I ever saw. I had to pack it a mile."

Sam loaded her plate with two legs, mashed potatoes, brown field peas, green jello salad, and slaw. Donna mashed up peas for her baby, who had a scrawny face and hair like duck down.

"I saw you with a girl in town one day last month," said Donna. "I was way across the square, but I could tell how tight that girl's shorts were. I could see her heinie clear across the square. Does she always dress like that?"

"Not in the winter," said Sam indignantly. "She *happens* to be my best friend."

"Let the child eat, Donna," said Mamaw. "She always *was* touchous."

They talked about blue mold on their tobacco crop. Her other grandparents had a nicer house, Sam thought. The Hughes house had old linoleum and no dishwasher.

Mamaw drank some iced tea and said, "I could kick somebody. Back in December we could have signed up for five dollars a bushel for wheat, but Joe here had to wait and see what it would bring at harvest. He thought it might go higher, but instead wheat was so good this year the price went down, and we got three dollars and ten cents a bushel. So we liked eighty cents making three thousand dollars on the wheat, when we could have made five thousand."

"She's went on and went on," complained Pap. "How was I to know? You got to take a risk sometime."

"He could have signed up for a guaranteed five dollars a bushel back in December," Mamaw said.

"But who would have thought wheat would be so good this year?" Donna said brightly. "I'd have done the same thing."

As they ate, Sam was aware of the studio portrait of her father that was standing on the old oak dish cabinet. She remembered always seeing the picture there. He had longer, darker hair than he had in the picture she had at home, and no Army hat. He had on a blue suit. His face was tinted pink, like something an undertaker would do to a dead body. His hair had a slight curl at the middle of his forehead. She squinted her eyes and tried to see him at the table with them. He would be a grown man, like Tom. He wouldn't be like Tom, though, living in a garage apartment. He'd be discussing blue mold and whether to take risks on wheat prices. Irene wouldn't have gone to Lexington. Sam would be jiggling a baby on her knee, like Donna.

Donna and Mamaw were talking about Donna's sister-in-law, who had just moved into a new brick house with her husband and two children. Donna was raving about the house and all its appliances. "And that baby has everything you can name. Jean didn't take any hand-me-downs. And they've got a video-cassette recorder and a bedroom suit that cost a thousand dollars. She doesn't think a thing about eating out."

Sam felt sick. She ate two slices of cake. It was white, with boiled icing, like something from Irene's white dinner, years ago.

After they ate, Mamaw showed Sam the pictures she had come to see. There were only a few besides the school pictures. She studied the small portraits, with "Burns High School" and the year printed below each one. He changed from a skinny, freckled little boy into a lanky, earnest teen-ager. Nowadays the school pictures were in color, and the kids posed in casual settings, by a swimming pool or under a tree, but these old-fashioned pictures were dark, cold, staring portraits. He was smiling in only two of them.

"This one's my favorite," Mamaw said, pointing to a picture in which his cowlick showed. "He was about sixteen there. He was the best boy! That was the year he made me that end table in shop."

"That was the year I was born," Donna said. "I don't have the slightest memory of him, my own brother. Ain't that a shame?"

Sam helped with the dishes. Pap was taking a short nap before he went back to work fixing some fences, and Donna was in her room with the baby. Her husband worked at Union Carbide, and they lived with Mamaw and Pap.

Sam set warm, dry glasses in the dish cabinet. The furniture-polish smell was in the cabinet. On top, her father stared down at her. She had looked at his likeness so often lately he was beginning to seem real, someone who might have some strong opinions about her.

Mamaw's hands didn't stop working at the dishes in the soapy water as she answered Sam's questions about Dwayne. She said, "You take after Irene's side of the family, Sam. You've got Dwayne's eyes, but you've got Irene's ways. And her cheekbones. I used to get so tickled at her. She'd do anything. She come out here once with Dwayne before they married, and she had a kite with her, and if she didn't go out in the pasture in her high heels and fly that kite I'm not here!" Mamaw laughed and dripped soapsuds down her elbows. "Dwayne was so taken with her. He thought she hung the moon."

"What did she think of him?"

"She was good to him." Mamaw swabbed a greasy plate with the dishrag. "Well, of course, he was my boy, but he was the thoughtfulest son you could ever have. That's a mother's privilege to think that, Sam. And he would have made a good farmer. Irene wanted him to go to New Orleans and work on a ship. Irene always wanted something big, anything to be different. But he wouldn't have done that. He would have come right back here. He was like that. He could talk about what-all he was going to do, but when it come down to it he was a mama's boy. He looked out for his mama and daddy. He wouldn't have gone off like Bill Holsum's boy did."

"He was a good boy," said Pap, appearing in the kitchen. "He never took a drink, didn't smoke."

"Did you get your nap out?" Mamaw asked him. "You wasn't laying down long."

"Y'all was beating your gums, and I couldn't sleep."

"Joe, tell Sam about Dwayne. She's here wanting to know more about her daddy. There's not a day I don't think of something loving he did. Like that flower box he made for Irene that time."

"He sure did love Irene," said Pap. "And I really do believe she loved him. Oh, they was young, and when you're that young you don't really know what you feel, but I saw how she was after the news come. It broke her heart."

"Irene was living at home with her folks then, and you was on the way, Sam. She was as big as a barn."

"We didn't see a whole lot of her," Pap said. "But after the news came they brought her over here, and everybody just set around and waited."

"It was so hard without the body," said Mamaw. "When somebody dies, you're supposed to prepare the body and watch over it. It's something that brings you all together, but he wasn't here. It was three days before we got him, and while we were waiting everybody was so lost. We just run around like a chicken with its head cut off. And the neighbors brought food. Oh, they just kept a-bringing good things to eat. It went on so long the people that brought food had to go home and cook some more for us. Lutie Cunningham brought a ham and a gallon of potato salad and three pies. I never will forget that. In a way, it was a relief when we finally got him in the ground." She laughed, a sort of whimper.

"It was a closed casket," Pap said. "The Army told us not to look."

Maybe it wasn't really him, Sam thought. Maybe he was still missing in action.

"That killed me," Mamaw said. "But they wrote and told what a help he was to his country. I take comfort in that."

"What good did he do for the country?" Sam asked. "Everybody knows it was a stupid war, but fifty-eight thousand guys died. Emmett says they all died for nothing."

"Well, Emmett can talk. He didn't die," Mamaw said indignantly. "Dwayne was fighting for a cause, and back then people didn't go around protesting. He believed in his country, and he was ready to go over there and fight."

"If you could go back to that time, would you let him go or would you send him to Canada?" Sam asked.

"Oh, Sam," Mamaw said, staring down at the linoleum. "People don't have choices like that."

"Did any stuff come with the body?" Sam asked. "I mean like his personal stuff. His clothes and things."

Mamaw nodded. "There wasn't much. I gave away the

clothes, and I made Irene take the flag, but she wouldn't take anything else. I didn't understand that."

"Mom said there might be a notebook."

"There was a little diary. It's around here somewhere."

"Do you care if I have it?"

"I can't imagine what you want with it. There's not much in it. He told a lot more in his letters. He wrote the lovingest letters. I wouldn't take anything for them. But I'll look for that notebook when I get done here."

Sam went with Pap out to the barn to look for wire.

"What's wrong with that cat's ears?" she asked, pointing to a sore-eyed cat with scabby ears.

"I trimmed 'em. He had ear canker. If you trim it off, it'll heal, so I clipped about a quarter inch off of each one."

"I never heard of that."

"You do the same thing to rabbits. Why, I've seen cats with their ears trimmed down to a nub." He laughed, a hoarse chuckle. "Sam, you don't know nothing!" He took his work gloves, a hammer, and some nails from a tool shed next to the barn.

"Our cat never had ear canker," said Sam. "He's got fleas, though. They're about to drive Emmett crazy."

"That hound's got mange. I've got to mix up some sulfur and saltpeter and burnt crankcase oil and paint him when I get a chance," Pap said.

"Won't that kill him?"

"I doubt it. Sam, can you reach me them wire pliers on that shelf behind that sack of fertilizer?"

Sam was exploring in an old stall where she remembered her grandfather once raising a calf. This would have been where her father had raised calves when he was a boy. There were no cows here now. She handed Pap the wire pliers.

"We got too much fertilizer this year," he said, shaking his head.

Sam walked down a dusty lane with her grandfather. She was seeing the place her dad knew. She was seeing where her mother lived once for a few weeks, where Sam started growing in her belly. Her roots were here, and she had been here often enough for the place to be familiar, but not enough to really know it. She felt she was seeing it for the first time.

"I remember when Dwayne first brought Irene out here," Pap said. "She was just a skinny little squirt like you. Nothing embarrassed her. She went around asking me the name of everything. She got a kick out of Emma's hen-and-chickens cactuses, said they was like pincushions. Imagine that. She picked the biggest bunch of flowers. She went back in the fields along the fence rows and picked daisies and Queen Anne's lace and black-eyed Susans and I don't know what-all. I never would have thought of picking weeds like that. She was raised on a farm, so I was surprised she'd thought of picking them."

"She always liked flowers," Sam said. They were talking about Irene as though she were the one who had died, and when they talked about Dwayne they weren't specific. You should always be specific, Sam thought.

"Country kids are just like the city kids now," Pap said. "They've got more. And they have cars, so they can go running around. Used to, Saturday was when you went to town, but now they take off and go any day of the week."

They talked about Sam's new car for a while, and then Pap said, "Everybody always thought it was something that Dwayne left us such a gift. When you were born, I remember how proud everybody was." He hammered a nail into a fence post. "Everybody expected a boy, of course, but we loved you just the same."

"Everybody wished I was a boy," Sam said, crushing a clover head in her hand. "Did you know my daddy picked the name?" she asked. "He thought it was in the Bible."

"No. I didn't know that. Why, you learn something new every day. Well, I'll say!" He stroked his chin thoughtfully.

While her grandfather worked on the fence, Sam walked down by the creek. She had remembered some wild goose-plum trees in the creek. She found them, but she didn't see any fruit. The trees had honeysuckle vines on them. On a vine she saw a large green stinkbug with an orange spot and a figure eight on its back. Water striders pranced on the shallow pools of clear water in the creek bed. She used to call them Jesus bugs because of the way they walked on water. She looked around the farm, trying to see it in a new way, trying to see what her father had known, the world he knew before he went to Vietnam. These were his memories, what he took with him over there. She thought she could comprehend it. Everything he knew was small and predictable: Jesus bugs, blue mold, hound dogs, fence posts. He didn't know about the new consolidated county high school, rock video, *M*A*S*H*. He didn't know her.

At the house, the dog, outside his pen now, bowed lazily, then lay down in a patch of dirt he had dug in the shade near the flowerbed. His back was covered with scabs. Sam recognized many of the flowers—tall blue stalks, pink droopy flowers, big round yellow faces—but she had no names for them. The rosebushes were insect-eaten. The lilies had dried up. The August sun was beating down. Sam recognized a plant with seed pods forming from some of the flowers. She remembered that when they turned brown those seed pods would explode, scattering their seeds. She remembered the plant's name—touch-me-not.

"I found that diary," Mamaw called to Sam from the porch. "You can have it, but I don't reckon it'll tell you anything. He just set down troop movements and weapons and things like that. It's not loving, like the letters he wrote back. Those was personal. Irene didn't even want this little book, but you can have it if you want it."

Sam reached for the brown spiral notebook. Mamaw was standing on the porch, and Sam was below her on the steps. Sam remembered reaching just this way at graduation when the principal handed her the rolled diploma. But inside the ribbon was a blank piece of paper. The real diplomas were mailed later, because they had come too late from the printer.

Mamaw said, "I remembered that I couldn't even read all of it because I couldn't figure out his handwriting, so I don't expect it'll tell you anything, but at least you'll have something of his." She shooed a cat out the door. "Do you want us to take you out to the graveyard later?" Mamaw said.

"No, not today," Sam said, her eyes on the cat. "I've got to go somewhere."

"Whereabouts?"

"Paducah. I've got to go to Paducah."

28

The mall was not crowded that afternoon. Shoppers called to each other across the wide corridors. A woman cried, "Wanda, you heifer! Wait for me!"

A man tried to pick Sam up. She was sitting on a bench beside some plants at the center of the two wings of the mall, reading her father's diary. She had a Coke and some chocolate-chip cookies. The man was wearing a Confederate-flag T-shirt that said I'M A REBEL AND DAMN PROUD OF IT. Sam gave him such a mean look that he backed off.

The diary was hard to read. Mamaw was right about his handwriting, but Sam had always been very good at figuring out handwriting. It was a talent of hers. Dwayne had written in pencil, and the words staggered off the lined paper. Sam guessed he had written in the dark. His writing was small and squinched. It was true that there was a lot of perplexing gibberish about troop movements and lists of weapons—stuff that wouldn't have interested his parents, who would have wanted to see notes on the weather or the crops. But after several pages of brief notations like "May 3. Two klicks west, dug in late, shells coming in" and "Sappers spotted, M-79 grenade launchers, 40 rounds spent," all of which made little sense, the diary got more interesting:

> *July 3.* Spent all day cutting trees up a hill. Got there and saw another hill and more trees. My hands are cracked and bleeding. Shelling at dark.
>
> *July 4.* Letter from Irene. Baby kicking strong.
>
> *July 5.* Smoked cigarettes in the dark, hiding them in

helmets. Helmets used for everything but to shit in. Depressed but got out of it remembering our purpose here.

July 6. Marched all day. I was on point again. Getting used to it, the way you hold your rifle just so, so that you're always on the ready. Thinking about rabbit hunting. Miss those fall days.

July 7. C-rats, ham and lima beans coming out of ears and butt. We've all got direah. Cut trees, waded swamp. We need rain but my feet stay wet. Hot Shot in a rage. He works us like a team of dogs, but we're one fine team. Dug in late, overslept watch. Slept like a baby.

July 8. Useless day, holed up, waiting. Hot Shot says it won't be long. Still got the scours.

July 9. Ambushed. It was over in two seconds but seemed like two hours. My knees still shaking. Bobby G. got hit in the leg but not bad. Doc patched him up. We got two V.C. I think one of 'em's mine, but Jim C. claimed it too. We had a big day, big deal over whose it was. No letters. Irene seems too far away to be real. But it's all for her and the baby, or else why are we here? Joe's got 5 notches on his machetty. He's a short-timer. I'm sure I'll get one soon. It's the law of averages. Joe's asking for trouble though. He'll volunteer to walk point. He ain't afraid of Nothing. And Bob goes along so quiet like he knows more than the rest of us. He wouldn't say shit if he had a mouth full of it. I'm tired tonight. A good kind of tired. We got two. Two weeks out and finally we got two. We had cigarettes and felt wild.

July 13. Hot Shot says we're getting closer. We walked all day through swamp grass. Eddie was in front of me, making a trail in the grass, like a speed boat. He's solid black but he's okay. I never knew a nigger that quiet. He's not a show-off.

July 14. Chopper dropped off mail and socks. Letter from Irene. The pencil makes swishing noises and sounds so loud I'm afraid it'll draw Cong like flies. It's so dark you can't see anything but burning cigarettes. Chopper brought Luckies. You can hide a cigarette almost inside your mouth. Joe does it, makes me think of a flame eater at the carnival. If I saw a gook and didn't have any ammo, I'd take a cig. and twist it in his eyes and burn 'em out. Hot Shot says we're getting closer. It can't be long now. There's supposed to be a whole hidden base up north of here, but it seems like we're going in a circle. The choppers find them and tell us where to go so we can root them out. It seems like we might turn around and find he's following *us*. It's like what John was telling me yesterday. I said it was like rabbit hunting and he says yes but there's a difference. An animal behaves by instink. A rabbit runs in a jagged line to fool you. A deer runs fast to get away. They're made that way—by God—to protect themselves, to get away from their enemies. But they don't come hunting *you*. What if a rabbit came after you? Sneaking after you and popping out behind a bush with a big M-60? I can't think of any animal but a panther that would do that (but not with a M-60). Daddy grew up on Panther Creek and he always told tales of hearing that panther cry. It was like a woman crying, they said. Irene crying. I try to play like she's here in this hole with me but it won't work. When I get her in my mind good she floats away and I hear something, like a leaf swishing, or somebody breathing, or the guys on watch trading places, and I'm right back here. And I wouldn't want her to be here and see this. I can't forget what I'm here for.

July 17. Two days ago, we come upon a dead gook rotting under some leaves, sunk into a little swamp-like place. They probably hadn't found it because it was covered up with big banana leaves. Interesting to see the body parts broken down, like we studied in biology. It had a special stink. Dead gooks have a special stink, we know by now. Bobby G. poked a stick around in it and some teeth fell out. Darrel's carrying one for good luck. He says now he'll have special gook stink on him and that will protect him. Uncle B. used to go deer hunting with deer piss on him.

July 18. Hot Shot's so mad he could pop. Darrel had his gear all scattered around and Hot Shot cussed him out, said he had to be ready to up and move at drop of a hat. What if Charlie dropped in sudden? It would be like Sundays when company came and Mama went around grabbing all of Pap's clothes and all the toys strowed all over the living room. You got to be ready, said Hot Shot. Organization. We're relaxing too much. Nothing to do. No gooks. Somebody let out a big fart like a firecracker and you could hear it all the way to Hanoi. Just sending Charlie a warning, Darrel said. It made me think of cherry bombing people's mailboxes on Halloween. Great guys here. Hot Shot works us hard, like a team of mules, or over here they have water buffalos. You can't whip buffalos around the way you can a team of mules, or a team of G.I.s. We're one fine team. If Hot Shot didn't get so mad we wouldn't be half as good as we are. He really knows how to run us. Just like Coach Jones in basketball. We're talking him into re-enlisting. We say the free world needs him.

Aug. 4. Darrel got it. It was over with before we knew what was happening. Goddam, it was awful. I'll never forget it. Darrel went off in the bushes to take a shit and they got him. Pop-pop. We opened fire all around but didn't get anything. We just stood there firing and firing and Darrel had blood shooting out of his back and his mouth. The chopper lifted him out but it was too late. He lost too much blood. The medic was covered in his blood. If we run across some gooks, they're going to be gook puddin when I get through with them! Darrel was a good guy. This shouldn't have happened to him, of all people. That tooth wasn't any protection, that's for damn sure. Talk about scary.

Aug. 6. Chopper brought hot A's, turkey and dressing and cranberries. It wasn't Mama's but it tasted like manna from heaven and it did come out of the sky. We had cigarettes and went wild.

Aug. 8. Hot Shot's ready to climb trees he's so mad. He's burned up about Darrel and says we can't be that dumb again. If Hot Shot didn't get mad, he couldn't keep us going. I've dumped most of my pack, but I'm sore all over and I've got bites and scabs and direah and another guy has malaria but they won't take him out. Can't stop now though.

Aug. 10. Unreal thought. A baby. My own flesh and blood. Too tired to write.

Aug. 12. Feet look like boiled chicken's feet. We're almost there.

Aug. 14. Big surprise. Face to face with a V.C. and I won. Easier than I thought. But there wasn't time to think. It was so simple. At last.

Aug. 16. It's getting bad. My feet's killing me. They look like they're rotting off. It's dark and this notebook is balanced on my knee, makes me think of Mama riding little Donna on her knee. Ride a little horsey. Ride downtown. Ride a little horsey. Oops! Fall down. No cigarettes. The last time the bird brought Luckies we said we're lucky. Everybody laughed. Lucky to be alive. When I get back to the World, this will be like a dream, but right now the World is a dream. It's like trying to put those round pegs in the square holes in that test we did in school. If we get out of this alive, it'll be a miracle. Long gone, ain't I lucky? Long gone, from Kentucky. Song Irene always liked.

Sam felt sick. Her stomach churned, and she felt like throwing up. She could see and smell the corpse under the banana leaves. She had never seen banana leaves, but she thought she knew what they were like. Bananas had a sickly-sweet smell when they were too ripe and the insects stirred around them. She could smell that. She ate a chocolate-chip cookie, thinking it would settle her stomach. She recalled the dead cat she dug up once in Grandma's garden, and she realized her own insensitive curiosity was just like her father's. She felt humiliated and disgusted. The diary made her wonder what she would do in his situation. Would she call them gooks? She thought of how Emmett loved on Moon Pie, and she could not believe Emmett could have done what Dwayne had done in the war, yet she knew he must have. Even if Emmett was sorry, he didn't do anything to make up for it, the way the guy her mother knew had, the guy who killed the whole family. She recalled Richard Pryor on TV saying he asked the murderer on Death Row at the Arizona penitentiary, "Why did you kill the whole family?" The murderer's answer: "They was home!"

Her father hadn't said how he felt about killing the V.C. He just reported it, as though it were something he had to do sooner or later, like taking a test in school.

Mamaw and Pap must not have even read the diary. If they had read it, they would have realized that he smoked and drank and murdered. Maybe they read it but didn't want to remember their son that way. So they forgot. Or they made up a more pleasant story. Or they pretended they couldn't read his handwriting. But why did Mamaw give the notebook to Sam? Had Irene read it? Maybe they just took it for granted that in war there was killing. That was it. They didn't question it. Mamaw would probably find the fact that he smoked more upsetting.

She left the mall and drove toward home. She wanted the road to go on and on, so she could clear her mind, so she could think about what the diary meant. Or maybe there was nothing to figure out. Maybe she should just forget about her father and dismiss the whole Hughes clan along with him. They were ignorant and country anyway. They lived in that old farmhouse with the decayed smell she always remembered it having—the smell of dirty farm clothes, soiled with cow manure. In their bathroom earlier, she had almost slipped on the sodden rug that lay rotting around the sweating commode. In the living room, the television was missing a leg, and a complicated old antenna—all claws and a fan of rods—sat in a corner, looking like a monster from outer space. The contraption was an effort to pick up cable so that Pap could catch the Wildcats' basketball games. Mamaw picked peas in a rusty bucket with a rag plug stopping up a hole. Sam couldn't get the sensations out of her head: the mangy dog, the ugly baby, the touch-me-nots, the blooming weeds, the rusty bucket, her dumb aunt Donna. The cat with its ears clipped made her want to cry. And the diary disgusted her, with the rotting corpse, her father's shriveled feet, his dead buddy, those sickly-sweet banana leaves. She had a morbid imagination, but it had always been like a horror movie, not something real. Now everything seemed suddenly so real it enveloped her, like something rotten she had fallen into, like a skunk smell, but she felt she had to live with it for a long time before she could take a bath. In the jungle, they were nasty and couldn't take a bath.

She didn't know how she could face Emmett now.

29

Moon Pie, lounging under Mrs. Biggs's forsythia bush, yawned at Sam when she slammed the car door. Emmett was usually home at this time of day, fixing supper, but the door was locked. He wasn't expecting her back from Mamaw's until tomorrow. Luckily, she had a key with her. When she opened the door, a harsh, overpowering chemical smell rushed at her, instead of the usual stale smell of cigarettes. What in the hell? Emmett couldn't have put his head in a gas oven, she thought. Their stove was electric. Her second thought was Agent Orange, although this didn't smell like oranges. She gulped a deep breath of air from outside and rushed in. When she called "Emmett!" her air rushed out. She gulped some more fresh air and raced around downstairs, calling for him. Then she found the source of the smell. In the center of the living room, between the TV and the couch, a spray can had been set on a kitchen chair. She snatched it up and read the label. It was a flea bomb, one of those spray cans that could be locked in a spray position. It was empty now. Emmett had set off a flea bomb and left the house, as though he had thrown a hand grenade inside and run away. It was just like him to do something secretive like that, without even mentioning it. It made her furious. He was so paranoid about those fleas.

She paced up and down the porch and tried to think. She had opened both doors to get cross-ventilation. She was so angry she could shit bricks. Then she had an idea. She went to the car and ripped a blank page out of her father's diary. She wrote Emmett a note and left it on the refrigerator, under a tomato magnet. The note said, "You think you can get away with everything because you're a V.N. vet, but you can't. On the table is a diary my daddy kept. Mamaw gave it to me. Is that what it was like over there? If it was, then you can just forget about me. Don't try to find me. You're on your own now. Goodbye. Sam."

Sam took a deep breath of fresh air and raced upstairs. The air in her room was tolerable. She opened the window, then searched the closet for her sleeping bag and backpack from Girl Scouts. She crammed some shorts and T-shirts into the pack, then grabbed some jeans and her cowboy boots. She got Emmett's space blanket and poncho from his footlocker. Downstairs, with a new breath from outside, she searched for food to take with her. They didn't have any ham and mother-fuckers, so she took pork and beans. G.I.s lived out of cans. They even had canned butter. She put a can of potted meat and some Doritos and granola bars in the pack, along with the Granny Cakes and the can of smoked oysters she had bought. She loaded a six-pack cooler with Pepsi and cheese and grape juice. She found some plastic utensils she had saved from the Burger Boy. Her job was supposed to start in two weeks. Where would she be in two weeks?

She imagined that the smell was Agent Orange. Her lungs were soaking up dioxin, and molecules of it were embedding themselves in the tissues, and someday it would come back to haunt her, like the foods that gave Emmett gas.

Probably dioxin wasn't in flea bombs. But for all anyone knew, they could have a chemical just as deadly. Those chemical companies didn't care.

On the way out of town, she had the appalling thought that Moon Pie might have sneaked back in the house. But she was almost sure he was still under that bush when she pulled out of the driveway.

If men went to war for women, and for unborn generations, then she was going to find out what they went through. Sam didn't think the women or the unborn babies had any say in it. If it were up to women, there wouldn't be any war. No, that was a naive thought. When women got power, they were just like men. She thought of Indira Gandhi and Margaret Thatcher. She wouldn't want to meet those women out in the swamp at night.

What would make people want to kill? If the U.S.A. sent her to a foreign country, with a rifle and a heavy backpack, could she root around in the jungle, sleep in the mud, and shoot at strangers? How did the Army get boys to do that? Why was there war?

Her dad had no sense of humor. At least Emmett had a sense of humor. Dwayne couldn't spell, and his handwriting was bad.

Emmett's fear of fleas was silly. Sam wasn't even afraid of spending the night at Cawood's Pond, sleeping out on the ground. Cawood's Pond was so dangerous even the Boy Scouts wouldn't camp out there, but it was the last place in western Kentucky where a person could really face the wild. That was what she wanted to do.

Along the secondary road leading to the pond, bulldozers had been at work, dredging the outer reaches of the swamp. Sam drove up the bumpy lane and left the car in the center of the clearing. Her shoes crunched on the gravel. Down the path to the boardwalk, she paused at a stump. Inside the hollow, a million tiny black ants were working on a bit of plastic, ripping it up into nonbiodegradable tidbits and marching off with it. Emmett imagined the fleas were like that, crawling all over him while he slept. She thought he must have been having a flashback when he tossed in the flea-bomb grenade and ran away. The fleas were the Vietnamese. How often had she heard the enemy soldiers compared to ants, or other creatures too numerous to count? She remembered someone saying that the G.I.s would fight for a position and gain it and then the next day there would be a thousand more of the enemy swarming around them.

The Vietnamese used anything the Americans threw away—bomb casings and cigarette butts and helicopter parts and Coke cans. It was like Emmett rigging up things in the house. It was Vietnamese behavior, she thought, making do with what he could scrounge. The Vietnamese could make a bomb out of a Coke can.

Emmett had helped kill those Vietnamese, the same way he killed the fleas, the same way people killed ants. It was easy, her father wrote. But the enemy always returned, in greater numbers. Pete had practically bragged about killing. Men were nostalgic about killing. It aroused something in them.

The fleas would come back. People in cities had roaches, super-bugs resistant to chemicals.

At Cawood's Pond, bugs rose up like steam from the swamp water.

Emmett set off the flea bomb just as casually as he would have launched a mortar into the sky, the way the soldiers did in the war, the way he pumped that firing button on the Atari.

She remembered when he used to shout in his sleep. He was after Charlie. There weren't any Vietcong to hunt down now, no hills to capture, no bases to defend, but he was still doing it. He was out to kill, in spite of himself, like a habit he couldn't break. It was sick. He was all the time reliving that war. Men wanted to kill. That's what men did, she thought. It was their basic profession.

Granddad killed Japanese soldiers in World War II. Her father had been killed because that was the way the game was played. Some lived and some died. There was no other conclusion to be drawn.

Women didn't kill. That was why her mother wouldn't honor the flag, or honor the dead. Honoring the dead meant honoring the cause. Irene was saying, Fuck you, U.S.A., he's dead and it meant nothing. He went to fight and he got killed and that was the end of him. Sam thought, To hell with all of them—Lonnie, her dad, her uncle, her grandfathers, Lorenzo Jones. Tom. Maybe not Tom.

She waited on the boardwalk, sitting there for a long time, quietly, until the birds flew by unselfconsciously. This was what Emmett did, as he watched and waited, like a spider hiding in a web. A big bird whooshed through the swamp like a reconnaissance chopper, and she caught a glimpse of brown. Then she heard a blue jay squawking. The blue jay was teasing a squirrel. She saw some sparrows. She wanted to know what the big deal was, waiting for birds. It was what hunters did.

She was a runaway. There was no runaway hotline out here. Emmett had run away too, to Lexington, so she felt justified. It wasn't as though she were running away to New York to be a prostitute in a dope ring. Her English teacher who thought Thoreau's retreat to Walden Pond was such a hot idea would probably approve. If it was in a book, there was something to it. But in Sam's opinion Thoreau was paranoid.

That rotting corpse her dad had found invaded her mind—those banana leaves, reeking sweetly. She knew that whenever she had tried to imagine Vietnam she had had her facts all wrong. She couldn't get hickory trees and maples and oaks and other familiar trees, like these cypresses at Cawood's Pond, out of her head. They probably didn't have these trees over there. Rice paddies weren't real to her. She thought of tanks knocking down the jungle and tigers sitting under bushes. Her notions came from the movies. Some vets blamed what they did on the horror of the jungle. What did the jungle do to them? Humping the boonies. Here I am, she thought. In country.

Cawood's Pond was famous for snakes, but it also had migrating birds—herons, and sometimes even egrets, Emmett claimed. She saw the egret so often in her mind she almost thought she had really seen it. It was white, like a stork. Maybe her father had seen egrets in Vietnam and thought they were storks. The stork bringing her. Emmett went over there soon after, as though he were looking for that stork, something that brought life. Emmett didn't look hard enough for that bird. He stayed at home and watched TV. He hid. He lived in his little fantasy world, she thought. But Sam meant to face facts. This was as close to the jungle as she could get, with only a VW.

A blue jay fussed overhead. A fish splashed. She leaned over the railing of the boardwalk and watched the Jesus bugs. The place was quiet, but gradually the vacancy of the air was filled with a complex fabric of sounds—insects and frogs, and occasional whirring wings and loud honks of large birds.

The insects were multiplying, as though they were screwing and reproducing right in the air around her. A gnat flew into her eye. She went back to the car and put on her jeans and boots. She hadn't brought any Bug-Off. With the space blanket and her backpack and the picnic cooler, she followed a path through the jungle. The cypress knees, little humps of the roots sticking up, studded the swamp, and some of them even jutted up on the path. She had to walk carefully. She was walking point. The cypress knees were like land mines. There would be an invisible thread stretched across the path to trigger the mine. She waded through elephant grass, and in the distance there was a rice paddy.

She dropped her things in a clearing and returned to the boardwalk for a while, sitting on a pillow she had thought to bring from the couch, a little square of foam rubber covered with dirty green velour. She watched for snakes. They would be out in the water—water moccasins, no doubt—and their triangular heads would leave a V mark in the water. A large turtle perched on a log. It was probably too late in the day for snakes, she thought. Snakes needed sun to heat up their blood. She remembered that from a *National Geographic* special.

Before dark, she hauled her stuff farther down the path and fixed up her camp. She had to search for a flat place that wasn't interrupted by cypress knees. She found a tall oak tree that had a flat clearing under it. This area had once been water, but now the water level was lower and the ground had dried out. Even the mosquitoes seemed less annoying here. The tree had a bank of moss and a curtain of ferns. She spread out the space blanket and waited for dark while she ate pork and beans and some cheese and crackers, with a Pepsi from the cooler. In the dark, the snipers couldn't find her. She would be invisible, and no one could find her. No one, she thought, except a creature with an acute sense of smell.

Here she was, humping the boonies.

The smells returned. The flea bomb, the banana leaves, the special gook stink.

If she were a soldier, she would be wading through that swamp, with snakes winding themselves around her legs.

There were patches of ooze, like quicksand, that swallowed up people in the swamp. But she was on solid ground under this tree. There couldn't be a sinkhole next to a tree.

She pictured Emmett standing silhouetted against the Vietnam sky, standing at the edge of a rice paddy, watching a bird fly away. In the background, working in the fields, were some peasants in bamboo hats. Emmett kept watching the bird fly into the distance, and the *beat-beat-beat* of a helicopter interrupted the scene, moving in slowly on it. The peasants did not look up, and Emmett kept staring, as though the bird had been transformed into the chopper and had returned to take him away. Then in one corner of the scene a bomb exploded, sending debris and flame sky-high, but the peasants kept working, bending over their rows of rice.

Did rice grow in rows? Was it bushy, like soybeans? No, it was like grass. It was like wheat growing in water.

She felt so stupid. She couldn't dig a foxhole even if she had to, because she didn't have the tools. And could she actually dig a foxhole? She didn't know. The way Emmett had worked on his ditch for so long had irked her so much that she hadn't taken it seriously. But it might be handy to know how to dig in. It occurred to her that in this swamp any hole would fill up with water.

In Vietnam, the soldiers wouldn't have had a safe boardwalk. They would have waded through the swamp, with leeches sucking on them and big poisonous jungle snakes brushing their legs, and the splash of water would have betrayed their positions. They had to creep. They had to go with the natural sound of the water and hold their breath if they saw a snake. A startled peep could mean the end. They couldn't afford to be cowards. She wondered if there were alligators in Nam. Vietnam had a monsoon climate, Emmett had said. Sam remembered monsoons from geography.

She ate a Granny Cake. Each bite was a loud smack, like a breaking leaf. The bullfrogs had started bellyaching, like Emmett with a gas attack. It was amazing how long you could sit out in the wild and still not see many animals. They know I'm here, she thought. Even the squirrels know I'm here. Squirrels are always on the other side of the tree. You go around the tree and they sneak around to the other side. That's why you need a squirrel dog to hunt squirrels, Granddad Smith had told her. A fice is best, he said.

And then something happened. It started with a chirping sound, and then some scrapes. She could see movement through some weeds on the side of the entrance to the boardwalk where the bank sloped down to the swamp. She saw a face, a face with beady eyes. It scared her. It was a V.C. Then she saw a sharp nose and streaks around the eyes. It was a raccoon. As she watched, the raccoon came into view, and then she saw a baby raccoon, and then another. They were large, almost grown, but still fuzzy. They climbed down the bank and stood in the water and drank. The mother nuzzled them. Behind her, two others wriggled down the bank.

For a long time, Sam watched as the babies chirped and the mother poked her nose at them, trying to round them up, to go back up the bank. She led two of them up and returned for the others, but then the first two followed her down again. It took her about ten minutes to get them rounded up. Twice, she stared straight at Sam. And when she had all the babies together, she led them away, through the underbrush.

After a while, there was a pattern of recognition in the night noises. There were voices, messages, in the insect sounds. "Who's next?" they said. Or "Watch out." She had read about a lizard in Vietnam that had a cry that sounded to the American soldiers like "Fuck you! Fuck you!" She recognized the owls. Like the V.C., they conducted their business at night. Sam crouched on the space blanket and thought about what people would think if they knew where she was. Lonnie would be totally disgusted with her. His mother would think Sam had lost her brains. Grandma would have a heart attack just at the idea of the snakes. Sam enjoyed thinking of their reactions. Maybe her mother would think the idea wasn't so ridiculous. Her mother had done braver things. A frog belly-ooped. Sam remembered that Emmett used to go frog-gigging with Granddad at his pond. She heard rustling weeds and chirps and water splashing.

There weren't any people out here, so there was really nothing to be afraid of.

First watch. She wouldn't sleep. She'd stay on watch. The G.I.s stayed awake in the frightening night, until they fell asleep like cats, ready to bolt awake. It was hot inside the sleeping bag, but outside the bag the mosquitoes plucked at her skin, whining their little song. When she had come to the pond before, with Lonnie and Emmett, it had seemed safe. Did the soldiers feel safer with each other? Of course, she could retreat to the VW. VWs were watertight, so they would be bugtight too.

It hit her suddenly that this nature preserve in a protected corner of Kentucky wasn't like Vietnam at all. The night sky in Vietnam was a light show, Emmett had said once. Rockets, parachute flares, tracer bullets, illumination rounds, signal flares, searchlights, pencil flares. She tried to remember the descriptions she had read. It was like fireworks. And the soundtrack was different from bugs and frogs: the *whoosh-beat* of choppers, the scream of jets, the thunder-boom of artillery rounds, the mortar rounds, random bullets and bombs and explosions. The rock-and-roll sounds of war.

It was growing darker. She wouldn't find that bird in the dark. She recalled the poem from school about the man who had to wear a dead albatross around his neck. The man in the poem was sorry he had shot the albatross, and he went around telling everybody at a wedding about it, like a pregnant woman thrusting her condition on everyone. Dawn would be like that. Sam's mother had been like that earlier this year. "You'd think she was the only person on earth who had ever had a baby," Grandma had said. But women would never really behave like that guy with the bird around his neck. Women were practical. They would bury a dead bird when it started to stink. They wouldn't collect teeth and ears for souvenirs. They wouldn't cut notches on their machetes. Sam kept thinking about the albatross, trying to remember how the poem went. Then chills rushed over her. Soldiers murdered babies. But women did too. They ripped their own unborn babies out of themselves and flushed them away, squirming and bloody. The chills wouldn't stop.

In the deepening dark, she struggled against Dracula images invading her mind. The soundtrack in the back of her mind, she realized, was from *Apocalypse Now*—the Doors moaning ominously, "This is the end . . . the children are insane."

It must have been years since she had gone so long without listening to a radio.

Dawn washed over the swamp, along with a misty fog. It was cool. The clatter of birds was like a three-alarm fire. Everything seemed alarmed by the new day. Sam lay very still on the space blanket and looked around her slowly. Her watch said five-fifteen. The soldiers would have been up before first light, creeping around, pulling up camp. She had survived.

She had many large bites on her body. One on her leg was bright red and inflamed, like a rash. She peed on a honeysuckle vine, and some splashed on poison ivy. She splattered a nondescript, hard-shelled bug crawling along.

As quietly as she could, she got some grape juice out of the cooler. She drank the juice and ate a granola bar. If she were a soldier, she'd drink hot chocolate or coffee from her canteen cup.

She cleaned up her camp. She was learning to be quiet. She could fold her sleeping bag silently. She closed the lid of the picnic cooler in slow motion. She had survived. But she didn't know what to do. She wished that bird would come. If the bird came, then she would leave.

The quality of dawn was different from the quality of dusk. Dusk lingered, and went through stages of dimness, but dawn was swift and pervasive. There must be some scientific principle behind that, she thought.

Before long, the sun blasted through the swamp. Sam actually saw some glowing rays hitting the path like those rays in religious paintings, like the ones in Aunt Bessie's *Upper Rooms*. Sam didn't think there was any upper room. Life was here and now. Her father was dead, and no one cared. That outlaw was dissolved in the swamp.

At seven-thirty, she heard noises. Low scratchings of gravel—maybe a dog, or some deer. She sat behind the tree, out of sight of the clearing, and waited as the noises grew louder. She wondered if it was Emmett, looking for her. Or was it a hunter? If a hunter saw her move, she might get shot. Hunters would shoot anything that moved. They were always shooting each other, mistaking each other for turkeys or deer.

There were peculiar new rustlings, something creeping, a sort of shuffle. It couldn't be a rapist, she thought. Rapists didn't go out into the wilderness, where there weren't likely to be any women to rape. They were calculating. Sam was defenseless. She looked around for rocks and sticks. She felt inside her backpack for a weapon. She had the can of smoked baby oysters with a roll-key opener. Hurriedly, she worked to create a weapon with the sharp edge of the can. The smell of smoked oysters sickened her. Too late, she realized the smell would give away her position. She tried to remember what she had been told about self-defense. Jab his eyes out with a key and knee him in the balls. She could take the open can, with its dangerous edge, and smash oysters all over his face and cut his nose.

The birds grew quieter, and the footsteps were on the boardwalk. She should have made her camp farther in the woods.

What an idiotic thing to happen, she thought—to face the terror of the jungle and then meet a rapist. It would be like that scene in *Apocalypse Now* where the soldiers met a tiger, the last thing they expected in the guerrilla-infested jungle.

30

The footsteps on the boardwalk grew louder. Sam closed the zipper on her backpack, inching it along. She intended to leave the path and creep through the jungle back to the car. But it seemed a cheat to have a car for escape. She should have had a foxhole, with broken branches over it, to hide in. But the V.C. would know the jungle, and they would see where she had been. They would see the picnic cooler. The V.C. rapist-terrorist was still at the boardwalk. A bird flew over but she didn't dare glance at it. Its shadow fell on the bushes.

Here she was in a swamp where an old outlaw had died, and someone was stalking her. In her head, the Kinks were singing, "There's a little green man in my head," their song about paranoia. But this was real. A curious pleasure stole over her. This terror was what the soldiers had felt every minute. They lived with the possibility of unseen eyes of snipers. They crept along, pointing the way with their rifles, alert to land mines, listening, always listening. They were completely alive, every nerve on edge, and sleep, when it came, was like catnapping. No nightmares in the jungle. Just silent terror. During the night, she had stayed awake in the dark swamp, watching and waiting. She could make out faint rings of lights and winking lightning bugs. She put herself in Moon Pie's place. In Emmett's place. She had fantasized Tom there with her in her sleeping bag, the way her father had tried to imagine her mother. But Tom floated away. She was in her father's place, in a foxhole in the jungle, with a bunch of buddies, all breathing quietly, daring to smoke in their quiet holes, eating their C-rations silently, their cold beans. She remembered Emmett eating cold split-pea soup from the can. She felt more like a cat than anything, small and fragile and very alert to movement, her whiskers flicking and her pupils widening in the dark. It was a new way of seeing.

Now she felt no rush of adrenaline, no trembling of knees. She knew it was because she didn't really believe this was real, after all. It couldn't be happening to her. In a few moments, everything would be clear and fine.

Her breathing was silent. Not even her eyes moved. She could see bushes stir as the rapist approached. He had left the boardwalk and was heading down the path in her direction. Her only hope was to remain hidden, with the can of oysters ready to cut his eyes out. The greasy oysters leaked onto her fingers.

A leaf moved, a color flashed. Someone whistled a tune, "Suicide Is Painless." This was a joke, after all, for it was only Emmett, in an old green T-shirt and green fatigues. He was empty-handed. His running shoes were wet with dew and his hair was uncombed. She stood up, feeling like a jack-in-the-box. In Vietnam, this scene would never have happened. It would always be the enemy behind a bush.

"Hey, Emmett," she said.

"What are you doing here?"

"How did you know I was here?"

"I saw your car out there."

"I know that. But how did you know my car would be here?"

"Just a guess."

"How'd you get here?"

"Walked."

Her knees still weren't trembling. She hadn't been scared. She marched ahead of him on the path, and he trailed after her. She had her backpack, and he had grabbed the cooler. She said, "It was crazy to walk all the way out here."

"Jesus fuckin'-A Christ, Sam!" Emmett yelled suddenly. "You worried me half to death! Crazy? I'd say it was crazy to camp out here. I thought you'd gone off the deep end. Man, I thought you'd lost it."

Sam reached her car and opened the door and set her stuff in the back seat. The windows had mist on them. The car inside seemed damp and cool. It must not be watertight, after all. Emmett was haggard and unshaved, and his T-shirt was dirty. The smoke from his cigarette flooded the swamp, obliterating the jungle smells.

"You scared me," he said. "I was afraid of what you might do. You might have considered that some people would be worried about you."

"Ha! I'd talk if I's you. At least I left a note."

"I was worried. I was scared you'd get hurt."

"You didn't have to come after me."

Emmett sat on a front fender and put his hands on his face. He was trembling, and his teeth chattered. A bird flew by and Emmett didn't look up. It was a Kentucky cardinal, a brilliant surprise, a flash of red, like a train signal.

"What were you doing out here?" Emmett asked.

"Humping the boonies."

"What?"

"I wanted to know what it was like out in the jungle at night." Sam scraped the dew off the bumper with her boot.

"This ain't a jungle. It's a swamp, and it's dangerous. I thought you aimed to stay at the Hugheses' last night."

"I didn't want to. Where were you?"

"I went over to Jim's. He's back from Lexington. I thought it would be a good time to set off that bomb, with you gone. But I went back to round up Moon Pie at dark and I went in and found your note."

"Did you leave Moon Pie in the house to breathe those fumes?"

"No. I took him to Jim's. He hated riding in Jim's truck."

"When I found that stupid flea bomb, I thought you'd flipped out again."

"I had to get rid of those fleas."

"Those fleas don't even bother Moon Pie, and you know it."

He smoked his cigarette down and ground it out on the gravel. He said, "I found out something yesterday morning after you left."

"What?"

"Buddy Mangrum's in the hospital. His liver's real bad."

Sam kicked at the car. "I hate Agent Orange! I hate the Army! What about his little girl?"

"She's home. That operation went O.K., but I don't know how they're going to pay all the bills. If he dies, maybe his wife will collect some benefits, but I doubt it."

Emmett leaned against the VW hood, its prim beige forehead. He said, "Jim and me went up to the hospital for a while, but we didn't see Buddy. We hung around in the waiting room a long time arguing about Geraldine Ferraro." Emmett smiled. "I guess Jim's afraid Sue Ann might decide to run for President or something." Emmett seemed old and worn out. He said, "I know why you were out here. You think you can go through what we went through out in the jungle, but you can't. This place is scary, and things can happen to you, but it's not the same as having snipers and mortar fire and shells and people shooting at you from behind bushes. What have you got to be afraid of? You're afraid somebody'll look at you the wrong way. You're afraid your mama's going to make you go to school in Lexington. Big deal."

"I slept out here in the swamp and I wasn't afraid of anything," she said. "Some people are afraid of snakes, but not me. Some people are even afraid of fleas. I wasn't afraid of snakes or hoot owls or anything."

"Congratulations."

"And when you came, I thought it might be a hunter, or a rapist. But I wasn't scared. I was ready for you." She had left the can of smoked oysters behind, but her hands still smelled.

Emmett lit another cigarette and the sun came up some more. The fog was burning off. Emmett's pimples were crusted with yellow salve. Bile was yellow. Maybe his bile was oozing up from his liver. His liver would go next.

"I wanted to see that bird," she said. "That bird you're looking for." He shrugged, and she went on. "I saw a cardinal. And some raccoons. And a blue jay teasing a squirrel."

"Good for you."

She breathed deeply and kicked at the fender. She was bored

with Cawood's Pond. How could that outlaw have stayed out here in hiding? What did he eat? What did he do for recreation? She said, "How did you know I was here?"

"I called around."

"Nobody knew I was here."

"I thought you might have gone to Lexington, but I called Irene this morning and she hadn't seen you."

"You didn't tell her I was missing, did you?"

"No. I just talked about something else. I knew she'd mention it if you were there. I finally figured out you were here from your note. For one thing, I figured you'd go someplace to escape. And also someplace dramatic, because that's like you. Also, you took my poncho and space blanket. When I read that diary I tried to imagine what I would have done, and this is what I would have done. Once when I was little and Daddy gave me a whipping because I didn't feed the calves on time, I ran away from home. I ran to the creek and stayed there till it got dark, and while I was there I thought I was getting revenge, for some reason. It's childish, to go run off to the wilderness to get revenge. It's the most typical thing in the world."

"That explains it, then," Sam said disgustedly. "That's what you were doing in Vietnam. That explains what the whole country was doing over there. The least little threat and America's got to put on its cowboy boots and stomp around and show somebody a thing or two."

Emmett walked down the path to the boardwalk, and Sam followed him. She watched her feet, carefully avoiding a broken plank. He flung his cigarette into the water.

She asked, "What did you think of the diary?"

"I didn't sleep none after I read it."

"He couldn't even spell 'machete.'"

"Are you disappointed?"

She fidgeted. "The way he talked about gooks and killing—I hated it." She paused. "I hate him. He was awful, the way he talked about gooks and killing."

Emmett shook her by the shoulders, jostling her until her teeth rattled. "Look here, little girl. He could have been me. All of us, it was the same."

"He loved it, like Pete. He went over there to get some notches on his machete."

"Yeah, and if he hadn't got killed, then he'd have had to live with that."

"It wouldn't have bothered him. He's like Pete."

"It's the same for all of us! Tom and Pete and Jim and Buddy and all of us. You can't do what we did and then be happy about it. And nobody lets you forget it. Goddamn it, Sam!" He slammed the railing of the boardwalk so hard it almost broke. He would have fallen into the murky swamp. Emmett was shuddering again, close to sobbing.

"Oh, Emmett!" cried Sam. She was standing with her arms branched out, like the cypress above, but she was frozen on the spot, unable to reach him. She waited. She thought he was going to come out with some suppressed memories of events as dramatic as that one that caused Hawkeye to crack up in the final episode of *M*A*S*H*. But nothing came.

"Are you going to talk, Emmett? Can you tell about it? Do the way Hawkeye did when he told about that baby on the bus. His memories lied to him. But he got better when he could reach down and get the right memories." Sam was practically yelling at him. She was frantic.

Emmett said, "There ain't no way to tell it. No point. You can't tell it all. Dwayne didn't begin to tell it all."

"Just tell one thing."

"O.K. One thing."

"One thing at a time will be all right."

Emmett lit a cigarette and started slowly, but then he talked faster and faster, as though he were going to pour out everything after all. He said, "There was this patrol I was on and we didn't have enough guys? And we were too close together and this land mine blew us sky-high. We was too close. We had already lost a bunch and we freaked out and huddled together, which you should never do, so we was scrambling to an LZ to meet the chopper. And first we hit this mine and then this grenade come out of nowhere, and I played like I was dead, and I was underneath this big guy about to smother me. The NVA poked around and decided we were all dead and they left, and I laid there about nine hours, and I heard that chopper come and go, but it was too far away and it didn't spot me. I was too scared to signal, because the enemy was there. I could hear 'em. They shot at the chopper. What do you think of that? For hours, then, until the next day, I was all by myself, except for dead bodies. The smell of warm blood in the jungle heat, like soup coming to a boil. Oh, that was awful! They got the radio guy and the radio was smashed. I couldn't use it. I was petrified, and I thought I could hear them for a long time."

"That sounds familiar. I saw something like that in a movie on TV." Sam was shaking, scared.

"I know the one you're thinking about—that movie where the camp got overrun and the guy had to hide in that tunnel. This was completely different. It really happened," he said, dragging on his cigarette. "That smell—the smell of death—was everywhere all the time. Even when you were eating, it was like you were eating death."

"I heard somebody in that documentary we saw say that," Sam said.

"Well, it was true! I wasn't the only one who noticed it. Dwayne smelled it."

"He probably liked it."

"Oh, shit-fire, Sam! We were out there trying to survive. It felt good when you got even. You came out here like a little kid running away from home, for spite. Now didn't it feel good? That's why you weren't afraid. 'Cause it felt good to worry me half to death."

Sam said, "If you ran away when you were little, and you think it's childish to run out here, don't you think you do the same thing? Don't you think it's childish to do what you do, the way you hide and won't get a job, and won't have a girlfriend? Anita's a real pretty woman and it just kills me that you won't go with her."

Emmett's head fell forward with sobs. He cried. Sam hadn't

seen him cry like that. The sobs grew louder. He tried to talk and he couldn't. He couldn't even smoke his cigarette.

"Don't talk," she said. He kept crying, his head down—long throaty sobs, heaving helplessly. Sam let him cry. She heard him say "Anita." She was afraid. Now, at last. She went into the woods to pee and when she got back he was still crying. He sounded exactly like a screech owl. She touched his shoulder, and he shoved her hand away and kept crying—louder now, as though now that they were out in the woods, and it was broad daylight, and there were no people, he could just let loose.

His cry grew louder, as loud as the wail of a peacock. She watched in awe. In his diary, her father seemed to whimper, but Emmett's sorrow was full-blown, as though it had grown over the years into something monstrous and fantastic. His cigarette had burned down, and he dropped it over the railing.

They walked back to the car. Sam sat in the car and Emmett, still crying, sat on the hood. His bulk made the car shake with his sobs. Sam reached in her backpack and wormed out a granola bar. She resisted the temptation to turn on the car radio. An old song, "Stranded in the Jungle," went through her mind. A flash from the past. A golden oldie. It would be ironic if the car wouldn't start. But Cawood's Pond was beginning to seem like home. She and Emmett could stay out here. Emmett's ability to repair things would come in handy. He could rig them up a lean-to. He could dig them a foxhole. It still made her angry that she couldn't dig a foxhole. That woman Mondale nominated could probably dig one.

She had left the car door open. Emmett hung on the door and bent down to speak to her through the window. He said, "You ran off. When you ran off I thought you were dead."

"No, I wasn't dead. What made you think that?"

"I thought you'd left me. I thought you must have gone off to die. I was afraid you'd kill yourself."

"Why would you think that?"

"So many kids these days are doing it. On the news the other day, those kids over in Carlisle County that made that suicide pact—that shook me up."

"I wouldn't do that," Sam said.

"But how was I to know? You were gone, and I didn't know what might have happened to you. I thought you'd get hurt. It was like being left by myself and all my buddies dead. I had to find you."

"Thank you." She wadded up the granola wrapper and squeezed it in her hand. She said, "You've done something like that before, Emmett. When you went to Vietnam, you went for Mom's sake—and mine."

He nodded thoughtfully. He said, "It wasn't what you wanted, was it? It wasn't what Irene wanted. Then she got stuck with me because of what I did for her. Ain't life stupid? Fuck a duck!"

"Get in, Emmett," she said, reaching to open the door on the passenger side.

"No. I ain't finished." His face was twisted in pain and his pimples glistened with tears. He said, "There's something wrong with me. I'm damaged. It's like something in the center of my heart is gone and I can't get it back. You know when you cut down a tree sometimes and it's diseased in the middle?"

"I never cut down a tree."

"Well, imagine it."

"Yeah. But what you're saying is you don't care about anybody. But you cared enough about me to come out here. And you cared about Mom enough to go over there."

"But don't you understand—let me explain. This is what I *do*. I work on staying together, one day at a time. There's no room for anything else. It takes all my energy."

"Emmett, don't you want to get married and have a family like other people? Don't you want to do something with your life?"

He sobbed again. "I *want* to be a father. But I can't. The closest I can come is with you. And I failed. I should never have let you go so wild. I should have taken care of you."

"You cared," she said. "You felt something for me coming out here." She felt weak. Now her knees felt wobbly. She got out of the car and shut the door.

"I was afraid," he said. "Come here, I want to show you something." He led her to the boardwalk, and they looked out over the swamp. He pointed to a snake sunning on a log. "That sucker's a cottonmouth."

"I wish that bird would come," Sam said.

"You know the reason I want to see that bird?"

"Not really."

"If you can think about something like birds, you can get outside of yourself, and it doesn't hurt as much. That's the whole idea. That's the whole challenge for the human race. Think about that. Put your thinking cap on, Sam. Put that in your pipe and smoke it! But I can barely get to the point where I can be a self to get out of."

Sam picked a big hunk of fungus off a stump and sniffed it. It smelled dead. Emmett said, "I came out here to save you, but maybe I can't. Maybe you have to find out for yourself. Fuck. You can't learn from the past. The main thing you learn from history is that you can't learn from history. That's what history *is*."

Emmett flung a hand toward the black water beside the boardwalk. "See these little minnows? It looks like they've got one eye on the top of their heads. They're called topwaters. They're good for a pond. Catfish whomp 'em up. See that dead tree? That's a woodpecker hole up there. But a wood duck will build a nest there."

"How do you know all that?"

"I've watched 'em. There are things you can figure out, but most things you can't." He waved at the dark swamp. "There are some things you can never figure out."

He turned and walked ahead of her, walking fast up the path from the boardwalk. She followed. He entered a path into the woods and walked faster. Poison ivy curled around his shoes. From the back, he looked like an old peasant woman hugging a baby. Sam watched as he disappeared into the woods. He seemed to float away, above the poison ivy, like a pond skimmer, beautiful in his flight.

Part Three

1

Sam would have expected Emmett to be the one to flip out—or that pain to crack his head open—but to her surprise she was the one who went sort of crazy after Emmett came to find her at Cawood's Pond. On the road to Washington, she is still stunned, waiting for her head to clear, wondering what will hit next. Emmett is subdued, mellowing out again, withdrawing like a balloon losing air and collapsing into itself. Since that time at the pond, it has been awkward, and she and Emmett seem to be in separate orbits, waiting until they can orbit face to face.

On the way home from Cawood's Pond that morning, they stopped at Jim's and got Moon Pie, who squirmed in Sam's arms as Emmett drove. The house smelled only faintly of the flea bomb. Emmett's schedule was screwed up. It was already too late for breakfast at McDonald's. At three o'clock, he made potted-meat sandwiches with chopped sweet pickles, but Sam couldn't eat. The thermometer on the porch said ninety-five, but she still had on her boots and jeans, and the air conditioner was overworked. Emmett kept asking her what she was going to do, and he teased her about being hot, but she felt like a zombie. Emmett wanted to know if she wanted tacos or if she needed a doctor, and he fussed nervously around her. On some level, she knew she was behaving the way Emmett had acted a lot of the time, just strung out and dazed. She knew she was trying his patience, and in a way that felt gratifying. They had changed places, she thought. She had post-Vietnam stress syndrome.

She sat around all weekend staring at MTV. 99 *Luftballons*

kept dancing in her head—all those H-bombs going off. *Legs* by ZZ Top. *Panama* by Van Halen. *Flesh for Fantasy* by Billy Idol. So many videos were full of disasters, with everything flying apart, shifting, changing in the blink of an eye. The random images on the screen were swirling, beyond anyone's control; everything was falling, like their fragile house, but Bruce was still dancing in all that darkness, and the heart of rock-and-roll was still beating, in that song by Huey Lewis and the News. Joan Jett, in her shining black leather, was screaming with her band, the Blackhearts. Lonnie used to think they were called the Blackheads. Lonnie hadn't called. Dawn said she heard he was working at the Sunoco on Main Street.

Then Emmett announced a plan. They were going to see the Vietnam Memorial in Washington. He was so definite about it, as though he were an executive making a big decision that would mean millions of dollars for his company. And he even insisted on bringing Mamaw along. He said it would mean even more to her than it would to them. Emmett was so certain about everything that Sam felt powerless. Sam had never seen him swing into action like that. He checked Sam's car over, and he drove out to the Hughes place and persuaded Mamaw to go on the trip. He even went to the Burger Boy and arranged to take Sam's job himself so he could pay the money he owed the V.A. "You don't need that job," he said confidently. "You'll be going to Lexington." It was as though Emmett had found that bird he wanted to see. Grandma Smith said on the telephone, "Well, I'm glad Emmett's come to his senses. Maybe now we can get a crop out."

Emmett went to the hospital to see Buddy Mangrum. He told Sam he had seen Tom in the waiting room, and Tom had asked about the VW. At home, Sam petted Moon Pie, and the Luftballons rose to the sky. Boy George pranced around as if nothing on earth mattered except makeup and hem lengths. Weird Al Yankovic lost on *Jeopardy*. The Cars were driving a girl mad in *You Might Think*. Sam felt so spacey. She knew that what Emmett was doing was good, but she couldn't feel it yet. She didn't even have the energy to go running. She couldn't remember why she had been such a determined runner. Only when they started traveling did she begin running again. It was because they were in new places, and she remembered that she wanted to see the world.

America the beautiful. It is beautiful indeed, Sam thinks now on the road. The United States is so peaceful and well-organized. The farms are pretty, the interstates are pleasant. Even the strip mines are hidden behind a ridge on the parkway. It is a good country. But she keeps getting flashes of it through the eyes of a just-returned Vietnam soldier. The day they came back from Cawood's Pond, she felt she was seeing that way as they drove into town, past the rendering plant and the four-corners gas stations, and the lumberyard, and the stockyards. She didn't fit in that landscape. None of it pertained to her. They passed by the Burger Boy, McDonald's. She couldn't see herself working at the Burger Boy again. The soldiers must have felt like that, as though they belonged nowhere.

In Lexington, when she and Emmett and Mamaw stopped the first night, Sam's mother was puzzled by their trip, and Lorenzo Jones chattered about it as though it were a leisurely vacation. "Have you thought of going through colonial Williamsburg on the way back?" he asked. "It's really worth seeing. But you can't see it all in one day." He advised them to go to Washington on the Skyline Drive in Virginia, because it was so pretty, even though it was out of the way. Sam hardly spoke to him. He seemed like someone from the moon.

"You ought to go to New Orleans this year," he said to Mamaw. "The World's Fair's on, and there's the Superdome, and the French Quarter, and Bourbon Street. It's the home of Dixieland jazz."

Mamaw laughed loudly, "I've never been this far away from home in my whole life," she said. "It's too late to do all that in my old age."

"Why, you're not old, Mrs. Hughes!" he said.

"I'm fifty-eight," she said. "And I've got about twenty years' worth of worry tacked on to that."

"Well, I'll put it this way: you don't look old and you don't act old. Being old is a state of mind. Isn't that right, Emmett?"

Emmett said, "I felt as old as I was ever going to be fifteen years ago."

Lorenzo Jones was balding, and his pants fit loosely. He showed off his Jim Beam bottles and described the motorboat he wanted to get. Irene raved about Geraldine Ferraro. "Women can do anything now, Sam," she said. "If they go to college." She showed Sam the room where she would live if she moved to Lexington and went to U.K. It was painted pink, with a white bedspread. The house was nice, a brick ranch with eight rooms, and it had a shag rug and a microwave. Irene fixed supper in about two minutes.

Sam fed the baby and played patty-cake with her. The baby had developed a little more personality since Sam saw her last. She smiled and showed her tooth. When she clapped her hands, Lorenzo Jones acted as though the baby had solved a quadratic equation. He wrote it down in a baby book. It made Sam feel strange to see a grown man playing with a baby. Later, he changed the baby's diaper and made her giggle.

After supper, when the others were watching TV, Sam told her mother about the letters and the diary. She had brought the diary to show her.

"I'll read it after you go," Irene said. "I'd be too nervous to read it right now."

"Mamaw thought it wasn't anything but troop movements, but it was. You'll see. His handwriting is hard to read, but I can read it to you."

"I'd better wait. I need a quiet time by myself to read it. My nerves are ragged right now. I've been up late studying."

"Did you ever read this before?" Sam asked.

"No. It must have been in those things the Army sent. I remember it was the longest time before I'd even look at anything of his. I guess I told her I didn't want to see it. I didn't want to be reminded."

"I don't think she even read it. If she had, I don't know how she could live with herself." Sam's tone was bitter, and her mother looked at her with scared eyes.

"What's the matter with you, Sam? You've been acting strange ever since you got here. Aren't you happy with your car?"

"Yeah."

"I worry about you taking off like this. Be sure to watch out for trucks. They can flatten a bug."

"I will."

Irene said, "I found a picture of Bob to show you."

The hippie. Irene loved him more than she had loved Dwayne.

The picture was in a drugstore envelope of old black-and-white snapshots with wavy edges. They showed large scenes of people at a distance. The people were very small, hard to make out.

"That was the guy they called Captain Marvel," said Irene. "You can't possibly remember these people. You were only three when they were living with us."

"I remember that moon party."

"I don't remember which moon landing that was, but I remember us out in the yard looking up at the moon, knowing there were people up there. It was strange."

Sam studied the picture of Bob. A guy with dark, bushy hair and a bandanna headband. He had a small chin and a gap between his teeth. "How come they all left?" she asked.

"There was so much pressure in town for them to get out. They just weren't accepted. Emmett was wild. He was so moody then, and he hadn't settled down into those routines of his."

"Why did we go to Lexington?"

"Well, I was going crazy living in Hopewell. I was afraid I was going to have to be responsible for Emmett, so I tried to get out while I could."

"What was Bob like?"

"What I liked about him was his sense of humor. He always had something witty to say. I can't remember things he said, but he'd play with words. He called Hopewell 'Dopewell.' He was well read, and he had been married once, but his wife left him and started practicing witchcraft somewhere in California—*everything* was going on in California back then, and I was dying to go there. Emmett always said the sixties never hit Hopewell. I think he came back with the intention of bringing the sixties with him. But it didn't go over. Not in Hopewell. Dopewell." Irene sighed. "I still haven't been to California."

Irene showed Sam another picture of Bob, standing in the back yard under the maple tree. The tree was much larger now.

"I was crazy about him," she said sadly. "He had lived in England, and I always wanted to go to England. His family had money too." She fooled with the worn edge of the photo. "I got stuck. I had to take care of things at home. Not long after that, Emmett flipped out for a while, and then you probably remember that time he lost the feeling in his legs. The doctors said he was identifying with the paraplegics, but he didn't even know anybody like that then."

"I remember you trying to keep me quiet when he was sleeping." Sam remembered Emmett yelling out in the middle of the night.

"The war knocked all the ambition out of him. It's like he stayed a hippie. A case of arrested development. That's a term I learned in my psychology course!" Irene flipped through the pictures. "Here are some pictures of the whole bunch. These were taken out in California—Emmett and some people out there he hung around with. Look at this one."

In the photo, about twenty people were in a large tree that had good climbing branches spread out in all directions. The people all had long hair, and it was hard to tell the males from the females, except for the ones who had beards. They wore bell-bottoms and loose-fitting shirts. There were vests and beards and hats—straw hats and cowboy hats. At the left of the photo, near the end of a huge branch, Emmett was hanging like a monkey. His hair reached his shoulders.

"Emmett called them freaks," Irene said. "That's Susie. Jim. Bob. Estelle and D.R. That beautiful girl is Joan. Joan had some awful disease and went back to her parents in Ohio. She shook all over."

"They look like they're having a good time," Sam said enviously. "The sixties were a lot more fun than now. I was born too late." She was dying to find that Beatles record for her mother. "Whatever happened to Bob?" she asked.

Irene laughed. "That's what kills me. I went back to Hopewell because I could never depend on him to make a living? In Lexington we had this little apartment that was where this old woman died in the back of a guy's house, and it was filthy. It hadn't even been cleaned out after she died. Well, it wasn't five years till I heard Bob had a good job in his dad's office-supply company back in California. He's probably worth a fortune now. And he got married and had that kid I told you about. Nuclear Ragtime! Can you believe it?"

"I'm glad you didn't name me something that dumb." Sam could thank her father for that.

"I guess he tacked on the Ragtime part to give it a kind of kick, so people wouldn't think the child's name meant nuclear bomb."

"Like Olivia Neutron-Bomb?"

"Yeah."

Sam said, "You mean if it hadn't been for Emmett, I might have grown up rich in California?"

Irene laughed, a painful laugh. "You don't understand how it was back then. Everything's confusing now, looking back, but in a way everything seemed clear back then. Dwayne thought he was doing the right thing, and then Emmett went over there and thought *he* was doing the right thing, but then Emmett got soured on it and got in the anti-war movement and thought that was right and got involved with those hippies. Most of those guys escaped the draft somehow." She paused and reached for a cigarette from a pack on the kitchen counter. "Everybody always thinks they're doing the right thing, you know?"

Smoke circled the table where they were sitting. From the den, the predictable sounds of a car chase held Mamaw, Emmett, and Lorenzo Jones enthralled.

"I shouldn't be smoking again, but Heather's almost weaned," Irene said, tapping the cigarette on a saucer. She went on. "It was country boys. When you get to that memorial, you look at the names. You'll see all those country boy names, I bet you anything. Bobby Gene and Freddie Ray and Jimmy Bob Calhoun. I knew a boy named Jimmy Bob Calhoun that got killed over there. You look at those names and tell me if they're not mostly country boy names. Boys who didn't know their ass from their elbow. Oh, God, what a time that was." She puffed on a cigarette. "It wasn't a happy time, Sam. Don't go making out like it was."

"I brought you a present," Sam said. She had decided to give the cat bank to her mother after all. She ran to the car and brought in the box.

Her mother looked at the cat bank as though it were a tiny UFO that had just zoomed in her door. Her expression changed to recognition, then to joy.

"I love it!" she cried. "Oh, Sam, this is the sweetest thing anybody ever gave me."

Then she burst into tears, and the punk maharajah cat just smiled, staring. Sam stared too, in amazement.

2

They are in Maryland. Sam is at the shopping mall down the road from the Holiday Inn. The transmission has been repaired—for $258.69—and Emmett and Mamaw are waiting for her at the motel. At the record store, she flips through the Beatles albums: the *White Album, Sgt. Pepper's Lonely Hearts Club Band, Abbey Road, Meet the Beatles, Magical Mystery Tour, Let It Be.* No new album. There's nothing in the 45s either. The new song must be a bootleg tape, the chatty, rotund clerk suggests. But he hasn't heard of it. Sam's gaze lingers on the *Born in the U.S.A.* album, displayed near the counter. On the cover, Bruce Springsteen is facing the flag, as though studying it, trying to figure out its meaning. It is such a big flag the stars don't even show in the picture—just red-and-white stripes. Her mother's credit card could buy that album. Impulsively, Sam buys it, realizing too late that the vinyl will probably melt in the hot car.

The shopping mall is gigantic. Sam recognizes a store that sells punk clothes. The same store is in Paducah. She realizes it must be part of a chain. In the store, the punk outfits bring out that urge in her to be outlandish—she could wear something weird to the memorial—but they are all too expensive. She finds some black leather-look panties that are only six dollars, and she decides to buy them, even though she does not know who will ever see them. She also buys a hot-pink tank top, something like Anita's red one. As she waits for the sales clerk to check the number of her mother's credit card, she imagines herself a returned soldier, twenty-four hours away from the steamy jungle, entering this store. Emmett told her that the first place he went to when he came back was a clothing store in San Francisco. He stood there, surrounded by dress pants and fine shirts and sportswear, and he just froze. He no longer had any concept of who he was supposed to be, he said. It was days before he could get out of his uniform and buy a simple change of clothes.

The clerk is explaining that if the Visa number is in the booklet, it means the card has been stolen. Sam doesn't say the card isn't hers. She signs her mother's name. Her father never heard of credit cards. She feels a surge of anger growing in her.

The mall is split by a median strip of tropical plants, thriving under skylights. The palm trees are tall, and vines—familiar houseplants—are climbing them. Sam stands transfixed by the trees and the thick foliage. They become the jungle plants of Southeast Asia. And then they change to cypress trees at Cawood's Pond, and the murky swamp water, infested with snakes, swirls around her. All of these scenes travel through her mind like a rock-video sequence. She wishes she knew the song that goes with it.

As they drive into Washington a few hours later, Sam feels sick with apprehension. She has kept telling herself that the memorial is only a rock with names on it. It doesn't mean anything except they're dead. It's just names. Nobody here but us chickens. Just us and the planet Earth and the nuclear bomb. But that's O.K., she thinks now. There is something comforting about the idea of nobody here but us chickens. It's so intimate. Nobody here but us. Maybe that's the point. People shouldn't make too much of death. Her history teacher said there are more people alive now than dead. He warned that there were so many people alive now, and they were living so much longer, that people had the idea they were practically immortal. But everyone's going to die and we'd better get used to the notion, he said. Dead and gone. Long gone from Kentucky.

Sometimes in the middle of the night it struck Sam with sudden clarity that she was going to die someday. Most of the time she forgot about this. But now, as she and Emmett and Mamaw Hughes drive into Washington, where the Vietnam Memorial bears the names of so many who died, the reality of death hits her in broad daylight. Mamaw is fifty-eight. She is going to die soon. She could die any minute, like that racehorse that keeled over dead, inexplicably, on Father's Day. Sam has been so afraid Emmett would die. But Emmett came to Cawood's Pond looking for her, because it was unbearable to him that she might have left him alone, that she might even die.

The Washington Monument is a gleaming pencil against the sky. Emmett is driving, and the traffic is frightening, so many cars swishing and merging, like bold skaters in a crowded rink. They pass cars with government license plates that say FED. Sam wonders how long the Washington Monument will stand on the Earth.

A brown sign on Constitution Avenue says VIETNAM VETERANS MEMORIAL. Emmett can't find a parking place nearby. He parks on a side street and they walk toward the Washington Monument. Mamaw puffs along. She has put on a good dress and stockings. Sam feels they are ambling, out for a stroll, it is so slow. She wants to break into a run. The Washington Monument rises up out of the earth, proud and tall. She remembers Tom's bitter comment about it—a big white prick. She once heard someone say the U.S.A. goes around fucking the world. That guy who put pink plastic around those islands should make a big rubber for the Washington Monument, Sam thinks. She has so many bizarre ideas there should be a market for her imagination. These ideas are churning in her head. She can hardly enjoy

Washington for these thoughts. In Washington, the buildings are so pretty, so white. In a dream, the Vietnam Memorial was a black boomerang, whizzing toward her head.

"I don't see it," Mamaw says.

"It's over yonder," Emmett says, pointing. "They say you come up on it sudden."

"My legs are starting to hurt."

Sam wants to run, but she doesn't know whether she wants to run toward the memorial or away from it. She just wants to run. She has the new record album with her, so it won't melt in the hot car. It's in a plastic bag with handles. Emmett is carrying the pot of geraniums. She is amazed by him, his impressive bulk, his secret suffering. She feels his anxiety. His heart must be racing, as if something intolerable is about to happen.

Emmett holds Mamaw's arm protectively and steers her across the street. The pot of geraniums hugs his chest.

"There it is," Sam says.

It is massive, a black gash in a hillside, like a vein of coal exposed and then polished with polyurethane. A crowd is filing by slowly, staring at it solemnly.

"Law," says Sam's grandmother quietly. "It's black as night."

"Here's the directory," Emmett says, pausing at the entrance. "I'll look up his name for you, Mrs. Hughes."

The directory is on a pedestal with a protective plastic shield. Sam stands in the shade, looking forward, at the black wing embedded in the soil, with grass growing above. It is like a giant grave, fifty-eight thousand bodies rotting here behind those names. The people are streaming past, down into the pit.

"It don't show up good," Mamaw says anxiously. "It's just a hole in the ground."

The memorial cuts a V in the ground, like the wings of an abstract bird, huge and headless. Overhead, a jet plane angles upward, taking off.

"It's on Panel 9E," Emmett reports. "That's on the east wing. We're on the west."

At the bottom of the wall is a granite trough, and on the edge of it the sunlight reflects the names just above, in mirror writing, upside down. Flower arrangements are scattered at the base. A little kid says, "Look, Daddy, the flowers are dying." The man snaps, "Some are and some aren't."

The walkway is separated from the memorial by a strip of gravel, and on the other side of the walk is a border of dark gray brick. The shiny surface of the wall reflects the Lincoln Memorial and the Washington Monument, at opposite angles.

A woman in a sunhat is focusing a camera on the wall. She says to the woman with her, "I didn't think it would look like this. Things aren't what you think they look like. I didn't know it was a wall."

A spraddle-legged guy in camouflage clothing walks by with a cane. Probably he has an artificial leg, Sam thinks, but he walks along proudly, as if he has been here many times before and doesn't have any particular business at that moment. He seems to belong here, like Emmett hanging out at McDonald's.

A group of schoolkids tumble through, noisy as chickens. As they enter, one of the girls says, "Are they piled on top of each other?" They walk a few steps farther and she says, "What are all these names anyway?" Sam feels like punching the girl in the face for being so dumb. How could anybody that age not know? But she realizes that she doesn't know either. She is just beginning to understand. And she will never really know what happened to all these men in the war. Some people walk by, talking as though they are on a Sunday picnic, but most are reverent, and some of them are crying.

Sam stands in the center of the V, deep in the pit. The V is like the white wings of the shopping mall in Paducah. The Washington Monument is reflected at the center line. If she moves slightly to the left, she sees the monument, and if she moves the other way she sees a reflection of the flag opposite the memorial. Both the monument and the flag seem like arrogant gestures, like the country giving the finger to the dead boys, flung in this hole in the ground. Sam doesn't understand what she is feeling, but it is something so strong, it is like a tornado moving in her, something massive and overpowering. It feels like giving birth to this wall.

"I wish Tom could be here," Sam says to Emmett. "He needs to be here." Her voice is thin, like smoke, barely audible.

"He'll make it here someday. Jim's coming too. They're all coming one of these days."

"Are you going to look for anybody's name besides my daddy's?"

"Yeah."

"Who?"

"Those guys I told you about, the ones that died all around me that day. And that guy I was going to look up—he might be here. I don't know if he made it out or not."

Sam gets a flash of Emmett's suffering, his grieving all these years. He has been grieving for fourteen years. In this dazzling sunlight, his pimples don't show. A jet plane flies overhead, close to the earth. Its wings are angled back too, like a bird's.

Two workmen in hard hats are there with a stepladder and some loud machinery. One of the workmen, whose hat says on the back NEVER AGAIN, seems to be drilling into the wall.

"What's he doing, hon?" Sam hears Mamaw say behind her.

"It looks like they're patching up a hole or something." *Fixing a hole where the rain gets in.*

The man on the ladder turns off the tool, a sander, and the other workman hands him a brush. He brushes the spot. Silver duct tape is patched around several names, leaving the names exposed. The names are highlighted in yellow, as though someone has taken a Magic Marker and colored them, the way Sam used to mark names and dates, important facts, in her textbooks.

"Somebody must have vandalized it," says a man behind Sam. "Can you imagine the sicko who would do that?"

"No," says the woman with him. "Somebody just wanted the names to stand out and be noticed. I can go with that."

"Do you think they colored Dwayne's name?" Mamaw asks Sam worriedly.

"No. Why would they?" Sam gazes at the flowers spaced along the base of the memorial. A white carnation is stuck in a crack between two panels of the wall. A woman bends down and straightens a ribbon on a wreath. The ribbon has gold letters on it, "VFW Post 7215 of Pa."

They are moving slowly. Panel 9E is some distance ahead. Sam reads a small poster propped at the base of the wall: "To those men of C Company, lst Bn. 503 Inf., 173rd Airborne who were lost in the battle for Hill 823, Dak To, Nov. 11, 1967. Because of their bravery I am here today. A grateful buddy."

A man rolls past in a wheelchair. Another jet plane flies over.

A handwritten note taped to the wall apologizes to one of the names for abandoning him in a firefight.

Mamaw turns to fuss over the geraniums in Emmett's arms, the way she might fluff a pillow.

The workmen are cleaning the yellow paint from the names. They sand the wall and brush it carefully, like men polishing their cars. The man on the ladder sprays water on the name he has just sanded and wipes it with a rag.

Sam, conscious of how slowly they are moving, with dread, watches two uniformed marines searching and searching for a name. "He must have been along here somewhere," one says. They keep looking, running their hands over the names.

"There it is. That's him."

They read his name and both look abruptly away, stare out for a moment in the direction of the Lincoln Memorial, then walk briskly off.

"May I help you find someone's name?" asks a woman in a T-shirt and green pants. She is a park guide, with a clipboard in her hand.

"We know where we are," Emmett says. "Much obliged, though."

At panel 9E, Sam stands back while Emmett and Mamaw search for her father's name. Emmett, his gaze steady and intent, faces the wall, as though he were watching birds; and Mamaw, through her glasses, seems intent and purposeful, as though she were looking for something back in the field, watching to see if a cow had gotten out of the pasture. Sam imagines the egret patrolling for ticks on a water buffalo's back, ducking and snaking its head forward, its beak like a punji stick.

"There it is," Emmett says. It is far above his head, near the top of the wall. He reaches up and touches the name. "There's his name, Dwayne E. Hughes."

"I can't reach it," says Mamaw. "Oh, I wanted to touch it," she says softly, in disappointment.

"We'll set the flowers here, Mrs. Hughes," says Emmett. He sets the pot at the base of the panel, tenderly, as though tucking in a baby.

"I'm going to bawl," Mamaw says, bowing her head and starting to sob. "I wish I could touch it."

Sam has an idea. She sprints over to the workmen and asks them to let her borrow the stepladder. They are almost finished, and they agree. One of them brings it over and sets it up beside the wall, and Sam urges Mamaw to climb the ladder, but Mamaw protests. "No, I can't do it. You do it."

"Go ahead, ma'am," the workman says.

"Emmett and me'll hold the ladder," says Sam.

"Somebody might see up my dress."

"No, go on, Mrs. Hughes. You can do it," says Emmett. "Come on, we'll help you reach it."

He takes her arm. Together, he and Sam steady her while she places her foot on the first step and swings herself up. She seems scared, and she doesn't speak. She reaches but cannot touch the name.

"One more, Mamaw," says Sam, looking up at her grandmother—at the sagging wrinkles, her flab hanging loose and sad, and her eyes reddened with crying. Mamaw reaches toward the name and slowly struggles up the next step, holding her dress tight against her. She touches the name, running her hand over it, stroking it tentatively, affectionately, like feeling a cat's back. Her chin wobbles, and after a moment she backs down the ladder silently.

When Mamaw is down, Sam starts up the ladder, with the record package in her hand.

"Here, take the camera, Sam. Get his name." Mamaw has brought Donna's Instamatic.

"No, I can't take a picture this close."

Sam climbs the ladder until she is eye level with her father's name. She feels funny, touching it. A scratching on a rock. Writing. Something for future archaeologists to puzzle over, clues to a language.

"Look this way, Sam," Mamaw says. "I want to take your picture. I want to get you and his name and the flowers in together if I can."

"The name won't show up," Sam says.

"Smile."

"How can I smile?" She is crying.

Mamaw backs up and snaps two pictures. Sam feels her face looking blank. Up on the ladder, she feels so tall, like a spindly weed that is sprouting up out of this diamond-bright seam of hard earth. She sees Emmett at the directory, probably searching for his buddies' names. She touches her father's name again.

"All I can see here is my reflection," Mamaw says when Sam comes down the ladder. "I hope his name shows up. And your face was all shadow."

"Wait here a minute," Sam says, turning away her tears from Mamaw. She hurries to the directory on the east side. Emmett isn't there anymore. She sees him striding along the wall, looking for a certain panel. Nearby, a group of marines is keeping a vigil for the POWs and MIAs. A double row of flags is planted in the dirt alongside their table. One of the marines walks by with a poster: "You Are an American, Your Voice Can Make the Difference." Sam flips through the directory and finds "Hughes." She wants to see her father's name there too. She runs down the row of Hughes names. There were so many Hughes boys killed, names she doesn't know. His name is there, and she gazes at it for a moment. Then suddenly her own name leaps out at her.

SAM ALAN HUGHES PFC AR 02 MAR
49 02 FEB 67 HOUSTON TX 14E 104

Her heart pounding, she rushes to panel 14E, and after racing her eyes over the string of names for a moment, she locates her own name.

SAM A HUGHES. It is the first on a line. It is down low